THE RIVER MOUTH

THE
RIVER
MOUTH

KAREN HERBERT

 FREMANTLE PRESS

Karen Herbert spent her childhood in Geraldton on the midwest coast of Australia, attending local schools before moving to Perth to study at the University of Western Australia. She has worked in aged care, disability services, higher education, Indigenous land management, social housing and the public sector, and is a board member of The Intelife Group, Advocare Inc., and President of the Fellowship of Australian Writers WA. Karen lives in Perth, Western Australia, with her husband, Ross. *The River Mouth* is her first book.

For Joanne and Katie, my sisters.

CHAPTER 1

Sandra

This is what Sandra knows.

She is forty-nine years old and she can see the river mouth from her kitchen.

When the sandbar is open, the river stains the sea brown for as far as she can see.

Ten years ago, her son was killed below the limestone cliffs at the riverbank.

Last week, her best friend's body was found off a remote road in the Pilbara.

Her friend's DNA matches the DNA scraped from under her son's fingernails.

CHAPTER 2

Colin

Twenty-five days before Darren dies

Colin's last class was tech drawing, so he got to the bus stop first. He put his bag next to the stop sign to claim his place at the front of the line and retreated to the basketball court fence to wait in the shade. The bus would be a while. It had to pick up the little kids from the primary school. He watched the other students as they dribbled across the school oval. Some of the first years still thought it was fun to run headlong down the grassed slope from the quadrangle to the ovals. No-one had shamed it out of them yet, at least not the boys. Colin doesn't know how girls work that kind of thing out. He couldn't see them beating each other up but he couldn't see them politely taking each other aside and explaining the rules of high school either. He sniggered as he saw two first year girls run down the slope, lose their balance, and go tumbling, skirts up and pink knickers on show. A group of boys whistled and jeered, and the girls picked themselves up and dashed for the bus stop, laughing and bags flying.

'Look at that ranga!'

The voice came from the opposite direction and Colin turned his head and saw Darren and Tim walking down from the English block, their shirts untucked and their bags dragging halfway down their backs.

'Who let you out of the zoo?' Darren put his fists up and danced at Colin as he approached. He was in a good mood, thought Colin, and then remembered Darren's last class was woodwork. Of course he was in a good mood. Anything that didn't involve putting pen to paper made Darren happy. Colin, taller by five centimetres, took him in a headlock.

'Your mum. She thought you needed some company in the wild.' He rubbed his knuckles into the top of Darren's head. 'Why's your head so small, Daz? You can tell you're descended from monkeys.'

Darren wrestled out of his grasp and punched him in the shoulder for his efforts.

'Ouch,' Colin protested, 'you're strong for a little squirt, aren't you?' He feinted at him and Darren ducked, laughing.

'Stronger than you, ya big orange ape.'

'Says the kid who gets sunburnt watching the telly.'

Darren and Tim took their bags to the line forming behind Colin's and walked back to the basketball fence.

'How's tech drawing?' asked Tim, looking down at his feet, his hands shoved into his pockets.

'Good.' Colin glanced at Tim and saw his face redden. It wasn't the tech drawing he was interested in.

'You gonna ace it again this term?' Darren, this time.

'Yep.'

'Fucking nerd.' He punched him in the arm, just hard enough to feel it.

'Fuck off, Darren.' Colin smiled anyway.

'Did you sit with Amy?' asked Tim, still examining his shoes.

'Yep.'

'Course he did; that's how he gets the marks,' said Darren.

'Yeah, right.'

The boys looked up and fell silent as four girls from their year walked past. Like the boys, they had untucked their shirts from their waistbands after the last bell sounded. As they passed, one of them hooked a finger into the elastic holding her hair and dragged it out, shaking her head. Her white hair fell to her shoulders and Colin caught the sharp smell of chlorine. He blushed and, like Tim, looked down at his feet.

'Want to go down to the river?' he asked, bending down to pick up a stick. He broke it in half and in half again.

'What, now?'

'Yeah.'

'No bathers,' said Tim.

'Go in your shorts.'

'Mum'll be pissed off,' Tim protested.

'They'll dry before you get home.'

That was true. It wasn't summer yet, but the afternoon was hot enough. The river hadn't broken through since it last rained, and the water level was high enough for bombies off the rope swing. They hadn't been down there for a swim since last summer. The water would be cool. Colin's mum worked Wednesdays and expected him to be home to put on dinner, but he'd have time if they were quick.

'I'll come,' said Darren.

The bus arrived and the three boys levered themselves off the fence. Instead of taking their places in line, they waited while the other kids boarded, forcing them to step over their bags. When they got on, they went straight to the back seat. The younger kids knew to leave it free for the year tens and this year the boys didn't need to defer to any senior school students. The ones from their bus had all left to do year eleven and twelve at private schools in the city. Colin would join them next year. Not Darren and Tim though. They would stay at the local high school.

The bus circled around the school grounds and turned toward the centre of town, passing car yards and the low white government administration building with its rose beds and lawns. A group of pre-school age children splashed barefoot in the shallow ornamental pool while their mothers sat on the grass under a jacaranda tree. Blooms were scattered on the lawn around them. Colin remembered begging to be allowed to play in that pool when he was a little kid and his mother flat out refusing. He wouldn't be seen dead doing it now. At the traffic lights, the bus turned right into the main street and the boys scooted across the seat to the windows.

'Oh my God, it's Mr Johnson.'

'He's carrying toilet paper! A twenty pack!'

They hollered out of the window.

'Well done, Mr Johnson, keep your bum clean!'

Mr Johnson, their maths teacher and local sporting legend, obliged by holding the bagged toilet rolls above his head in both hands and doing a victory lap around himself.

'You boys settle down back there.' The bus driver eyeballed them in the rear-view mirror.

'Yes Mr Stevens,' they chorused. The bus reached the end of the main street and they dropped back in the seat to watch the windsurfers in the bay. The southerly was pumping, and the blue water was washed out with white caps. Bulk carriers anchored out near the horizon. Colin could see three sails scudding in and out from the shore. He turned to Tim.

'Did you see Johnno in the paper on the weekend?'

Tim tore his eyes from the water, where a windsurfer had just stacked it attempting an aerial turn. He blinked before answering. 'No, what's he done now?'

'He won some state title for windsurfing.'

'Cool.'

'I thought he was Amy's swimming coach,' said Darren.

'Swimming, windsurfing. He's in the gun club with Dad too,' said Colin.

'What else is he going to do around here?' said Tim, sinking further into the seat and stretching his legs down the aisle. 'You can play sport, or play sport, or, I dunno, how about play sport. You might as well mix it up.'

The bus passed the fish and chip shop and the tennis courts, and bumped over the Wey River bridge. Tim led them down the aisle to the front door. The bus driver frowned at them.

'You know you're not supposed to stand up until the bus has come to a complete stop, boys.'

'Sorry, Mr Stevens,' said Tim.

The driver shook his head at Colin, who was the last to get off. Colin grinned at him and the driver reached across to swat the side of his head, a smile on his lips. Colin ducked and they both laughed as he swung off the bus.

'Tell your dad I want to see you at the club on the weekend.'

'Will do, Mr Stevens,' he replied. Mr Stevens was president of his dad's running club. His determination to get Colin to join was a standing joke. Wiry, and getting tall with it, Colin had an easy gait that ate up the ground. Mr Stevens wanted him to compete in the next regional competition, but Colin preferred team sports where he could hang out with his mates.

The boys shouldered their bags and walked back toward the bridge. Road trains thundered past them on the highway and they didn't speak until they turned down the road that ran along the river to the beach.

'So, are we swimming or not?' asked Darren.

'Not me,' Tim replied. 'Bring your boardies tomorrow. We'll all go after school.' Tim turned to cut across the vacant block and into his street. 'See you round.'

Colin looked up at the sky and shrugged, now indifferent. 'Nah, it's getting a bit windy now.' He felt Darren slump next to him and felt bad. He knew he was thinking Colin had backed out because Tim wasn't coming. They walked in silence toward Darren's house, shunning the new footpath on the other side of the road to walk on the grassed verges. They crested the last ridge before the beach and stopped, looking out at the sea and the choppy waves.

'Dad said I could take the tinnie out on the weekend if the wind dies down,' said Darren. 'Do you want to come? Saturday morning. Early.'

'Where are you gonna go?'

'Other end of the reef. Maybe up to North Point a bit.'

'Sure.' It would make up for him not going swimming this afternoon.

'Cool. See you tomorrow.'

Darren shot him a grin before he walked up to the front door of his house and pushed it open, a swagger in his hips. Through the open door, Colin could hear Darren's dad calling to his mum.

'Sandra! We're out of milk.'

Colin continued down the road. He didn't have to come this way to get home from school. He could have crossed back over the bridge and walked down the track on the south side of the river. It would take him straight down to his house but could get muddy if the water was high. This route took him across the sandbar at the river mouth to get home, which was hard going with a heavy school bag, but it meant he got to walk with Darren and Tim for a bit and there was always the possibility of stopping off for a while if none of them had been told to go straight home. Colin reached the beach, thought for a moment, then bent down, and took off his shoes. It was easier to go barefoot across the sand.

CHAPTER 3

Sandra

The two officers are Sandra's age. They stand side by side at the front door, the hard light of the afternoon behind them and the wind from the sea making their shirt sleeves flap. Their presence makes time stop and Sandra stands there, unmoving, taking them in while the south-westerly rattles down her hallway making the vertical blinds at the back of the house clatter. Her brain all at once is tired and she doesn't want to think about why they are at her door again after all these years. She can see from the way they stand there looking back at her that they share her weariness, the legacy of long working lives of patching up and admonishing the broken and the bad among them. Younger people – people at the start of their careers – stand taller, she thinks, unbowed by the burdens they have yet to carry, or even realise are in front of them. She looks over the officers' shoulders at the sea. It is choppy under the wind and the swell has picked up. Despite the hard-blue sky overhead, a bank of cloud has formed on the horizon. There is a cold front forecast. She pulls her cardigan tighter around her and, without speaking, stands aside and motions for them to come in.

Out of the wind and under the indoor light where they are not backlit by the sun, Sandra realises she knows one of the officers from high school. He was in the year above her and played in the school football team. As a teenager he'd matured early, she remembers, and came back from the summer holidays in year ten with a man's thighs and a head taller than his classmates. He was the first year ten to play in the Country Week team and everyone said the state league teams had their eye on him. He dated her friend's older sister, which at the time ruffled feathers among the parents. Sandra remembers the school ball photo at her friend's house and the dress her sister wore. It had a high lace collar around her throat, which Sandra coveted to the point of pain. She asked her mum if she could have one for her own ball but by the next year fashions had changed, and they couldn't find one the same. She settled for leg of mutton sleeves and lace gloves. The police officer – his name is Keith, she remembers now – is thicker around the waist than when he played football, but he has avoided the tight, hard belly of most working-class men of his age. His hair and skin are dark, and her memory flashes with the name they used to call him on the playing field. You wouldn't get away with calling someone that now. He asks if they can sit and she realises she hasn't said a word to them yet.

'Of course.'

She leads them to the couches by the back windows and watches them take in the garden and the shed that spans the width of the block. The shed dominates. It is too big for a suburban home, and these days mostly empty. Sandra has tried to mask it from the house with bushes and garden beds but there is no denying its glum, industrial presence. Keith, she realises, must already be familiar with her shed; he would've been there, back in the day. She turns away from it, goes back into the kitchen and returns with a jug of cold water from the fridge. She pours for both men, sliding the glasses across the table and leaving two trails of condensation.

Keith tells her Barbara Russell's body has been found out in the bush, near Wittenoom in the Pilbara. It was only one hundred metres from her car. She had broken down and wandered off. Two local kids found the body.

Sandra feels her face sink. Her cheeks hollow and her jaw tightens. Her thoughts go everywhere and nowhere, and she bites her lower lip against the tingling. She is conscious that the second officer is watching her reaction. She doesn't know him; he must have been posted up here just recently. Working in the hospital emergency department, she gets to know all the local police after a while, and she hasn't met this one yet. Now she can see his face, she realises he is younger than she first thought, maybe early thirties. Ten years older than her son would have been, at most. She does know Barbara, though. She has known her for years, since Barbara and Stuart moved up from Perth. She was her best friend.

The emptiness in her face tracks down through her neck and into her chest and she gasps to refill her lungs. With the air comes the first prickle of tears and she blinks hard to push them away. She feels numb and so very tired. She could, she thinks, put her head down on the couch and fall asleep, block out the two officers and their awful message.

Keith is explaining that Barbara had been missing for three days. Keith did go to the state league in the end, Sandra remembers, and played three seasons before he joined the police service and returned home, injured and unimpressed with city life. She thinks he still umpires for the local league. She can't recall if he ever married. She figures he is the one doing the talking because he is supposed to have the local connection. It is usual, Keith says, for the coroner to investigate and take a DNA sample in missing persons cases. Sandra nods and tries to focus. She hadn't known Barbara was missing, although she wouldn't expect to after three days. Barbara had been promoted to area coordinator and then district manager over the last five years and Sandra no longer saw her every day on the wards. She knew, of course, that Barbara had been away this week. They had been discussing the trip for six months now. Barbara was nervous, which was understandable. It seems reasonable under the circumstances, she thinks, that the coroner would be involved, but she doesn't understand why the police are telling her.

'We ran the sample through the database and got a match,' he says.

She nods again, trying to make sense of what he is saying. Then her brain clicks over, and she feels her heart thud. A buzzing starts up in her head. Her throat tightens again, this time against the bile rising up from her stomach and she wishes she had brought a glass of water for herself. The urge to lie down and close her eyes is overwhelming.

'Mrs Russell's DNA is a match with the DNA under Darren's fingernails.'

Sandra looks him. Keith is looking back at her with a face she can't read. His expression is too neutral to call apologetic, and too kind to call impassive. His face is just there. She supposes that is what they teach them in the academy. Stick to the facts. Keep it professional. Don't show emotion. She wonders what it is like for him, to come into her home and give such horrible news. At least he is not telling her that her son is dead. Another police officer did that ten years ago. In the scheme of things, she guesses today's chore is easy. She looks down at her hands. They are still and polite, folded in her lap. Her heart is hammering. She sees Barbara as she was that day, standing outside the nursing home, her bag over her arm, sweating in the heat and eyes dark with anxiety.

'What does this mean for the investigation?' she asks him. 'I mean, I know the case is not active, but ...' She trails off, no longer familiar with the jargon and not knowing what words to use.

Keith steps in. 'We will review the case file, look at her movements on the day, probably interview a few people.'

'But finding Barbara's DNA doesn't mean she did it. The shooter would have been a hundred metres away. You can't scratch someone from a distance.' Sandra frowns as she tries to gather all her thoughts back to her. They won't come together. Everything is flying away.

'No, it is not conclusive, but it does raise questions. We'll need to reopen the investigation, I'm afraid, Mrs Davies,' he says. 'I'll keep you in the loop and let you know if anything comes up.' He passes her a business card. 'Please call me if you have any questions.'

The two men stand to leave. Keith drains his water and puts the glass on the sideboard next to a photo of father and son. They are standing on the wharf in front of the boat.

'Good-looking kid,' he says. 'Do you see much of Greg?'

She tries to group her mind together for a smile but only half manages and feels herself grimace instead. People expect acrimony when it comes to her and Greg. She supposes it will all start again now. 'I do, yes. He's doing well.'

Keith smiles back at her, gently sympathetic. 'Good to hear.' As his partner walks down the hallway, he looks out at the yard, squinting as though he is trying to picture a scene one thousand kilometres away. 'You wouldn't have any idea what Mrs Russell was doing in the Pilbara, would you?'

'No,' she says. 'No idea at all.'

'It's just she was supposed to be at a conference in the city.' He looks back at the photos on the wall. 'At least, that's what her husband thought.'

Sandra stands at the front door as the police car backs out of the driveway. She lifts her hand as it heads down the road, away from the beach. Back inside the house, she pulls her mobile phone out of her pocket and dials a Pilbara number, looking out to sea as she waits for the other end to pick up. Her fingers tap on the rim of the photo and she glances down at it. Keith is right; he was a good-looking kid, in his own way.

CHAPTER 4

Colin

Twenty-four days before Darren dies

Tim swung high out above the river while Darren and Colin watched. At the top of the swing, he let go of the rope, tucked himself into a spinning ball as he flew an extra two metres and dropped with a smack into the water. The spray reached the riverbank and splattered the flat rocks that created the ledge where Colin stood, jutting over the water. Tim surfaced and shook his head like a dog.

'Whoo!'

'Mate!'

Colin reached out and hauled him onto the rocks.

'Legendary, man. You were as high as the bridge.'

'Your turn.'

Colin grabbed for the rope and wrapped his hands around the float they had knotted into the end. He walked backwards as far as the rope would allow, ran across the wet rock ledge, feet slapping, and launched himself across the water. The other end of the rope was attached to a solitary tree left to stand when the council had made a clearing on the south bank of the river, on the downstream side of the bridge. Like most kids who lived north of town, Colin and his friends spent long afternoons there, swimming in the river, riding their bikes on the tracks that cut along the river reserve, and, when the river was high, doing bombies into the water off the rope swing. At the top of the swing, you could see down the river toward the bend. Further on, and masked by bush, the river continued toward the sea before reaching the sandbar and making a last turn into the saltwater. The sandbar was another hangout. It was where they dumped their gear when they surfed the reef-break, and on the river side, the warm, tea-coloured water was good for mucking about when the surf was too choppy.

Colin swung out over the water as a double road train roared past on the bridge. The highway was the main route north and ended back where it started, circling all of Australia in a bitumen belt. The truck was travelling south, red dust on its undercarriage, and a sunburnt forearm leaning out of the driver's window. Colin turned his head away from the hot air and grit that blasted at him as it passed. Downstream, he caught a flash of movement under the trees near the bend and forgot to let go at the top. On the downward swing, he turned himself around, held his feet together and flexed. Darren and Tim cheered him on.

'Do it!'

He reached the tree trunk with a thud and pushed off hard with his feet, sending himself soaring back out above the water. He looked back down the river and called out. 'Amy!'

He missed the drop again and swung back down, feet out, ready to push off. This time, his left foot was too far to one side and didn't make a solid connection with the trunk. It slipped, scraping the knuckle on his big toe and sending him on a wobbling course out into the river. He released the rope early and let himself fall backwards into the water; his arms punched out in a victory V.

'Maaate!' called Tim as he came to the surface. Darren walked over to the rock ledge and pulled him out. 'Good save.'

'Hey.' The three of them looked down the path to the beach. It was Amy Jenkins, walking up the track under the trees.

'Hey,' she called again, raising one arm.

'Hey.'

'Hey, Amy.'

'Having fun?'

'You bet. D'you want a go?' Darren jumped to his feet and grabbed the rope, holding it out to her.

'I'd love to, but I don't have my bathers.'

'Go in your undies.'

'Yeah, as if, Darren,' Amy laughed. 'I see you haven't got your special ones on today.'

Colin snorted and Darren scowled. Amy's mum had a photo of Amy and Darren as toddlers, playing in the river near the sandbar in their underwear. Darren's undies had Superman on the front, and they all teased him whenever they were at Amy's house.

Amy sat down in the shade, plucking sourgrass. She'd changed out of her school uniform and was wearing shorts and thongs and Colin eyed her legs, envious of her tan. Even though it was late afternoon by the time they got to the river, his own skin was already turning pink. He found a dry spot out of the sun and investigated his toe. Red blood and river water ran together on the rock. Darren prepared to swing out.

'Watch this, losers.'

They watched him run up and launch, shading their eyes against the sun. He swung back down, pale soles upturned, and thudded his feet against the tree, copying Colin's move. At the top of the second swing he called out – *Geronimo!* – and swanned out away from the rope, arms wide and back arched, his hollow belly stretched tight under the lines of his ribs.

'Shit, he's not going to dive, is he?' Tim jumped to his feet. 'It's too shallow.'

Amy sucked in her breath and she and Colin joined Tim at the water's edge.

'Fuck, Darren. Darren! Roll!'

Darren continued his arc into the air, his body curving up and then downwards toward water. At the last minute, he flipped them the finger and tucked his knees to his chest, smacking into the water bum first with a spray that reached all of them as they stood, hearts thumping, on the bank. He surfaced, laughing.

'Gotcha, you dumb shits!'

'Fuck you, Darren,' Tim was angry. 'That wasn't funny.'

'Don't be such a pussy.'

'Fuck off, I'm going home.' Tim reached for his bag and slid his thongs onto his feet.

'Aw, come on, mate. It was just a joke. I was only fooling around.' Darren hauled himself out of the water and tipped his head to the right, shaking water out of his ear.

'Yeah, well I'm out anyway. See you tomorrow.'

Tim stalked back up the track. Darren shrugged, looking to Colin for support. Colin shook his head. *Let him go.* They watched as Tim climbed the embankment up to the highway. He didn't look back at them as he walked across the bridge.

'Right. I'm going again.' Darren grabbed the rope, ran out, and launched. This time, he curled and somersaulted, copying Tim's first jump. Colin helped him out of the water and grinned at him.

'That was a triple. Cool.'

'I know, right?' Darren grinned back. He shot a look over his shoulder at the bridge, but Tim was gone.

'Nice.'

Darren climbed onto the rock and found a dry spot in the sun. He stretched out with his eyes closed to the glare, goosebumps pimpling across his thighs.

'I was just having a bit of fun; why'd he have to get angry?'

'I know you were, mate. He was just worried about you, that's all. He really thought you were going to dive.'

Colin joined him in the sun to dry off. He'd need to go home soon; his mum had told him not to be late. Amy was back under the tree, plucking at the sourgrass again. She twisted off a piece and nibbled at the stem, screwing up her face as the juice hit the back of her tongue. Darren rolled onto his stomach to face her.

'You should be careful, walking down here by yourself, especially in those creepy trees over there.' He looked toward the bush where the track disappeared along the riverbank.

'Careful?' she screwed up face and looked back along the track. 'Why?'

'You know.'

'No, Darren, I don't.'

'The homeless guy. What if something happened in there? No-one would hear you.'

'Mr Arthur?' She snorted. 'He'll talk your head off, but he wouldn't hurt a fly.'

'You never know.'

'You never know what's going to happen anywhere,' she retorted. 'I'm safer down here with Mr Arthur than I am in my mum's car.'

'How do you figure that one out?'

'More people get killed in car accidents than by old drunk homeless guys. Statistically, I'm safer here.'

'Better not tell your mum that.'

'Anyway,' she said, 'you're more likely to get hurt than I am.'

'Bullshit.'

'It's true. Men are more likely to be assaulted by random strangers and women are more likely to be assaulted in their own homes.'

'That's crap. What about the Weymouth rapist?'

She rolled her eyes and shook her head. 'Case in point, dumb arse.'

'No, I mean, he's a random stranger.'

'We don't know that, though, do we?'

'So, you're saying it's someone we know?' Darren's voice rose at the end of his sentence.

'I'm saying it is more likely than the random truck driver theory,' Amy replied.

'That's enough, you two can have your lovers' quarrel, but I'm going home.' Colin reached for his socks and used them to clean his feet before putting his sneakers back on.

'What's wrong with you?' asked Darren, poking Colin in the leg with his foot.

Colin kicked him away. 'Nothing, I just have to be home.'

Darren was right. The she-oaks between the clearing and the river mouth was creepy. They made a whirring sound that sounded nothing like what leaves were supposed to sound like, rustling agreeably in the breeze. The she-oaks made the wind sound like it was heralding the onset of winter; a vicious one where wolves howled, and vegetables froze in the ground like in a little kids' book. And there were spiders in there. Big ones. The track to the beach ran right through the she-oaks and Colin always picked up his pace when he walked that way home. He caught Darren smirking at Amy and knew he was making fun of him. He stuffed his school clothes into his bag and stood up.

'I'll come too,' Darren said, jumping to his feet as well and gathering his own gear. 'Is the river mouth open?'

'It's shallow,' said Amy, who'd just walked up from the beach. 'You can get through it if you want to cross there instead of the bridge.'

'Not me, mate,' said Colin. 'I have to get milk for Mum on the way home. See you tomorrow at the bus stop.'

Amy said she would walk home with Colin and they both left, following the track up the embankment to the highway. Darren walked back toward the beach alone. By the time Colin turned to look back, he'd disappeared down the path and into the trees.

CHAPTER 5

Sandra

Sandra is on the floor of the sitting room upstairs, an archive box and a stack of files next to her. She sits cross-legged like she used to do at school assemblies on the quadrangle, the backs of her legs burning on the tarmac. Now she sits on carpet and has placed a wine glass on the upturned box lid. She stretches over and lifts it to her mouth as she flips a stack of papers with the other hand. She is looking for any mention of Barbara Russell. Barbara's son, Colin, comes up a lot, of course. He was at the river that day. Sandra has made notes about what Colin said he saw, what he did, and what the other people at the scene were doing. In her timeline of Darren's movements during the month before he died, Colin appears almost every day, catching the school bus, swimming in the river, hanging out at the tennis club. Some of these events she still remembers herself, like the afternoon the three boys came over after school and ate their way through an entire loaf of bread and finished her milk. She had to go to the supermarket afterwards or there would have been nothing for breakfast the next day. It was only two weeks before Darren died.

Barbara barely appears in her notes; it is like she had temporarily ceased to exist. Looking through the papers, Sandra finds little mention of her usual involvement in the boys' weekly routines. In those two weeks, there is no record of sleepovers at Colin's house, or lifts home from training in Barbara's car. She was preoccupied, Sandra knew, and she guesses that explains why there is just one mention of Barbara being at the club for the tennis finals on the day of the murder. Sandra had been on shift that morning. Barbara had been at that awful school assembly, of course, where the local police came to talk to the students about personal safety. That was three weeks before. Barbara and Sandra had both taken time off work and sat to one side of the students with the other parents while the police effectively imposed an after-dark curfew. No-one had paid any attention, of course, and all it had done was fuel some of the more outlandish rumours that were doing the rounds at the time.

Sandra uncrosses her legs and stretches her back. The black-and-white record doesn't capture a friendship, she thinks. Not even photo albums record the real stuff of life, only the good times, the picnics on the beach and the barbeques in the backyard. They don't bear witness to the chats at the school gate, the discovery of shared head lice, or the wine drunk after receiving negative blood tests. It was Barbara who was with her in the doctor's surgery – Greg was out on the boat – when Sandra was given the all-clear, and Sandra's arms that held Barbara when she started bleeding at work. What will happen when Sandra forgets the million kindnesses; will they vanish as though they never happened? She remembers a story about a man walking down the street, smiling. Eventually, he looks up, and sees that people walking toward him are smiling at him smiling. He looks over his shoulder and sees that the people walking behind him are smiling at the people who are smiling at him, and he realises that smiling is infectious. Sandra wonders if Barbara's kindness will also keep existing, passed on to strangers, uncredited but doing good in the world somewhere.

Sandra needs a break from sitting on the floor and takes her wine to the windows. Outside, the sea is pale blue and churning under the south-westerly. Windsurfers skitter across the waves. The she-oaks along the riverbank bend away from the coast. Underneath her window, a four-wheel drive ute heads for the beach, two boards on the tray. She watches it pull onto the gravel shoulder and nose its way down the track to park on the sand bar. Barbara died a long way from the ocean, she thinks, and grimaces at the thought. The vast inland hectares of the Pilbara are as foreign to Sandra as snow-covered mountains. She wouldn't know what to do with herself among the red rocks and spinifex grass. Barbara and Stuart had a painting on their loungeroom wall that Barbara said showed the waterholes and meeting places of the local people. The land, she said, was criss-crossed with tracks and studded with landforms – breakaways, valleys, and ancient rivers – that had their own unique stories and meaning. But when Sandra and Greg went camping up there, Sandra been appalled by the dry emptiness and night-time silence. There was no body of water and no sea breeze to cross over it, to bring its briny smell and deposit flecks of salt on her skin. In her own home, she sleeps with a window open to the sound of the waves and walks along the beach every day, her toes in the water. She can't bear to be away from the sea.

Sandra takes another mouthful of wine and considers what she knows. Most of her records from the investigation are about the three suspects: Arthur Zelinski, her own husband, and the Weymouth rapist. The local police questioned Arthur about every crime committed in the town as a matter of course, and no-one Sandra knew had thought he'd done it. He might have been poor and known to every law and order and health and human services agency in town, but he wasn't a murderer, or even a petty thief. And anyway, he was in the nursing home dying of cancer on the day of the shooting. Sandra knew he was because she'd seen him there.

Sandra's money was on the Weymouth rapist. They never found him, and the assaults stopped after Darren died. Sandra thinks the murder rattled him, and he left town. He's probably somewhere in far north Queensland, she figures, torturing kittens and watching porn on the internet. She returns to the floor and pulls out another stack of papers bound together with a fat bulldog clip. At the top of the bundle is a cold-case story run in the state-wide daily newspaper on the fifth anniversary of Darren's death.

Did the Weymouth rapist kill Darren?

Weymouth schoolboy, Darren Davies, might have been the last and most tragic victim of the Weymouth rapist, sources close to the five-year-old investigation told The Daily News *this week. Darren (15) was killed by an unknown shooter five years ago on the bank of the Wey River in broad daylight. None of the witnesses to the shooting saw the killer, who is thought to have been hiding in bushes downstream from the popular local playground when he fired the gun. A witness says Darren may have been shot by the Weymouth rapist after Darren disturbed him climbing out of a potential victim's window, just one week before Darren was killed. The assaults ended after Darren's tragic death.*

The witness, of course, was Colin, who rang Sandra in tears after the article came out. The reporter had been waiting outside the city office tower where he worked and had gone straight to the Weymouth rapist theory. Did Colin think it was possible? Hadn't one of Darren's friends been a victim? Was it true that Darren had seen an intruder trying to break into a house in the week before he was killed? Could he have identified the man? Colin had given him one-word answers and bolted back upstairs. Later that day, police officers had come to the building to question him. They were sympathetic, they said; they'd been contacted by the same reporter. Did Colin want to add anything to his statement from five years ago? Colin's colleagues, who hadn't known about Colin's connection with the shooting, were quiet for the rest of the day.

Sandra puts the article aside. It had reopened the investigation but failed to create any useful leads and there was still no trace of the Weymouth rapist. There had been assaults in the town since then, of course, but nothing to link them to the previous crimes. There had been three, all in the space of six months. Each victim was a teenager, two were schoolgirls, and all had been asleep in their childhood beds when they were attacked. In each case, the assailant climbed through the window, gagged them with a scarf, and left again the way he came in. He wore gloves and a balaclava and left no fingerprints, just the scarves, which the police traced to the pharmacy on the main street. His DNA was not on any police database.

It was true, what the article said about Darren, if Sandra's notes from the second investigation were correct. The three boys slept the night at Darren's house and had walked to the fish and chip shop on the highway for late night chips and gravy. They never told anyone about it because they weren't supposed to be out after dark. They'd chatted to Amy – who was working that night and who Sandra suspected was the real reason for their need for a snack – ate their chips in the park and then walked home. In a street two blocks back from the beach, Colin and Tim went for a pee in a vacant block. While he was waiting, Darren saw a security light come on at the side of a house. When the story broke five years later, Colin told the police Darren said there was a man standing on a chair, levering a window open with a crowbar. He was dressed in black and wearing gloves.

It all tallied with police records, although it was a mystery how the press found out. The residents of the house, a family with teenage children, had heard the noise and investigated. The mother found a window open and the father, who'd leapt to the front door swinging a cricket bat, had seen someone running away. The information he gave police produced an identity sketch that looked like any trades apprentice or farm worker in the district. At the press conference, the police commissioner explained that the information had been passed on to the investigating team at the time of the first investigation and they had been unable to establish any link between the incident and the sexual assaults. The local investigating officers concluded the incident was just an attempted robbery. The window opened out from the loungeroom, not the girl's bedroom, and the family had recently bought a new television from the store on the main street. The intruder was probably after that, looking to sell it for drug money.

Still, it felt too neat for Sandra. She thought it could easily be a coincidence the family had just bought the TV, and as for the window, even intruders can make mistakes. It was entirely possible the Weymouth rapist discovered Darren's identity and decided he had to be silenced. Despite what the police said, she had no doubt about how he got the gun.

CHAPTER 6

Colin
Twenty-three days before Darren dies

'There it is,' said Tim, pointing across the water to a bare white rock that jutted out halfway up the limestone cliff. 'That rock is at the top of the entrance.'

Darren and Colin looked at the opposite bank. They were standing at the bend in the river, a few hundred metres upstream from where the water took its last turn along the sandbar and out to sea. Here the river arced away from them, creating a marshy, open patch of ground with clumping grasses. It flooded when the river was high, and everyone called it the swamp. The lack of trees gave them a clear view across to the other side. The rock Tim pointed out was the only thing on the opposite bank not obscured by branches and was easy to see.

'Looks like it's above the path,' said Darren.

'Yeah, Matt said there's a secret path that comes off the main one closer to the bridge.' Tim's cousin was five years older and knew this section of the river better than any of them. 'He said you need to look out for an empty soup tin filled with dirt.'

Colin looked at the bush upriver from the white rock. It was impossible to pick out any pattern in the vegetation that would suggest a path. The bushes looked thick. They were wattles and would be full of hairy black caterpillar nests. Underfoot it would be rocky and steep. He looked down at his feet. He was wearing sneakers, but the boys were all still in their school uniforms. They'd get them dirty and then they'd get in trouble. At least it was the end of the week.

'OK, let's do it then,' he said. 'Beach or bridge?'

'Bridge,' said Darren. 'Mum might see us if we go past the beach. I'm supposed to be home before she goes to work.'

The three boys headed off, Tim leading them single file, picking their way through the swamp. It was criss-crossed with paths made by sheep from the small flock kept by the nursing home as they navigated the south bank between the bridge and the beach. At this time of the year it was also boggy, especially if they chose the wrong path, and the mud sucked at their shoes as they walked.

'This stuff's like quicksand,' said Tim, poking a stick into the side of the path.

'I heard a kid went the wrong way in here once and got sucked into the mud. All they found was one of his shoes.'

'You're so full of shit, Darren,' said Colin. He pushed him in the back, and Darren stumbled to the side of the path, his foot dropping into the sludge.

'Fuck!' Darren wrenched his foot out, panicked, and left his shoe behind. Colin bent down to pick it up and scraped it on the grass while Darren hopped about on one leg. Darren cuffed him on the back of the head when he handed it back. 'You'll keep.'

They cleared the marsh and came to the tree line where the ground was too high for the river water to settle on the surface. Under the she-oak canopy, it was cooler and quieter, the sounds of the traffic on the bridge fading away. Sourgrass grew in clumps where the sun filtered through to ground level and Tim plucked a stalk and chewed on it.

'Dogs piss on that stuff, you know,' said Darren.

Tim shrugged and chewed anyway. Off to the side of the path, Colin could see spider webs strung between branches. They were the thick strands spun by golden orbs and were sticky and itchy if you walked into them. He brushed his hands over his face automatically. His mum said the spiders were beautiful, but Colin lived in dread of walking into one in its web. He had visions of it scuttling down his back, under his shirt, with hairy spider legs and nasty jaws. He let Tim go first whenever they walked single file through the bush. He scratched at an itch on his leg and called out to Tim to pick up the pace.

Through the trees they could see the flat rocks and the rope swing in front of the arches of the bridge. The clearing was empty except for a stray dog that watched them emerge from the tree line then lifted its leg defiantly against a rubbish bin. Darren whistled to it and slapped his thighs, but it ignored him and disappeared under the shadows of the bridge. The boys skirted around the edge of the clearing and scrambled up the embankment to the footpath which they followed, keeping single file, across the narrow bridge. Road trains sucked at them as they roared past, making them reach for the railing and turn their faces away.

They slid down the opposite embankment on the north side and followed the river back toward the beach. The riverbank had been cleared here to make a grassed picnic spot, with gas barbeques and shelters. Colin had never seen anyone use them. The gravel carpark above the picnic area was rutted from the winter just gone. When the boys were still in primary school, a black-and-yellow Torana had been abandoned there and was progressively stripped of its wheels and doors until one day it disappeared. Colin's dad said the council would have taken it to the rubbish dump east of the highway.

When they got back into the trees, the path climbed upwards and the noise from the road faded away again. Tim spotted the tin when they were about three metres above water level.

'Got it, it's here!'

They pushed aside a purple flowering bush and could see a second path heading further up the cliff, clearly marked out through the winter grass. It climbed another metre and then levelled out to a limestone ledge, wide enough for the three of them to stand side by side. The white rock was above their heads and the cliff face bowed inwards, creating a shallow cave. Another three metres above was the footpath and the road that ran past Darren's house and down to the beach. The marshy riverbend, where they had stood earlier, was directly opposite.

'Far. Out.' said Darren. 'Right underneath our house.'

'Does he really live here?' said Tim, his eyes disbelieving.

'That's what your cousin says, doesn't he?' said Colin.

Darren was exploring the back of the cave, pressing his palms into the spiky limestone wall.

'Imagine if you could tunnel in here,' he said. 'You could go right under the road and come up at my house, connect it to the car pit in the shed. You could smuggle in all sorts of shit. No-one would ever know.'

'What, like cigarettes and booze?' says Tim. 'You could walk that in through the front door in your school bag if you wanted to.' He joined Darren inside the cave. 'It stinks in here.'

Darren ignored him, intent on exploring the wall. He found a dip in the back corner and recoiled. 'Fuck!' He fell as he scrambled backwards.

Colin laughed at him, sitting on his arse in the dirt. Darren didn't see the funny side.

'You go and take a look then.'

Tim was already in there.

'Aw, that's a bit sad,' he said, pulling his shirt up around his nose. 'Poor puss.'

Colin looked over Tim's shoulder. A dead cat lay in the cavity at the back of the cave. It was facing them, eyes open, the end of a pink tongue just visible. Ants had discovered the body and were crawling in and out of its ears. He picked up a fire-blackened stick and poked at the body. The black hair around the animal's belly and legs was sunken.

'Oh man, it has a collar.' He pulled his own shirt up. 'We should take it off and see if there's an address or phone number.'

'I'm not touching it,' said Darren from behind them.

'Why not? It's not like it's going to scratch you now, is it?' Tim looked at Colin and rolled his eyes.

'He's got a point,' said Colin. 'It's probably covered in germs.'

'I'll do it.' Tim bent over the body, holding his head as far back as he could and still reach the neck. He unhooked the collar and lifted it off and they went back out into the sunlight. There was no tag.

'I guess it's up to us, then,' he said.

'What is?' asked Darren, keeping his distance from the cat and the collar.

'To give it a proper burial.'

'Tim, it's just a cat.'

'It could spread disease,' said Colin, 'and Mr Arthur probably isn't so keen on sleeping here with a dead cat.'

'What do you care?' said Darren, pulling a face.

Tim ignored him. 'Your house is closest, Darren. We can get a shovel from your dad's shed.'

'Fine,' he snapped, defiant, but still followed them up the cliff to the house and back down again carrying the shovel. The way up to the road from the cave, it turned out, was a lot easier than the way up to the cave from the river. When they returned with the shovel, Darren slid it underneath the cat's body and lifted it out, turning his face away.

'Christ, that stinks.'

'Hold it downwind,' said Tim.

On the shovel, the cat's front leg twitched. Darren dropped the shovel and leapt away.

'Fuck, it's still alive.'

'No way.' Colin edged around Darren to look at the cat, now lying on its back, half on the shovel and half on the dirt outside the cave.

The three boys gathered around the body and Colin poked it again with the firestick.

'Oh man, it's breathing.' The bottom ribs fluttered up and down and then stopped, then started again.

'We have to kill it,' said Tim, 'put it out of its misery.'

'I'm not fucking killing a cat,' protested Darren.

'Look at the poor thing, we can't leave it like that.'

'Can't we just bury it anyway?'

'Alive?' Tim looked at him in disbelief. 'What sort of sicko are you?'

Darren shrugged.

'Oh, for Chrissake,' said Tim. 'Give me the shovel.' He lifted the cat back onto the blade and led them down the path toward the beach where the sand was soft. He put the body down on the sand and dug a hole.

'Go and stand there and turn the other way, both of you.' He pointed downstream.

Colin and Darren did as they were told and flinched at the crack as the shovel came down on the cat's head. Colin glanced across at Darren, who was hunched over, his hands in his pockets and tears running down his face.

'It's alright, mate.' He put his arm around his shoulders, and they stared across the water while Tim filled in the hole.

CHAPTER 7

Sandra

At the triage desk, Sandra receives a new patient file and a rape kit. The shift manager directs her to the private consultation room at the back of the emergency department and nods at the female police officer in the waiting area.

'Police are here and SARC are with the patient,' she says.

Sandra is on an early shift today, and so far, the department has been quiet, just the usual drunks picked up off the streets by the local police, a potentially serious anaphylactic reaction to a bee sting, and a farm worker whose mate has backed the ute over his foot. The bee-sting boy had an EpiPen on him but will need to stay in for observation. The farm worker has been sent to radiography. Sandra guesses he'll be wearing a moonboot for the next four months. The fortunate drunks are asleep on rare spare beds.

In the consultation room, out of sight of the rest of the department, a fifteen-year-old girl is sitting on the bed, her legs folded in front of her. An older woman is beside her, an arm around the girl's shoulders. The girl is leaning into her, her eyes closed, her arms hugging herself. A member of SARC – the sexual assault referral team – is sitting quietly in the corner.

'Ashleigh?' Sandra asks. Getting a nod from the older woman, she introduces herself and pulls a chair to the bedside. The girl is wearing ugg boots and a pink dressing-gown, which she has pulled tight around her body. Pyjama pants with a cartoon pattern stick out from under the hem. The upturned soles of the boots have worn through under the big toes and stained, synthetic sheep's wool pokes through.

'The triage nurse has told me what happened.'

The girl keeps her eyes to the floor. She releases one arm to tuck a strand of hair behind her ear.

'She's written it down in your file, so I don't need to go through it all with you again, but I'd like to take a look at you and make sure you're OK. Would you like your mum to stay?'

'She's my auntie.'

Sandra offers her chair to the auntie, who introduces herself as Robyne, and pulls the curtains across.

'I understand you're going to make a police report. Is that right?'

'Yes.' The girl hasn't moved and keeps her eyes to the floor.

'I'll need to call the police officer in from the waiting room, and then I need to take an internal swab and some photos. Is that OK?'

'Yes.' Sandra looks up at Robyne, who also nods her consent. Ashleigh untangles her arms and legs and shuffles her bottom across to lie back on the bed, shifting her eyes from the floor to the ceiling. Robyne slides the chair across the linoleum floor and reaches for her hand.

Sandra calls the female police officer, who positions herself outside the consultation room door, and works through the procedure in the rape kit. The girl is passive, responding to each of Sandra's instructions without comment. Robyne keeps her hand on the girl and her eye on Sandra. Fair enough, Sandra thinks. Robyne has been here before, nearly as many times as she's been asked to leave. At least once a week she is one of the people asleep on the spare beds. Sandra knows from Barbara that the family's problems with alcohol and violence go back two generations. She doesn't know Ashleigh's story, but she wouldn't be surprised if pathology matches the swabs with a known offender living in Ashleigh's community, if not her own home. She takes photos of the bruises on the girl's thighs, hips, and neck.

'Well done, Ashleigh. We're finished now. You can go after you've talked with the police.' She raises her head to the SARC representative, who unfolds her legs and stands. It is her turn to take over. The girl rolls onto her side, away from Sandra, and draws up her knees. Robyne goes out to make a cup of tea.

Sandra goes back to her desk, writes up her notes, and prepares the rape kit to go with the police to their pathology department. She will need to write up the official report to the child protection authorities before she leaves today. What was a quiet shift has become a busy one; she won't be seeing many patients for the rest of the day. It is time for her break though, and she checks with the shift manager and leaves for the staffroom. She has soup in the fridge, and she heats it up in the microwave and finds a table with another emergency department nurse who is also on her break. The woman gives her a careful smile as she sits down.

'That smells nice. I bet it's homemade.'

'Thanks, it's pumpkin,' Sandra replies. 'The secret ingredient is salt.'

They both laugh.

'I hear you.'

'I was sorry to hear about Barbara,' the woman says. Her tone is cautious, and she keeps her eyes on her plate. Sandra nods her thanks. She has been here before. Sympathy can be conditional, she knows from experience, and is best kept at arm's-length. They eat in silence for a while. Sandra had stayed up too late the night before, looking back through the papers from the original investigation. It had been light when she'd started and almost midnight when she'd finished. The bottle of wine had slipped down before she'd eaten dinner and she's glad now she resisted the urge to open another. She feels so tired. She could crawl into one of the spare beds herself.

'How's Ashleigh?' asks the other nurse. A safer topic.

'It's hard to know.' Sandra pulls herself back into the staffroom. 'She was quiet as a mouse.'

'Is she going to report it?'

Sandra nods again, her mouth full of bread and soup.

'Good. I hope she goes through with it.'

Sandra hopes so too, but she's seen it before, especially when the alleged offender is a family member and a breadwinner. No-one wants to bite the hand that feeds them. She supposes that's how they get away with it for so long.

'I see Robyne was with her,' says her colleague. 'Nice to see her sober for once.'

'It's been a while since she's been in here at all, hasn't it?'

'Now you mention it, yes,' the other woman acknowledges. 'Let's hope she stays good for a while.'

Sandra pulls a face. 'That poor family. Alcohol is a curse.'

'Alcohol? Meth is their drug of choice. I would have thought you'd known. Don't you remember the Worners were involved in that bust ten years ago? The old man was bringing it onto the beach north of town, but the police couldn't make anything stick other than possession.'

Sandra shakes her head. Ten years ago, she had more on her mind than worrying about small-time local drug dealers.

'He did three years, but nothing changed. The drugs kept coming in and by all reports he was straight back into it when he got out. I wouldn't be surprised if he's the one responsible for this tonight.'

The two women look at each other.

'You can't be serious,' says Sandra. 'What sort of man rapes his granddaughter?'

'Step-granddaughter, if you want to be technical about it.'

Sandra shakes her head, not understanding.

'She's his son's – Randall's – stepdaughter,' the other woman explains. 'Randall met her mum in the city when Ashleigh was still a toddler. The mum couldn't get off the grog, though, and left them both. Randall brought Ashleigh back up here. They live with old Cyril.'

'There's too much misery in this world for some people isn't there?' Sandra shakes her head in despair.

'She's had it tough, that poor kid. Where would she have ended up if her mum hadn't met Randall? At least up here she's had Randall's older kids as brother and sister.'

'Jaelyn and Wesley, right?' Sandra remembers they were at high school with Darren. 'They were nice kids.'

Later, as her shift is finishing, Sandra sees Ashleigh and Robyne walking out through the emergency department doors. She doesn't know what horrors Ashleigh might have seen living with her mum, but she can't imagine they could be much worse than living with a step-grandfather who can't keep his hands to himself.

Two police officers, Keith and the female officer who interviewed Ashleigh, are standing inside the exit doors. Sandra walks over to them.

'How's she doing?' she asks.

'Quiet, but she gave us a good report. The bastard climbed in through her bedroom window while she was sleeping.'

'You're joking.'

'Brazen.'

'That's what that guy did ten years ago, remember?' says the female officer. She's a long-time member of the local police service and Sandra has seen her regularly over the years, bringing in people for her to patch up. 'What happened with that?'

'The Weymouth rapist?' Keith replies. 'Yeah, he stopped after the campaign to get people to lock their windows at night. We never got him.'

'I hope he died in a fire. One of those girls was a friend of my kids.' The officer's face hardens, and she turns away to the water cooler in the corner.

'How are you doing after the news about Barbara?' Keith asks Sandra.

Sandra thinks about it for a moment. She's not sure how she's doing. She'd expected when the police finally found a firm lead, that she'd feel everything drawing together. The sense of closure her psychologist talked about. It hadn't come. In its place was just the ongoing uncertainty coupled with the sickening idea that someone she knew well might have been her son's killer. She looks up at Keith, who is waiting patiently while she ruminates.

'I don't know.'

'I figured you might say that. Why don't you come down to the station and I'll fill you in. Maybe even go over some old ground. It might help me to get my own head straight about the investigation back then.'

Sandra knows she looks surprised. 'Don't you have colleagues for that? Forensics is hardly my field.'

'It's just me on this one, I'm afraid. For the time being at least. Think of it as two birds with one stone. I said I'd keep you up-to-date.'

He looks sheepish and Sandra guesses he's given away more than he should about the staffing levels at the station. What the hell, she thinks, he looks like he's trying.

'Sure, but I'd rather not come to the station if that's OK with you. Too many bad memories.'

'I understand completely. How about I come to your place? I finish up in about an hour.'

'Sure, I'm not going anywhere. How about four thirty?'

'Done. I'll see you then.'

CHAPTER 8

Colin

Twenty-two days before Darren dies

Colin, Darren and Tim were watching Amy's tennis match from the fence. She was losing. Her strokes were powerful, but they could go in any direction. They watched her sidestep to line up a return forehand and swing her left arm across to prepare the shot. Colin waited for the drop. This was where she always went wrong. He held his breath.

'There she goes again,' said Tim as she lowered her forearm, the racket turned face down to the ground. She flipped it upwards too late and the ball travelled hard and fast off to the side of the court.

'She needs to learn to drop the racket on the edge, not face down,' said Tim. 'She should watch Agassi.'

'There's no point having those enormous shoulders if you can't hit straight,' Colin called over the fence as Amy returned to the baseline after losing the point.

'Says you who can't swim more than two hundred metres,' she retorted.

Amy was the only person the boys knew who could swim a lap of butterfly while they were still in primary school. She was brown from hours of training under the sun, her hair white against her tan and her eyes a washed-out blue. At school in the morning they were red from the chlorine and framed by lingering marks from her swimming goggles. In her navy-blue squad bathers, she was nothing but ropey muscle. Today she wore traditional tennis whites and Colin averted his eyes, self-conscious and embarrassed, when the skirt flashed up above her knickers.

Amy was playing on one of the courts closest to the canteen, which meant she had an audience. Mums and dads and grandparents sat on picnic rugs and camp chairs on the lawn, handing ice-cream money to children and shouting encouragement to the players. Colin could see his own mum sitting on the grass, her legs crossed in front of her under a long red skirt she had tucked around her ankles. Rebecca was stretched out on her stomach next to her, reading a magazine, her legs catching the sun. She was there under protest, Colin knew, and her short shorts were a deliberate finger to their mum. Colin's mum was ignoring her, talking with his maths teacher, Mr Johnson, her expression unreadable behind her sunglasses. Colin felt a twinge of panic; they'd sat a test last week and Mr Johnson would have marked the papers by now. He tried to read his mum's body language as she straightened her back and lifted her arms to tuck escaped strands of curly hair into the clip at the back of her head. Unconsciously, Colin ran his hand over his own curls. Mr Johnson closed his hands together like a book and Colin's mum smiled. Colin breathed out. Of course, Mr Johnson was the school coordinator for the student exchange programme and Colin had told his mum he wanted to go. She would be doing her social worker thing and getting all the details before she agreed. He guessed there would be a long conversation at dinner about it tonight. He turned back to the game and rested his elbows back on the fence, reassured.

Colin and Darren had already been knocked out of the competition early in the day. Colin could run and kick a football well enough, but anything that involved a racket, a bat or a stick stumped him. He stuck with it because his friends were here, and the canteen made good pies. He'd spent most of his time today leaning against the fence behind the baseline, talking sport and gossiping about school. The day before, the school principal had invited the local police to talk to the students about personal safety *in the wake of recent events*. The police officer was old, older than their parents, and he wore short sleeves. His arms were thick and red from the sun. When he spoke, his voice was big and deep, and he addressed them as *ladies and gentlemen*. They should all be aware from media reports by now, he said, that there is a suspected serial sex offender at large in the community. This caused a ripple of comment through the seated school population and he waited for it to pass. The police are doing their best to identify the person responsible for the recent home invasions and sexual assaults, he explained, however everyone must be alert and pay attention to their own personal safety. He paused again while the noise level rose and fell. He said students were to ensure they were home before dark and were not under any circumstances to walk around alone at night or in isolated areas by themselves during the day. They were to lock their doors and windows at all times. Anyone who had concerns about their personal safety should call the police or go to a house or shop displaying the Safety House symbol. At this, a snigger rippled through the seated students. Only losers and grannies had safety houses.

The principal thanked the officer and asked if any students had questions. A dozen hands went into the air. A year ten girl said she'd heard the offender was a truck driver who passed through the town once a week, so why couldn't the police put up roadblocks? The officer replied that he'd heard this rumour and it wasn't true. A boy in year nine said his dad told him that if someone really wants to get into your house, locking the windows won't make any difference. The officer asked the boy which house he would break into if he had a choice – one where he needed to smash the windows or one where he could just slide them open. The boy went red and looked at the ground. The principal said they had time for one more question and pointed to a girl in year eight. She'd heard one of the girls who was raped had satanic symbols painted on the walls of her bedroom. Was that true? The officer said no. The principal thanked the officer for his time and said anyone who was feeling worried or anxious could visit the school counsellor. A curly-haired man in a tweed jacket with leather elbow patches smiled and waved from the side. Some of the boys in Colin's class sniggered again. Most kids thought the school psychologist was only useful for getting out of maths tests.

'Window boy's dad is an idiot,' said Colin as they watched Amy win a rare point.

'Yeah' said Tim. 'I think they moved up here from the city.'

'There you go then.'

'Didn't your parents move here from the city, ranga?' said Darren with an elbow to Colin's side.

Colin elbowed him back, harder, and Darren staggered to the side, laughing and rubbing his arm.

Amy made an accurate return. She'd clawed her way back into the game with a series of rallies that had worn the other girl down. The umpire announced break point. She grimaced at them, nervous, as she returned to the baseline.

'You can do it, Amy,' called a woman's voice.

'Telling us to be home before dark is a bit of overkill, isn't it?' said Darren. 'I mean, it's OK for guys to go out; it's only girls he's interested in, right?'

The other girl fluffed her serve and Amy returned it with ease, pushing it to the opposite corner and out of reach. The boys clapped and she grinned at them on her walk back.

'I don't know. Maybe if you saw him and he thought you could identify him, he'd do you in.'

'He'd have to catch me first.'

Colin looked sideways at Darren. 'Who wanders around in the middle of the night anyway? I'm at home having dinner and doing my homework.'

'Yeah, well not everyone's a nerd like you, Mr Brainiac. Some of us have lives and no-one's going to put a curfew on me.'

Darren walked across to the canteen, an exaggerated swagger in his shoulders. Colin shook his head and looked at Tim, who just shrugged. Darren was manufacturing his outrage, but Colin thought he was right. It did seem over the top to make them all stay home after dark, especially when home was where the attacks had happened. He suspected Darren's parents might feel the same, but Colin knew there wouldn't be any point arguing the toss with his own parents. Whether he wanted to or not, there would be no night-time wandering for him until the guy was found.

Darren returned with three Cokes and three sausage rolls, which he handed out to Colin and Tim. Tim took his inside to get ready for his next game. As Colin watched him walk back across the grass, he saw Rebecca push herself upright and pick up the sausage roll and Coke that had been placed on the ground in front of her. She looked at him and smirked. He blushed, embarrassed for Darren.

'You don't need to feed us, you know,' he said biting into the meat and pastry anyway.

'I know,' Darren shrugged. 'But you're not getting any fatter on ham and salad sandwiches and I'm worried I'm gonna mistake your legs for matchsticks and light a fire with them.'

'Says you, who has to run around in the shower to get wet.'

'Nah, not true, mate. Look at these.' Darren shoved the rest of his sausage roll in his mouth, pulled up his shirt sleeve, and flexed. He was right, his biceps were looking solid.

'Yeah, I'll pay that.'

Darren grinned at him and cracked open his Coke. 'Are you still good for tomorrow?' he asked. The boys had delayed going out in the tinnie until Sunday morning. Darren's dad was going to pull pots off the northern reef and wanted Darren to go out and meet the boat. The boys could come aboard and have crayfish for lunch, he said. Colin had shrugged – everyone had crayfish for lunch, it was like chicken in their town – but it didn't bother him which day they went.

'Yeah, I'm good,' Colin replied. They watched Amy lose her next game and the match, then went to find where Tim was playing.

CHAPTER 9

Sandra

Driving home at the end of her shift, Sandra remembers the Weymouth rapist. The young women were assaulted in their beds over a ten-month period, all by someone who came in through their bedroom windows. The local newspaper ran the story on the front page, and the community locked itself down. Mothers cancelled sleepovers and collected their children from the school gate. Husbands cut sticks of dowelling to place in window runners. Neighbours came out at night with torches when dogs barked. The police took Arthur Zelinski in for questioning.

The worst was probably the first, at least for Darren's year group. Darren, Colin, and Tim had been at a back-to-school party at a friend's house south of town. The parents had cleaned out the garage and set up party lights and a sound system. The kids – a tentative selection of boys in surf brand t-shirts and girls in skater skirts – danced to the Hottest 100 and ate mini pizzas. Sometime around ten pm, the parents opened the garage door to let in the sea breeze and a few kids wandered onto the front lawn to practise flirting in private and semi-darkness. It was about that time someone climbed in through the open window of a house two doors down and raped a sixteen-year-old schoolgirl. By the time Sandra arrived at the scheduled pick-up time of eleven pm, the street was cordoned off and lit up with the flashing lights of patrol cars. The party music was off, and the kids grouped in a miserable huddle under the light of the front porch. The three boys hadn't said a word all the way home.

Sandra hadn't known any of the women and girls who were attacked, although she had heard about their injuries at the hospital. Of course, she hadn't paid the story any more attention after September of that year. Those first weeks, months, are missing from Sandra's memory. They're not missing in the sense that she can't remember what happened. She knows in detail what happened. The search team at the river, the interviews, the newspaper reports, the victim liaison officer who sat with her, the casseroles in her freezer, the arguments after the crime scene officers had left the property. It was busy. She was always doing something, talking to someone, providing information. The murder of a loved one, it seemed, could keep you occupied all day and every day. What is missing from her memories of that time is Sandra's own presence. They are like revisiting a book she once read. She is reminded about what happened, but only as something she was told by someone else, with no direct experience of her own. As she sits on the floor going through her files, she recognises the notes she made, remembers the content, but is surprised she made them. She has no recollection of writing them down. It is the same with the transcripts of her interviews. She recognises the words she spoke but doesn't remember speaking them. She thinks she remembers the interview room. It had green walls, a rectangular table, and four chairs. There was a one-way window in front of her and a security camera on the wall. But she doesn't know if this is a made-up memory, constructed from watching police drama on TV, or her own, real memory of what happened.

After a time, the investigation wound down and along with it went the calls from the newspapers and television producers. Sandra picked up more shifts at the hospital and turned her mind to the task of running a household that had only two adults. She spent less on groceries, learned to use smaller quantities in her cooking, and cleaned the house less often. There were only two loads of washing to do at the end of each week and no school clothes to iron. She no longer hosted sleepovers or spent Saturdays serving at the tennis club canteen. Sandra walked through the paring down of her life in much the same way she walked through the police investigation. She piloted herself through what needed to be done and didn't think too much about it. She guesses another person might think she would have been lonely – it was around that time that Greg left – but she doesn't recall feeling that way. Her nursing friends wanted her to get a dog, she remembers. She'd laughed about that with Barbara over a glass of wine and had been affronted when Barbara acknowledged it might be a good idea.

Sandra is nervous ahead of meeting Keith. She arrives home from work, showers, and then fusses about the house, dusting surfaces that are already clean, rubbing scuff marks off walls that have been there for ten years, and tidying away pots and pans she had left on the kitchen bench between uses. She sees the house through strangers' eyes and understands it has become a single person's home. She has a crocheted rug she puts across her legs when she watches television at night and it lies bundled up at the end of the couch, the only end that is ever used. On the floor is a pair of fluffy green bed slippers and the side table holds an old emery board and a pair of nail scissors. She puts all of them out of sight. At least there is no pile of discarded fingernails.

As she runs a dust cloth needlessly over the bathroom taps, she looks up at herself in the mirror. She turned forty-nine this year and she can see a sunspot on her right cheek bone she knows is invisible to everyone else but will darken in the next few years and be joined by others in time. They will be her testaments to a beachside childhood before the era of ozone layers and daily sunscreen. Her hair is the same colour it was on her wedding day, thanks to Teresa, her primary school best friend and forever hairdresser. She charges too much, but she is good at what she does and is discrete with her gossip. Sandra looks closer at the mirror. She will need to make another appointment soon. She hears tyres on the gravel outside the house and goes back downstairs to put the kettle on.

Fifteen minutes later, Keith sits on the same end of the couch he sat on five days ago. He leans his elbows on his knees and cups the tea in both hands.

'This is a nice place.'

Sandra is disappointed in him. It is a predictable opening line, one used by every police officer who has been here. It is an opener to asking about Greg's business, the current state of the fishing industry, and where the money comes from. Next, he'll be asking if Greg had any enemies who might want to hurt him.

'Yes, it is.' She figures she might as well play along.

'Nice to be near the beach,' he observes, turning his head to look out the kitchen window. She knows he can only see the sky from where he is sitting.

'Everywhere is near the beach in this town.'

She sees him wince at her tone. That was unnecessary, she tells herself. Be nice, he's only trying to help.

'But, yes, it is great to see the ocean from upstairs and walk to the water every day,' she adds.

'I suppose Darren and his mates spent a lot of time down there.'

'They did,' she acknowledges. 'On the beach, up the river, out on the water.'

'He surfed?'

'Yes, they all did. And he had the tinnie. He used to run about in the bay with his best friend on weekends.'

'That would be Colin Russell?'

'That's right. Barbara's son,' she adds, so he doesn't have to say it.

'Where's he now?'

'The city. He did a business degree and works as a financial planner. His wife is expecting their first baby.'

'You keep in touch then?'

'Barbara and I were best friends, she filled me in on how the kids were going.' Sandra hasn't seen Colin for five years, though. Not since the investigation was reopened back then.

'They've got an older daughter. Rebecca?'

'That's right. She works in the pharmacy on the main street. I see her when I go in there.'

Sandra has had enough of small talk and puts her cup down on the coffee table. Keith takes the hint.

'So, I've made a start on the case files. There's not much about Barbara other than recording she was Colin's mum. The investigating team obviously wasn't too interested in her; I guess they had other suspects to focus on.'

'Arthur Zelinski,' Sandra says, the tone reappearing in her voice. 'He was hauled in every time something happened around here.'

'You never thought he did it?'

'No. He's the local homeless guy, and through no fault of his own. He had an orchard on the Wey Valley road. One night – Darren would have been about ten – the whole place burned down, the house, the trees, everything. Arthur was lucky he wasn't inside at the time. He'd been drinking in the backyard. Police said he must have dropped a cigarette when he went inside to pee. Or something.'

'I remember it. Arson was ruled out.'

'Arthur was odd, even back then. Kids would make fun of his accent and his clothes behind his back, but people liked him. He helped old ladies across the street. You'd have had a hard time finding someone who would want to hurt him. He died not long after Darren.'

'The case file says he lived in a cave by the river.'

Sandra laughs. 'He drank in a cave by the river. I doubt it's even a cave, probably just a hollow in the limestone cliff. I've never seen it but it's just across the road from here if you want to go and look. The nuns let him sleep on their veranda until Barbara got him assessed for a nursing home bed. After that, he slept there on a mattress, on a bed, in a room. She was a good person. Always looking out for the lost.'

Keith takes in her comment silently. He looks toward the shed. 'Can I have a look?'

'Sure, but there's less now to see than when you lot looked last time.'

They cross the yard and Sandra rolls back the shed door. They stand in the open doorway, contemplating the space once filled with iceboxes, floats, ropes and stacks of pots. The detritus of the commercial crayfish industry.

'You were, what, twenty-one when you got married, right?' The question comes out of the blue and Sandra looks up at the spider webs in the corner. There will be redbacks in there, she thinks. She hasn't sprayed in years.

'You've done your homework,' she acknowledges. He doesn't reply, so she explains herself. 'Greg and I were together since we were sixteen.'

Keith looks at her.

'Yes, even when I went away to nursing school. He'd come to Perth each year when the season finished.'

'He worked on his dad's boat, right?' Keith narrows his eyes, remembering. 'I heard his old man gave him his own boat when you guys got married.'

Sandra nods. Greg had left school as soon as he was legally able and worked as a deckhand for his father. He got his skipper's ticket and when they got married, his parents gave him a boat and one hundred licensed pots. The licences weren't worth much back then, but the co-op became a publicly listed company two years later, sending the price skywards and lining the pockets of the local fishermen. It meant they could sell a few pots and build this house the year Sandra came back from university and started working at the hospital. She watches

Keith nod to himself slowly as he works it out. To his credit, he doesn't comment. Some people get snarky about what they think is easy money.

'You guys got married at the cathedral,' he says instead. 'I remember seeing the photo in the paper.'

'That's right, but I think the photo you saw was the one in the case file,' she corrects him. 'Greg was a suspect for a while.'

Keith ignores the invitation to talk about her ex-husband being a suspect. He wanders into the shed and pulls up the corner of a vehicle-shaped tarpaulin. 'You've still got the Torana here?'

Sandra just shrugs. Greg bought the car for Darren. He was going to give it to him when he got his licence. They'd been restoring the engine together.

'We used to stand around it at those barbeques you guys used to have,' says Keith, 'adjusting the carburettor and giving Greg useless advice.'

That would be right, Sandra thinks. Greg's barbeques were legendary. Everyone was invited, local police, fisheries inspectors, deckhands, their bank manager. Greg would light the fire and throw on a few crayfish from the boat, a farmer would bring an esky-load of chops, the old bathtub on the lawn would fill with beer, and later in the night a cop would pass around a joint from a bag of confiscated weed. Darren would drink too much Coke and play basketball on the driveway until he collapsed in a wired, cranky mess on the couch. The barbeques stopped after he died.

'You kept working when Darren came along,' says Keith. 'I wouldn't have thought you needed to do that.'

Sandra feels herself bristle. It wasn't anyone's business whether she needed or wanted to work, but the world seems to own your life choices when you're a working mother.

'I enjoy my work,' she replies, which is true. She did need to work, though, especially in the early days when there wasn't much coming in from the boat. Being debt-free is only one part of the household-finance equation; they still had bills to pay and a life to live. By the time the boat came good and Greg started making real money, she was part of the hospital, and couldn't see how she would spend her days if she wasn't on the wards.

'You know, they interviewed Barbara back then,' says Keith.

Like the question about Sandra's age, this one also comes out of nowhere, but Sandra had figured he would get to it eventually.

'She said she was working at the nursing home that day,' he says. 'The director of nursing confirmed it. That means she was eight hundred metres at most from the scene.'

Sandra sighs. She has told this story over and over. 'That's right. She was visiting Arthur. He'd just been admitted. I saw her there myself.'

'And why were you there?'

'Well if you'd read the file, you'd know I'd just come off shift at the hospital and I was visiting Arthur as well.' She's over this now and wants him to leave.

'Hey,' he held his hands in the air, palms front, 'I'm just double-checking. It's what I'm paid to do.'

Sandra deflates. 'Yes, I know. Sorry. It can be frustrating sometimes.'

'Yeah, I get that. It must be hard for you.' He smiles down at her and she can see he is genuine in his concern. 'So, she was still there when you left the nursing home and went for a walk down by the river.'

Sandra should have expected these questions and checked her notes before he arrived. She pauses before she replies.

'Yes.' She can see Keith has noticed her hesitation and is not surprised when he starts to dig.

'Do you usually go walking after work? I would have thought, being on your feet all day, you'd be glad to get off them.'

She gives him a look she hopes tells him he is welcome to leave any time now.

'Yes, I do, Keith, and I'd just visited a friend who was dying. Nature can be a good antidote.'

CHAPTER 10

Colin
Twenty-one days before Darren dies

The alarm went off before dawn and Colin considered bailing out. People had been up, walking around, in the middle of the night and although his room was at the far end of the house he still woke at the noise. He remembered his dad coming in to check on him and telling him to go back to sleep. Whatever. Night-time activity had become common in his house after Rebecca left school. It seemed to Colin she conducted her social life after midnight. He didn't know how she managed it as well as hold down a job, but he did know it pissed his parents off. He sat up and contemplated his feet at the other end of the bed, sticking out from under the sheets that he kicked off in the night. They flexed at him and he swung them off the bed and into his thongs. He pulled on boardshorts and a t-shirt and, as an afterthought, a jumper as well. Leaving his bed unmade, he rummaged through the fridge, let himself out of the front door and walked toward the end of the road and the sandbar.

Darren was pulling the tinnie across the sand by the time Colin made it to the other end. He helped him drag it into the water and they rowed out across the reef before lowering the outboard and pointing the boat north. Darren's face was pale, with dark rings under his eyes, and he smelled like he hadn't slept.

'You look like rubbish,' Colin observed.

'Yeah, I'm not a morning person.' Darren nodded at Colin's bag. 'Did you bring anything to eat?'

Colin pulled out a Tupperware container with the previous night's leftover roast chicken and half a loaf of bread. He tore a thigh off the carcass and passed it to Darren, who sucked the meat off the bone.

'Fuck I'm starved.' He tossed the bone into the sea and, one handed, opened the plastic bread wrapper, pulled out two slices and stuffed them into his mouth.

'No food at your place then?'

Darren looked cagey. 'No. Well, I might not have gone home last night.'

'What do you mean, *might not*?'

'I might have slept in the cave.'

'Bullshit.'

'Nah, no bullshit, it was cool. I took Dad's old swag. Mr Arthur was there. He had a fire and told me all about fishing in the river. He said you can get a good feed of bream and even big mulloway when the river mouth is open. He said he'll take me one day, and we'll cook it on the fire. You should come too.'

Colin didn't believe him. Darren could be a bit too eager to impress sometimes. Maybe he went to the cave last night, maybe he didn't. Maybe he did make a fire, maybe he did talk fishing with Mr Arthur once – Mr Arthur would talk your ear off if you let him – but Colin couldn't see him staying out the whole night. Darren was reckless, but he wasn't that brave. Sitting in the prow of the tinnie, facing back the way they came, and watching Darren steer the boat over the reef, it occurred to Colin that it had been a while since Darren had done anything seriously stupid. At primary school, he was famous for climbing onto the school roof and refusing to come down if he got into trouble in class, and two years ago he'd been lucky to get away with just a broken arm trying to walk across the Wey Bridge on the handrail. He'd fallen in, of course, and missed cracking his head open on the rocks by centimetres. That was back when Rebecca was still at school and consented to hang out with them at the river. She'd been there that day and had bound Darren's arm to his chest while Colin ran home to get his mum.

Darren turned the boat west and soon Colin could see a line of orange-and-yellow floats in the water. Mr Davies' bigger boat had been cutting fast across the bay, leaving a white wake behind it, and was now pulling up as it approached the end of the line. Colin could see the deckhands preparing to haul the first pot out of the water. Darren manoeuvred the tinnie alongside and they both climbed on deck, the working men reaching down to help them up. Darren's dad came out of the wheelhouse, his eyes squinting against the glare, and shook Colin's hand. He was tanned from working on the boat, his blonde curls made pale and coiled by the sun and the salt.

'Welcome aboard, son. This your first time on a cray boat?'

'Yes, Mr Davies.'

'I hope you've got sea legs. No chundering on deck; if you have to throw up, do it over the side.' He smiled and the deckhands laughed. 'And you fellas look after him. He could teach you some valuable manners. It's *Mr Davies* from now on. Got it?'

They all laughed again. Colin grinned back at him. He didn't get seasick and knew he was lucky for it. He had been to Rottnest on the ferry once and his dad had spent the second part of the trip throwing up off the back of the boat. His mum had refused to go with them. The island had a bad history, she said. It wasn't right to go there for sightseeing. She'd stayed back in Fremantle and gone shopping with Rebecca instead.

'Darren tells me you're going to leave us next year. He said you got a scholarship to some fancy school in the city,' said Darren's dad, passing him a can of lemonade. Colin juggled the can in his hands as his fingers at once began to ache against the too-cold aluminium.

'That's right, Mr Davies. I'll be boarding during school term. Coming home in the holidays.'

'I suppose you'll go to university afterwards. People say you're smart enough. Sandra reckons you want to be an engineer, is that right?'

'Yes, Mr Davies, I want to build boats.'

'Working boats, I hope; not those floating mansions for rich toffs.'

'Oil tankers.'

'Good for you.' The older man passed him a paper plate with two whole boiled crayfish and nodded toward an esky. 'You know what to do with these don't you? There's bread and butter and salt and pepper in the esky. Throw the scraps overboard.'

Colin and Darren sat on the side of the boat and ate their crayfish sandwiches, squinting back at the coastline. The flat-topped hills behind the town were still green from the winter. In less than a month, they would be drying off, turning brown and raising dust in the wind. A plane approached from the south, dropping over the suburbs, and disappearing into the flat paddocks between the town and the hills.

'It'll be hot out at the airport today,' observed Darren's dad behind him, making him jump. He didn't hear him come up behind them. 'The sea breeze isn't expected in until late afternoon.'

'It'll be a howler when it does,' said one of the deckhands from the back of the boat.

'Well you'd better move your arse and get those pots up then,' replied Mr Davies, 'or you'll be chucking your guts up all the way to the wharf like you did last week.'

The deckhand blushed and glanced at the boys, embarrassed to be called out in front of kids. Mr Davies grinned.

'It's alright son, it happens to all of us when we start off. It's lucky I bought you some lemonade too, eh?'

Colin and Darren downed the last of their sandwiches, threw the carcasses overboard and put their rubbish in the bin. Darren stripped off his shirt and edged his way around to the back of the boat, where he leapt over the side, tucking his feet to his chest and hitting the water hard. He came back up calling Colin to join him. Colin wasn't so sure. He wondered how deep it was below the boat and what else lived there that might be scavenging for crayfish carcasses. He looked past Darren at the dark blue ocean and the white sand dunes along the bay shore. There was a lot of water between him and the beach.

'Go on son,' said Darren's dad, 'nothing out here is interested in having you for lunch. And we won't leave you behind.'

Colin looked back over his shoulder at the older man, his feet planted wide as he coiled rope. He was shirtless under the sun and his pale blue eyes were unreadable as he watched him hesitate. Colin stripped his shirt off, closed his eyes and jumped.

The water was colder than he expected, much colder than at the beach, and it pushed him from side to side, ceaseless. When he opened his eyes, the side of the boat rose high and seemingly motionless above him. There would be no way he could get back up there without a rope or a ladder. He couldn't see Darren and he felt his chest tighten. The chop of the waves was higher than it looked from the deck and he had to work hard to lift his head to look around for his friend. When he spotted him, Darren had already made it to the front of the boat and was circling around to the other side, leaving Colin alone in the water between the boat and the horizon. Panicked, he swam after him, keeping his head out of the water.

'Hey, wait up!'

Colin was the stronger swimmer, despite what Amy said, and caught up with Darren on the shore side of the boat. Here, where he could see the coast again, he felt his chest loosen.

'How's your trousers?' taunted Darren, smacking water up into his face. 'Do you need some of Mr Johnson's bog roll for your bum?'

Colin grabbed his wrist. 'Give me your hand and you can wipe it for me.'

He kicked to lift himself out of the water and used his other hand to push Darren's head under the surface. He let go and swam hard to the back of the boat before he came up for air, Darren chasing after him. They climbed back onto the deck, both laughing with the relief of being out of the water.

When it was time for the boat to move on, they went inside to change out of their wet gear. The sea breeze had come in, making their skin pucker with goosebumps, and the swell picked up. The boat was beginning to roll from side to side. Colin stood on the deck with his face to the wind, waiting for Darren who was still down below with his dad, wondering if he'd ever stand like this on a boat that he'd built himself. Maybe doing engine trials off Fremantle, sailing past Rottnest, or even the Middle East. It would be cool to sail through the Suez Canal on an oil tanker. He imagined himself standing in the wheelhouse, looking out across the Sinai Desert on one side and the irrigated crops on the other.

Mr Davies came back up on deck and walked over to him.

'Looks like the sea suits you, son. Maybe you should build yourself a cray boat and come fishing.'

'I dunno, Mr Davies,' he replied. 'It seems like too much hard work. Mum says I'm not good at getting up early.'

'Never mind what your mum says, nothing's hard work when you love doing it.' The older man shook his hand again and dropped the other, heavy, on Colin's shoulder. 'Thanks for coming out. Make sure you remember who fed you fresh crays when you're rubbing shoulders with the rich city folk.'

Darren came back up on deck with a sports bag holding their clothes. His dad took it from him while they climbed back down to the tinnie, then passed it across.

'Remember what I told you, straight home. Don't get that bag wet.'

They did as they were told and turned the tinnie for the river mouth, silent as they headed across the waves. Colin was tired now, worn out by the sun and the salt water. Two dolphins breached in front of the bow and neither of them commented. He wished they'd brought an extra water bottle. They approached the reef and Darren navigated them through the gap and surfed the boat back to the shore, raising the motor. Colin jumped out too early, found himself in chest height water, and struggled to pull the boat in. Darren joined him and together they dragged it high onto the sandbar and flipped it over. Colin helped him strap the outboard onto the brick trolley he used to cart it to and from the beach. They said their goodbyes – they'd both be at the bus stop tomorrow morning – and Colin trudged back across the sandbar. He was sunburnt and thirsty and the sand was soft. All he wanted to do when he got home was shower and sleep. He hoped there was enough milk in the fridge for Milo. He squinted against the sun. A police car was parked in front of the house and his dad was talking to the officer outside the front door.

CHAPTER 11

Sandra

After Keith leaves, Sandra takes her own advice and laces up her sneakers and heads for the river. Pocketing her keys and mobile phone, she walks east toward the bridge, high above the water. On the south bank, the nursing home is the biggest building between the bridge and the beach. The white figure of the Virgin Mary faces the river, holding her arms out to visitors as they make their way to the entrance beneath her cupola. Her features are indistinct from this side of the river, but the familiar figure is recognisable, serene-cheeked and eyes downcast. Sandra is reassured by her presence and she fingers the pearl crucifix hanging around her neck. To the Virgin's left and right, Spanish arches in groups of three line the upper-floor facade. There is no seeing into the deep, shaded balcony behind them; the orange sandstone has been cut thick and the walls keep the rooms cool even in late summer.

As she walks, Sandra sees a figure in red round the corner of the building and cross the gardens. It looks like a woman. She opens the gate to the paddock between the nursing home and the river and starts down the track toward the cliffs in long, even strides. Sandra knows the track takes you to the riverbank and the path she herself will walk this afternoon under the trees and toward the beach. It is a popular walk. Like Sandra, the woman has the hood of her jacket up and she soon disappears as the track approaches the tree line. Sandra adjusts her own hood against the wind and veers to the right, leaving the side of the road and crossing the river reserve toward the bridge.

She is still annoyed at Keith's questions. The pursuit of unlikely suspects frustrated her ten years ago and she doesn't want to rehash pointless inquiries again. Arthur, Greg, and now Barbara. The evidence against them was circumstantial and they all had alibis for the time of the shooting. Being the father, Greg had been a suspect from the start. Sandra thought that was lazy; an obvious target for an investigation team that couldn't think of a motive apart from parental abuse. He'd been on the boat, with the crew, all day and they'd come into port an hour before the shooting. People had seen them. Then they'd unloaded the catch. It annoyed her that, despite the lack of evidence, despite searching her house and finding nothing, Greg had stayed in the investigating team's top three persons of interest until they were disbanded. She wonders if it is the same with all child killings: keep the father in the frame even if you can't think of a reason, until the real perpetrator is found.

Sandra crosses the bridge and walks down the embankment on the south side. The flat rocks are dry in the sun and the rope swing is tucked into the lower branches of the tree. The woman in the red jacket passes below her, heading under the bridge and upriver. She raises her arm in greeting without breaking stride. She looks familiar but Sandra can't place her. Perhaps someone from the hospital or an old school mum. Sandra is used to being bypassed. She knows people find it odd that she walks here. It seems the general community expects her to avoid the place. She doesn't know whether that is because she is supposed to be too traumatised to come here or they think she is uncaring, too hard. She suspects the way she conducts her grief has been judged and found wanting. She returned to work too soon. She paid too much attention to her appearance. She let herself go. She didn't look after her husband's grief. She didn't return all the casserole dishes. This last one is true; she returned most of them, but she still has one or two in her kitchen for want of an owner to come and claim them. People generally don't write their names on the bottom of their bakeware.

Sandra follows the trail through the trees, running her hands through the she-oak needles that overhang the path, and passes the track that branches off to the left and up the cliffs to the nursing home. She sees it is washed out from the recent rain and looks unstable. There are fresh marks in the dirt where someone, probably the woman in red, has slid on their heels. She continues along the riverbank, eventually emerging into the stretch of marshland before reaching the sandbar. There is still a narrow channel of water to the sea and a woman in her late twenties is sitting on the sand watching her daughter play in the shallow stream. She looks up as Sandra approaches, then stands, her arms opening as she recognises her. Sandra pauses for a moment, taking in the solemn face, then crosses the water. They embrace, close and silent, breathing quietly. When they pull apart, there are tears in the younger woman's eyes.

'I wasn't going to call you yet,' she says, wiping her face on a cuff. 'I thought I'd give it some time.'

'Me too.'

'Maybe we were just meant to meet like this.' Her face holds a youthful wish to believe in fate.

Sandra nods, her throat too tight to let out more words. The sudden emotion is unexpected, and she is embarrassed to find herself blinking away her own tears. They both fold their legs and sit on the sand.

'Jessica, not too close to the sea, OK?'

The child looks up, noticing Sandra for the first time, and waves. She runs to them, short legs working hard in the soft sand.

'I've got a stick, Auntie Sandra. Look.' She holds it out for inspection then carries the stick to the river side of the sand bar and drops it in the water. It floats on the current down to the sea. Laughing, she chases it and picks it up before it reaches the waves and looks back for acknowledgement. Sandra claps then takes the younger woman's hand while Jessica runs back to the river to repeat the trick.

'How are you doing, Rebecca?' she asks. She looks into her eyes, searching her face. Rebecca's chest falls as she exhales, and she looks at her lap.

'Truthfully? I don't know.' She fidgets with her scarf and Sandra waits. 'It's hard enough having her gone, but to think she might have been the one who, you know, I just can't deal with it.' Sandra gives her hand a squeeze as her tears start.

'I thought we'd had our tough times,' she said, looking back up at Sandra's face. 'After all we went through; the lies I told; Darren; Sam. I really thought there were no sad things left for us. And now this.' She frowns. 'Do you really think she could have done it? I know Mum was good at keeping secrets, but to cover up something like that for all this time ...'

Sandra shakes her head. 'It's one thing to keep your identity from your family, but that doesn't mean you've concealed a murder.'

'Did you know?' Rebecca asks. 'Did you know Mum was adopted?'

Sandra thinks about this. She knows Barbara was not going to tell

Rebecca and Colin the full story until she returned from the Pilbara. She wanted something to give them. Names and photos. Sandra doesn't know how much Stuart knows either and how much of the story has now been lost with Barbara's death. She might know more when the agency calls her back.

'I knew she didn't grow up with her birth mother and father,' she says to Rebecca. 'And I know she wanted to find them. But I don't know any more than that.'

Rebecca nods, accepting. 'Will you help me find out?'

'Of course, I will, love. Of course.'

By the time Sandra gets back home, the sun has dropped below the waves and she can feel the arrival of the night-time air. She puts water in a saucepan for rice and lights the stove. Yesterday she bought vegetables and chicken to make a stir fry and she takes these out of the fridge and starts chopping. Halfway through, she goes back to the fridge and pours herself a glass of white wine before returning to the chopping board. She worries about Rebecca. Pretty and socially adept as a toddler, much like little Jessica is now, she had struggled at school and the knock to her confidence had turned her inwards. Barbara would despair at her daughter's lack of enthusiasm for movie nights or sleepovers with friends. At least she had an interest in sport – the mainstay of social life in the town – and during netball season spent most of her Saturdays at the courts, playing and umpiring. When Rebecca started high school she discovered a cohort of girls who didn't care about her grades, but with them she also learned how to sneer at other social conventions, like wearing the school uniform, coming home on time, and not speaking back to her parents. Again, Barbara had despaired, not knowing how to mother an angry teenage girl. Sandra remembered her own mother had simply ignored her when she acted up, and this is what she counselled her friend. It had worked, but only up to a point, she thinks, her lips tightening in dismay. She wonders if things would have been different if she'd counselled otherwise.

Sandra pours another glass of wine and takes the glass and her meal upstairs, where she sits on the floor next to her papers. She gathers the bundle marked *Greg* into her lap and pulls off the bulldog clip holding them together. The first pages are her notes on Greg's testimony, given at the inquest. They confirm what she remembers. He'd left the house before dawn that day, driven to the wharf and left the harbour at, he thinks, five am. They'd checked pots off the point, at the reef out from the river mouth, and north of the bay. No-one had left or come onto the boat during that time. They'd docked back at the wharf at two thirty pm. Sandra had made a note here in the margin that Rochelle Patten had seen the *Reef Walker* from her window in the Port Authority tower and confirmed Greg was onboard and had stayed on the wharf to unload the catch. The ambulance was called to the river at three thirty-five pm so, assuming a delay of five minutes between the gunshot and the call, Greg would have had an hour to get to the river after docking. Technically, it was possible. Weymouth was a small town and at that time of day you could drive from the fishing boat wharf to the bridge in twenty minutes. But no-one saw Greg's car at the river that afternoon, he had no motive, and he would have needed to unload and register the catch and hose down the boat. It couldn't happen.

Sandra takes another mouthful of wine and flips through the papers. At the back of the bundle is a photo of Darren as a toddler. He is at the sandbar, where Jessica was playing this afternoon, standing with his skinny legs in the water. It was his first time. She remembers the shock on his face, his narrow eyes widening as he felt the sand on his bare feet. He'd held her hand and looked at her for reassurance while he bent down to touch it, his fingers sinking in. Of course, he'd brought it to his mouth. He cried when she laughed at his reaction, spitting out the grains and rubbing his face against her t-shirt. To distract him, she'd taken him over the sandbar to the river side, where the water was flat and warm. This he also approached with suspicion. He investigated, his grip still tight around her finger, and gasped when a tiny wave – a ripple, really – brushed his toes. She smiled her encouragement when he looked up at her, checking, and was rewarded when he lifted one small foot and stamped it into the water. He laughed out loud and did it again, then let go of her hand and ran into the river, where he fell over and she had to lift him upright while he spluttered, his thin arms outstretched and clawing for her to pick him up.

CHAPTER 12

Colin

Twenty-one days before Darren dies

Colin's dad and the police officer turned to watch him as he walked toward them. Whatever Darren did last night, he wanted to tell them, I wasn't part of it. He was hot and sweating by the time he got to the front door and he knew his face would be red.

'Hi Dad.' He stopped. It seemed like the right thing to do. 'What's up?'

'Granny went for a bit of a walk this morning,' his dad replied. 'The police brought her home.'

'Oh.' He could feel his relief on his face and blushed again.

'She's a tough old girl, your gran,' the police officer said, squinting at him.

'Where'd she go?' Colin perked up once he knew the officer was not about to throw him in a cell and interrogate him.

'Down to the river, under the bridge. She said she was going to the bank; said she needed to withdraw some money for dinner tonight.' He looked at Colin and smirked. Colin figured he didn't know much about old people.

Stuart's dad explained. Colin could hear his patient voice. 'Sometimes she tries to pay the staff at the nursing home. She thinks she's at a restaurant.'

'She must be getting some decent food then,' the officer replied, still looking at Colin. 'I might have to book a table one evening myself.'

He doesn't get it, Colin thought.

Colin felt his dad's hand cup his shoulder. He knew what that meant. *Let it go. Not everyone understands.*

The police officer shook Colin's dad's hand, taking his leave, and then offered his hand to Colin.

'I hear you and Darren Davies have been out on the water this morning.'

'Yeah, we went up to North Point.'

'Did you meet the boat; have some crays for lunch?'

'Yeah,' Colin nodded, enthusiastic now remembering his morning and his feat in circumnavigating the boat in the open water. 'And we went swimming off the back.'

'Nice. I hope you didn't bring any undersized ones back with you.'

'Nah, just a bag of Darren's dad's stuff. Oh shit.' He looked up at his dad. 'I left my clothes in the bag. Darren's got them.'

'It's alright son, we'll go around there later and get them.'

'Darren's dad said I should build cray boats instead of oil tankers,' he told them. 'He said then I could go fishing in my own boat.'

The two men smiled at each other, the indulgent smile adults use when they think their kids are being stupid, but cute. He was used to it.

'I think there might be more money in oil than crayfish, Colin.'

'Mr Davies is rich, though, isn't he?' he asked his dad. 'He's got two boats and Darren said he'll help him out to buy his own when he gets his skipper's ticket.' He watched the two men exchange glances.

'Well, all I know is I'm not one of the rich ones,' said the officer, looking back up the road toward the sandbar. 'I've got to go. You look after your granny, son.'

He took his leave for the second time and they watched him do a U-turn in the road and drive away. Inside the house, Colin found his mum in the kitchen taking a tray of scones out of the oven. She was barefoot, her feet and ankles tanned and skinny, and wearing her usual loose layers, the yellow swirls covered in flour. Her red hair had a streak of white where she had tucked a strand back in with dough-covered hands. She'd always been a messy cook. She leaned over the tray and kissed him as he walked past to the fridge and he reached across to pick the dough out of her hair. Colin had his mum's hair, red, thick, and curly. She wore hers long and fastened with a clip at the back of her head. He needed his cut every month to avoid becoming the only red-haired afro teenager in town. He'd inherited his dad's white skin though, which wasn't fair because Rebecca's is dark, and she doesn't burn in the sun. Like Darren, he gets sunburnt from thinking about going outside.

'Hi bub, how was the boat?' his mum asked, wrapping the scones in a tea towel. 'Did you have fun?'

'It was good. We saw dolphins in the bay.'

'That's a good sign. Did you get a feed of crays?'

'Yeah, Darren's dad cooked them on the boat, and we had them on bread.'

She studied his face and ran her floury hands up and down his arms. 'You're not too burnt, that's good. No more sun for the rest of the weekend, though. OK?'

'Yes, Mum.'

He filled a tall glass with milk and dropped in tablespoons of Milo, which floated on the surface. He stirred it slowly until he reached the perfect ratio of dissolved to floating grains and scooped the sludge from the top into his mouth.

'When you're done there, you can take these scones down to your sister. She's in the games room with her friends.'

'Where's mine?'

'Right under your nose. Nice and hot.' She tapped the plate she'd slid across to him while he was concentrating on his Milo and then leaned over to kiss him on the forehead. He leaned his head out of range, a smile on his face, and she grabbed him, laughing, and pulled him in close. He tried to push her away, but she was strong, his mum, and locked him tight to her breast, rocking them both from side to side. Her ankles were skinny, but under her tunic her torso was broad and deep. She still outweighed him.

'Don't try to fight it, my son,' she chided. 'You know your mum can out-wrestle you.'

Colin wriggled his arms up between them and used his elbows to push her arms apart. He broke free, puffing from exertion and laughter.

'Not for long you can't. I'll always get away.' He put his fists up and shadow-boxed at her while she made a show of trying to grab his wrists.

'Only if I let you.'

Colin took his scones and Milo to the kitchen table. He wasn't in a hurry to go downstairs to Rebecca and her friends. Rebecca was two years older than Colin and studying to become a pharmacy assistant at TAFE. She was alright on her own, still happy to hang out and play board games and eat pizza, but when she was with her friends she could be evil. He could hear from their voices that Melissa and

Lauren were here. Rebecca could be especially nasty when Melissa was around. Melissa would say something mean about her own brothers and sister – she had three and she was the oldest – and Rebecca would have to match it. And she couldn't be trusted with secrets anymore. At the tennis club last year, Melissa had come to the fence where Colin and Darren were watching Tim and Amy lose a mixed doubles game. She was wearing a tartan skater-girl skirt and a white crop top. It was an outfit all the girls copied, even Amy, and left Colin not knowing where to look. He resorted to staring at a point in the middle distance when they talked to him, bobbing their heads from side to side to catch his eye. Rebecca and Lauren trailed behind her. Melissa had looked backwards and forwards between Colin and Amy and sighed, her crop top wobbling as she pushed the breath out.

'Why don't you just ask her out, Colin?'

'What? Who?' Colin asked, although he knew what she meant. He'd flushed, feeling the heat in his forehead, and continued looking across the fence at the game.

'We all know, Colin,' she put her hand on his arm, a maternal gesture that didn't match her tone. 'Rebecca told us.'

'Just go away, Melissa.' He shook her hand off.

'Well I think it's sweet. Two nerds in love.' She put her hand back.

Darren, who had been fidgeting next to him, snapped.

'He said go away, Melissa. Just fuck off.'

'I wasn't talking to you, you little freak.' She stepped into him, the crop top alarmingly at face height. She was taller, and Colin guessed probably heavier, than both of them. Rebecca was behind her, two frown lines visible over the top of her sunglasses. Darren stepped forward so they were toe to toe, his chin raised.

'Yeah, well I'm talking to you, you fat cow, and I said fuck off.' He planted his hands on her shoulders and shoved her backwards, making her stagger into Rebecca, who took her weight and set her upright.

'You'll pay for that, freak,' she spat back at him. 'That's assault.'

'Hey Melissa, let's go,' said Rebecca, steering her away. 'He's not worth it.' She pulled a face at Colin as they marched off and he flipped her the bird. That evening, she'd made popcorn and the two of them watched *Mission: Impossible* on video beneath a rug on the couch. He figured it was some sort of apology.

Colin finished his scones and took the plate back into the kitchen where his mum was cleaning up.

'How's Granny? Dad said she'd wandered off.'

'She's fine,' his mum replied. 'She thought she needed money again.'

'Can't they stop her from leaving? What if something happened to her down at the river? Wouldn't they be responsible?'

His mum turned from the sink and wiped her hands dry with a tea-towel.

'They can, but it means moving her to the dementia ward where they lock them in. Dad's not real keen on it.'

'Why not? It means she'll be safe.'

Colin's mum pressed her lips together. He knew what that meant. Mum and dad didn't agree. Colin's parents didn't discuss their differences in front of their children and always presented a united front. There was no point trying to divide and conquer. Colin suspected this was mum's doing – part of the whole social worker training thing – but he could tell when they didn't agree on something. Pressed lips also meant the subject was not open for discussion. He picked up the plate of scones and took it downstairs.

Colin's parents' house was built on a block that sloped down from the road toward the beach. From the street it looked like a single-storey bungalow but the bottom floor, which was dedicated to a games room and his dad's workshop, was hidden from view and only became apparent from inside when you saw the stairs sinking below the floor. The upstairs was a large open-plan kitchen and living area with views out to the ocean between the trees. From the kitchen table, you could see all the way to the river reserve at the north end of the street and out into the bay. The bedrooms were on the south side, down a hallway that separated his and Rebecca's rooms from his parents. Colin's room faced the street. It was the biggest and used to be Rebecca's, but when she found out that Melissa had a sea view, she'd pleaded with him to swap, offering to do his chores for the rest of the year. That had lasted a month, Rebecca claiming that she'd never commit to something so ridiculous.

Downstairs, the games room opened onto the backyard and had hosted Colin's and Rebecca's birthday parties over the years. Childhood photos lined the face-brick walls and a cabinet against the far wall displayed their dad's gun club trophies. Colin dragged his feet down the steps. He could hear Melissa's voice in the room below.

'He is so into you.'

'It's kind of embarrassing,' he heard Rebecca reply.

'No, I think it's sweet. I bet you could get him to do anything for you.'

'He could be your own personal slave,' said Lauren. 'Please, Rebecca, let me carry your bag! Or he could prank that teacher who failed you in English. Graffiti her letterbox.'

'He is cute though,' said Melissa, 'like an elf with his pointy chin and button nose.'

'Yeah, I suppose,' his sister said, 'but in the way your little brother's best friend is cute.' They all laugh. 'Ugly, but interesting!'

Colin stumbled on the stairs and they heard him.

'Colin, is that you?' Rebecca called out. 'Were you listening to us?'

Rebecca appeared at the bottom of the stairs. She wore her favourite pink track pants and a surf brand t-shirt, her hair piled on top of her head in a messy red jumble.

'Oh my God, you were, you were eavesdropping. Mum! Make Colin go away.'

She put out her hands for the plate and crossed her eyes at him. Relieved he didn't have to enter the room, he passed them to her and fled.

CHAPTER 13

Sandra

It is Saturday afternoon and Sandra is at the Town Beach Hotel with two colleagues from the hospital. They have known each other since high school, the same high school their children went on to attend. Sharon's and Nat's girls were older than Darren, of course – it took longer to adopt a child than it did to get pregnant – and they'd both given birth to two more. Sandra had envied them with their households full of kid things. She'd have liked a girl as well. She'd heard so many stories about couples adopting and then a miracle baby appearing. That was never going to happen for her and Greg, of course. These days, she got her girlchild-fix from Jessica. Barbara was happy to share. *A kid can't have too many grandmothers*, she'd always said.

Sandra, Sharon and Nat had all gone on from high school to study nursing in the city, living in the university colleges for a year before moving into a share house together. It was a dive. A 1930s bungalow two blocks back from the campus with an outdoor dunny and a cracked green Art Deco hand basin in the bathroom. In the kitchen, the stove-top oven was wedged into the old fireplace, which threw down soot when the wind blew from the north. The owner, a biology professor from the university who was on sabbatical in the United States, had locked his own furniture in the garage so they made do with parking on the front lawn. Sandra chose the sleepout as her bedroom for the privilege of paying less than the others. The old veranda boards sagged under the swirling red-and-brown carpet and the thin cladding failed to keep out the cold in winter and the heat in summer. She slept on a second-hand futon mattress held off the floor by planks of wood on bricks. They'd pinned a cooking roster to the fridge, studied, partied, done their prac, and then all of them came back to the local hospital and married local boys. Sometimes, when they are on shift together, picking gravel out of the legs of another farmer's son who had fallen off the back of a work ute, they look at each other and laugh. You can't take the girl out of the country after all.

'How was the high-school girl who came in yesterday afternoon? What's her name? Mathilda?' Sharon asks, fussing with her hair. She was always the prettiest and has stuck with the gypsy boho look they all cultivated in their youth. Today, she is wearing a long, Mexican-patterned dress, complete with off-the-shoulder neckline, braided leather wrist bands and cowboy boots. Her hair is blonde and messy, piled on top of her head and fastened with jewelled clips. Sandra loves her and feels sad that her tan is becoming marked with lines and dark spots.

'Not great,' replies Nat. She has been looking after the girl on the ward. 'Her dad gave her a solid thrashing. No major injuries, but she's pretty sore.'

'Did she get discharged home?'

'To her mum's, yes. This morning.' Nat frowns. 'The dad lives on a block out of town. He was in the year below us at school.'

'I heard it happened on the school oval,' says Sharon, now rummaging in her bag. It is a striped cotton sack, the type that is imported from India and sold in shops alongside crystals and incense. It smells of patchouli.

'At the bus stop,' Nat clarifies. 'Apparently, he pulled in and started screaming at her, calling her a slut and all sorts of awful things.'

'Shit. I suppose all the other kids saw.' Sharon pulls out a lip gloss and rubs it across her mouth. She holds it out to Nat and Sandra and they both shake their heads.

'Yep.'

'Poor kid,' says Sharon, dropping the tube back in her bag. Her lips shine. 'What's the dad's problem?'

'Well, get this,' Nat lowers her voice and looks over her shoulder. The bar is filling up, but no-one is paying them any attention. 'Apparently a mate of his was driving past the school and saw her walking to the back of the oval with a group of boys. He rang the dad, who then left work and came up to the school.'

'What an arsehole. Both of them. What business is it of the dad's mate anyway?' Sharon is now fiddling with her glass and recrossing her legs. Sandra suppresses a smile.

'It gets worse,' Nat says. 'I did a physical exam and her knickers were torn and she complained she was sore.'

Sharon stops her fidgeting and gives Nat a sudden, sharp look. The two women hold each other's gaze, eyes narrowed.

'What?' Sandra watches a whole conversation pass between them and knows she is missing something.

'She said the boys had made a circle around her, then got her down on the ground and took turns at digitally raping her,' says Nat, not taking her eyes off Sharon.

Sandra's two colleagues slump back in their chairs and stare at each other.

Sharon picks up her glass and shakes her head. 'How long ago was it? Ten years, twelve years?'

'I can't believe it's still happening.' Nat's face is drawn, her mouth turned down in disgust.

Sandra looks from one to the other. 'What, has this happened before?'

'You wouldn't have known, Sandra, you didn't have girls,' said Sharon.

'When Olivia was fourteen, she told me about a group of boys at school who used to single out girls down on the back oval behind the science building,' Nat explains. 'They'd get her away from the other girls and take turns at putting their fingers inside them.'

'Darren never said anything about it.' Sandra feels her throat tighten and the skin on her arms prickle. She lifts her glass, then puts it down again without drinking, concentrating on aligning it directly over the circle of condensation it had left behind.

'He probably didn't know, love,' says Sharon, patting her on her knee. 'And it might have happened, well, you know, afterwards.'

The three women sit in silence, staring out of the window at the sunset. On the footpath outside, a group of teenage boys, too young to come into the pub, walk past with backpacks slung across their shoulders. They are at various stages of growing their hair long. Sandra imagines their mothers begging them to use a comb. The bags clink as they pass the window. They'll have convinced someone, an older brother or cousin, to buy for them and will be heading for a corner of the park.

'Well, it's obviously not the same boys doing it now,' says Sandra.

'No,' says Sharon. She turns to Nat. 'Are you going to report it?'

'I already have; it's mandatory under the new laws.'

They fall silent again, looking out at the darkening ocean. The noise level in the bar has dialled up and meals are coming out of the kitchen. A waiter passes with two plates of fish and chips. She delivers them to an older couple who Sandra guesses will eat half and bag up the rest for lunch tomorrow. At the table on the other side, a family with a teenage girl and two primary school age boys are sharing two plates of nachos. The girl has dressed up and the rest of the family are in jeans. She is bored and embarrassed and glances around the room, tugging at her skirt. She swats away one brother as he tries to put a corn chip up her nose. It's tough being a teenage girl, Sandra thinks.

'What do you know about Barbara?' Nat changes the subject and Sandra wonders what gossip she's heard on the wards. Both Nat and Sharon know she and Barbara were close friends.

'Not much,' she replies. 'Just that her car broke down out in the bush near Wittenoom and she died of dehydration. It was probably a stroke that did it.'

'What was she doing out there? Wasn't she supposed to be at a conference in Perth?'

'That's what I heard,' said Sharon.

Sandra shrugs. It was Barbara's story to tell, not hers.

'I heard the police did a DNA check,' says Nat, blurting it out and then looking down at her hands. 'Apparently they found a match.'

There is no avoiding it, Sandra thinks.

'Yes, the police told me,' she confirms.

'Shit.' Nat and Sharon look at her, stricken. Nat opens her mouth to speak and then closes it again.

Sandra knows what they are thinking. The Mystery Woman. It was all over the papers. When the investigation was reopened after the reporters ambushed Colin, evidence was sent to the United Kingdom for specialised testing. Scrapings from Darren's fingernails produced DNA from an unidentified woman. Police said at the time Darren would have had *extremely close and probably violent* contact with the woman for the DNA to be present in the scrapings. Desperate to keep the story running, the newspapers made a lot of the activities in the water on the day of the murder, speculating that Darren might have scratched one of his friends accidently, the way kids do when they are mucking about. Was there *overly rough horseplay* between Darren and his female friends? they'd asked. The daily newspaper even staged a re-enactment of the kids taking turns on the swing, bringing child actors in from the city to play Darren, Tim, Colin and Amy. The police took DNA swabs from each of them. Amy was interviewed again by police and asked if she and Darren had any physical contact that day. Only while she was applying CPR and trying to save his life, she'd told them. As if the story wasn't gruesome enough, it took a turn for the worse when a rumour started circulating that the DNA was from an Indigenous woman. Police refused to confirm or deny the rumour, but the slander was sufficient to set off another season of arrests for public drunkenness, pub brawls, and angry letters to the editor. It hadn't been the town's most shining hour.

'I thought the theory always was that Darren had been involved with some girl at school,' says Nat. 'You know, from one of the families east of the highway, and they'd had a fight.'

Sandra winces. They all know *east of the highway* means the suburb where most of the town's Indigenous families live.

'It could mean anything,' offers Sharon. 'I mean, Colin was Darren's best friend and Darren was always around at Barbara and Stuart's place. And DNA isn't proof. Remember that case in the United States? The one where the guy was convicted on the DNA evidence but ten years later someone else confessed? It was too late for him; he'd already been executed.'

None of them are familiar with the case and they sit in awkward silence. Nat, always their diplomat, breaks the silence for them.

'When is the funeral?' she asks.

'Tomorrow.'

'How's Rebecca coping?'

Sandra sighs and thinks about the chance meeting at the river mouth. Nothing is ever straightforward. Rebecca was looking well, as well as can be imagined in the circumstances, and has been doing OK in the last few years. The high-school friends who caused Barbara so much grief abandoned Rebecca after she became pregnant and she found herself a new, nicer group at ante-natal classes. She is still working part-time at the pharmacy and now she's halfway through a social work degree, just like her mum. Her son, Sam, recently turned ten. He's a nice kid, does well in school, plays football, and has never given his mum any trouble. The next few years might be tricky, Sandra thinks, but Rebecca has learned how to use the supports around her. Two weeks ago, Sandra would have been confident that not too much could derail Rebecca now, but Barbara's death has the potential to set her back.

'I don't know,' she answers, unwilling to reveal that she ran into her at the beach the day before. 'I guess I'll see all of them at the funeral.'

CHAPTER 14

Colin

Fourteen days before Darren dies

The following Sunday, Colin, Darren, and Tim stood by the riverbank ten kilometres inland looking uncertainly at the narrow stream dribbling through the paddocks. Tim had talked them into it at the barbeque at Darren's house on Friday night. His dad said he would drive them out to the hills, and they could hike back home along the river. It would take three hours and the river ran through a gully on the way. There was a ruin in there that was haunted. Tim's cousin's girlfriend was at the barbeque and said she'd seen the ghost one night when she'd camped there with some friends. They'd made a fire inside a ring of stones in the courtyard between the house and the old stables where it was out of the wind, and drunk beers and shared a joint. She said she saw it through the flames: an old woman walking past the windows of the second storey. It couldn't have been anyone pranking her because they'd tried to get up there themselves that afternoon and termites had eaten away the only staircase. She showed them the scrape on her shin where she'd tried to climb the wall. Tim's dad said they could check it out for themselves if they wanted.

Colin and Darren had agreed to go, although they didn't think they would see any ghosts during the day. They'd asked their mothers, who'd been sitting on camp chairs on the lawn between the shed and the house, drinking wine since the sun went down. Rebecca, who was sitting with the women, had laughed at them but their mums gave them instant permission, happy to have them out of their hair for half a day, Colin figured. Constable Samson, who'd arrived in the patrol car, had overheard them, and called a warning from the shed where he was standing over the Torana with Mr Davies and some of the other officers from the station.

'Don't you kids go lighting any fires while you're up there. We've got enough on our hands without you lot making more work for us.'

The men chuckled knowingly and tipped their beers to their mouths. They'd left the shed light off, preferring to hang a utility torch from the open bonnet, and the firelight from the barbeque cast their shadows against the back wall. It made them look taller and longer limbed than real life men and Colin thought uncomfortably of the backlit dancing skeletons in *The Lion King*. He'd been ten when he'd seen the movie at the cinema with his mum but the mad hyenas in the firelit cave still frightened him and he'd slept with a night-light on afterwards. From the shed, he could hear talk about windows and scarves and *if I catch the bastard*, and he retreated to the basketball hoop in the driveway and the ball they'd abandoned before dinner. Behind him, there was a sudden clattering noise and a thud, and someone swore.

'Shit, who left that there?'

'Where'd it go?'

The utility light swung hard shadows across the grass as the men searched the engine bay.

'It's probably fallen right through,' said Mr Davies. 'Darren, come here and fetch this spanner out from under the car.'

Colin bounced the ball on the driveway as Darren scurried over to the shed and wriggled on his belly underneath the Torana. He could see his skinny white legs sticking out from under the car, the soles of his feet facing upward, grey with dirt.

'Can you see it?'

'Yeah, Dad, got it.' He wriggled out again, backwards, dragging a flattened cardboard box with him. Colin saw him give his dad an anxious glance and shuffle the cardboard back into place.

'Sorry, Dad, sorry, don't want to get oil on the floor.' Darren stood up, holding the spanner above his head and grinning at the men around him. A smear of oil stained the front of his shirt. He handed the spanner to Constable Samson, who took a playful swipe at him.

'Now bugger off,' said his dad.

Later that night when the ice was melting and all that was left in the old bathtub was Coke and lemonade, Constable Samson let Colin call the station on the two-way in the patrol car.

'Tell them Constable Samson says the boys are on the move,' he instructed him.

'Tell *Senior Constable Samson* the roads are clear and to stick to the speed limit,' said the officer on the other end of the line.

On the Sunday morning, they packed water bottles, sandwiches and matches into their backpacks. Tim's dad drove them out of town along the tarred main road and turned off just after the airport. They rattled along the gravel for another ten minutes then he pulled over and pointed them to a line of trees.

'That's the river through there. Look out for snakes and don't go leaving any farm gates open.'

They said a chorus of thanks and climbed out of the car. Tim's dad did a U-turn and headed back the way he'd come.

The river was not a big one, just three metres wide, its banks cutting between wheat and canola. The boys walked along the flat sand under mallee and melaleuca trees, dragging sticks in the water and talking sport. After an hour, the banks dipped below the paddocks, and rocks emerged. Banksia scrub replaced the crops as the ground on both sides of the river became gravelly and climbed up and away from them. It was harder going here, having to navigate the uneven ground, and they sweated as they lost their shade, walking into the afternoon sun. Then the river did a dogleg and opened out and they saw the ruin at the far end of the gully where the cliffs fell away again to paddock. They could make out the L-shape of the main building, and the stables at the back. None of the buildings had roofing iron and the wooden beams were exposed to the sky. Darren gave a low whistle.

'Big place.'

'Dad said it was the original homestead for the whole area,' said Tim.

'They must've been loaded.'

'Dad reckons they owned all the land from the hills to the sea.'

'How did your cousin find out about it?' asked Colin.

'Dunno,' Tim shrugged. 'But that's where Matt and his girlfriend camped, right in the middle there.'

'How'd they get here?'

'Matt's ute.' Tim pointed south behind the house. 'There's a road that comes in from the highway.' Sure enough, they could see a track between the paddocks, not more than two wheel ruts, snaking toward a gravel road that connected the house to the highway they'd driven in on an hour before. 'He said no-one ever comes here. The owner lets the paddocks to the Wilsons on the other side of the scarp.'

The boys contemplated the house and the gully.

'Let's go then,' said Darren. 'Give this ghost a fright.'

They had to leave the riverbank in places to get down to the ruin. Colin went first, lost his balance on the slippery gravel, and tumbled, scraping his ankle bone, and coming to a stop halfway down. He slid the rest of the way on his butt, controlling the fall by digging in his heels. Darren laughed.

'Stylish mate.'

Colin grinned back. It hurt where his skin was torn but he let the blood drip on its own, not wanting to look more of a dweeb than he did already.

'Come on then, let's see you do better.'

Darren took the slope face first at a run. Before he reached the gravel, he launched himself into the air, arms cartwheeling, legs working. As the ground fell away from him, he appeared to gain height where he should have been coming back to earth. Colin felt a swish of disorientation as Darren hung in the air, suspended and untouchable, then rushed into the ground. His body bounced along the stones and came to rest against a clump of spinifex grass. His shorts were torn, and the heels of his hands were bloody. He was laughing. Colin shook his head.

'You're going to get yourself killed one day, you know that.'

Darren stood up and dusted off his butt. 'Live fast, die young, leave a beautiful corpse.'

'Except that logic doesn't work in your case, freak-face.'

'Look who's talking, Mr Blood Nut.'

Colin looked back up the slope to find Tim.

'Over here.' He was walking down from the right, picking his way through the larger rocks on the other side of the gravel scree. 'I like my essential body fluids on the inside.'

Now they were lower down into the gully, it was an easy walk to the ruin, which looked sadder and more ordinary than it did from a distance. The sun was lower in the sky and the walls cast hard shadows to the east of the building. Here, green-and-black moss covered the bottom courses of stone. The vegetation was thicker and tangled with evidence of past order. The trunks and branches of untended fruit trees twisted in on themselves and Colin could see the remains of brick pavers that had once made garden paths. Rusted wire loops marked out forgotten garden beds and patches of Paterson's curse ran down to the riverbank. That and the capeweed were the only plants flowering. With the dry and dusty air of the paddocks behind them, the boys breathed in a riper, wetter smell, and were silent as they explored deeper into the ruin, picking their way through empty doorframes into ground-floor rooms.

Most of the second-storey walls were still intact but Tim was right, the staircase was gone, the wood most likely scavenged, and the pile of limestone rubble inside wasn't high enough to reach the floor joists above their heads. They wouldn't be able to get up there without a ladder. Using Tim's torch, they traced the outline of fireplaces. Colin counted two upstairs and two downstairs. Welcome swallows swooped in and out of the second-storey windows, chattering, their nests pressed into the walls. Darren found a broken one on the ground where the floor cavity would have been if the boards hadn't been removed. They felt the soft feathers that lined the inside of the cup-shaped mud but there were no bones. Any nestlings were gone, flown away or fallen out long before their house fell down. The boys moved across to the western wing that created the long arm of the L. Bedrooms were lined up along a veranda, like a roadside motel. Someone had scavenged the floorboards here as well, and wattles were filling the end room, their branches reaching out of the west-facing window.

'Can you imagine if you did this place up?' asked Darren. 'It could be a palace.'

'It would cost a freaking fortune,' said Tim.

'Not if you did the work yourself,' Darren replied. 'You could live out here while you did it.'

'Yeah, and shit in the bushes.'

'Nah, there'll be an outdoor dunny around here somewhere.'

They went searching and found the familiar shape behind the stables. Like the rest of the buildings, its wooden door had been repurposed elsewhere. They threw stones down the hole and counted until they heard the thud.

'I need to piss,' announced Darren, and Colin and Tim left him to it to explore the stables. They smelled of damp and chaff. The stalls were stacked with rusting farm equipment and a row of hooks held oily bridles and rotting girth straps. Colin found a stack of horseshoes in the corner and tried without success to hang them on the hooks.

'What's taking him so long?' asked Tim from one of the stalls. He'd set himself down on an old petrol tin and was rummaging in his backpack.

'Dunno,' Colin replied. 'Scared of falling in?'

Tim snorted.

'What's with him and Rebecca?' he asked. 'Why're they so tight?'

'What d'you mean?'

'I saw them out the front of the house at the barbeque the other night, sitting on the kerb. They were having a regular session.'

'Smoking?' Colin knew Rebecca smoked, although their parents didn't. She'd be in trouble if they found out.

'Something like that, yeah, I guess.'

Colin grimaced. Darren could get a bit silly when Rebecca was around. He was probably trying to impress her with some stupid scheme. He would prefer not to know.

From back up the gully, he heard a popping sound. He looked at Tim, who looked back at him, eyes wide.

'What the hell?'

Tim shrugged. *No idea.*

Darren appeared in the doorway; his face tight. 'There's some fucker out there with a gun!'

The shots came again, three this time, the last followed by a ping as the bullet connected with its target.

'Shit!' Darren vaulted over the stall door, and the three of them squatted in the corner.

'You're fucking kidding me,' Darren whispered. 'I though you said no-one came here,' he hissed at Tim.

'How was I to know there'd be some lunatic out here with a gun?' he replied.

Colin looked at Darren. He was white and there were red rims around his eyes.

'What the fuck are we going to do?'

Tim threw him a scornful look. 'Are you going to cry? For Chrissake, Darren, keep your pants on.'

'It's probably just someone out here for target practice,' said Colin. 'They'll shoot off a few rounds and go home.'

'Yeah, but what if they don't?' said Darren. 'What if it's some psychopath? What if he knew we were going be out here and now he's hunting us, trying to flush us out so he can get a clear shot? What if it's the Weymouth rapist? What if it's your fucking cousin and he planned it all along?'

Tim paled and looked as though he was going to vomit.

'No-one's planned anything,' said Colin, wanting to avoid smelling Tim's regurgitated breakfast. 'We just sit here and wait. They'll bugger off sometime and then we'll just go home.'

They sat, tense and miserable and slowly getting cold against the walls of the damp stable. Colin passed Tim his cheese sandwich, which Tim ate quickly, all things considered, and then passed around his packet of chips. After a long, hissed debate, they agreed to risk the sound of opening their Coke cans and drank those as well as finishing the rest of the sandwiches in Tim's and Darren's backpacks.

They realised they hadn't heard any shots for half an hour and decided to make a move. While they were discussing whether to leave or abandon their rubbish, Colin heard footsteps coming across the courtyard between the stables and the house. He motioned for them to drop. As he ducked, he caught sight of a figure walking quickly past, red hair tucked under a black baseball cap. He waited, counting the steps in his head, and guessing how many it would take to make it to the corner of the house. He stuck his head up, gave the OK to the others, and they crept out of the stables in the other direction. Rounding the corner of the house where they had first arrived, they silently made their way toward the river. As they hurried westward along the bank, Colin turned back to look at the stables, catching the corner of his mum's car as it trundled back down the track to the gravel road and the highway.

CHAPTER 15

Sandra

People don't wear black to funerals anymore, thinks Sandra. She can see a lot of navy and grey. Plenty of denim. White shirts. Busy ties. No black except for her and her mum. Her mum nudges her elbow and Sandra turns to watch the cortege pull into the cemetery entrance and the family's limousine roll in behind. The flowers on the coffin are white roses and both vehicles are black. Sandra can see Stuart and Colin Russell sitting side by side in the second vehicle, both looking down at their laps. Rebecca is there too, with her husband, facing them. She would have taken the day off from work. At the sight of the family, Sandra's mum, Joan, takes a white handkerchief out of her pocket and presses it to her eyes. This will be hard for her, Sandra thinks to herself. Her mum was fond of Barbara and Stuart. They always made a point of sitting with her at barbeques, making sure her drink was topped up and her plate full. She will fight any suggestion that Barbara was involved in Darren's death. Sandra knows she has already taken a casserole to Stuart.

Stuart knows about the investigation, Sandra thinks as she watches him glide past, and she feels a sudden burst of pain for him. It is one thing to have a family member murdered, and another entirely to consider the possibility of having a murderer in the family. How does a person make sense of that? How does Stuart reconcile thirty years of marriage to a person who might have murdered his son's best friend? To view their shared history through a horrible new lens. He must wonder what clues he had missed. Whether her occasional unkindness was a result of momentary maternal fatigue or the surfacing of something darker. A latent capacity for evil.

Sandra doesn't believe people are evil, not even people who

murder children. She believes human beings are essentially good and sometimes some of them go wrong. She has seen in the hospital emergency department what her species can do when they go wrong: awful things, which cause grief and pain and life-long suffering. The two girls just last week, Ashleigh and Mathilda, both harmed by people who should have kept them safe. Ashleigh is not pregnant, thank goodness, but who knows how the assault will affect her behaviour and her relationships now? Sandra's colleague had been right; the swab was a match with her grandfather's DNA. Old bastard. She's surprised the girl reported it. She suspects it was the auntie's doing. Robyne has a good heart when she's sober, and Sandra hopes she stays that way while she has Ashleigh in her care. Maybe it will be a chance for both to rediscover their belief in human kindness. Sandra doesn't know what Stuart Russell believes.

They join the rest of the small group of mourners and trudge up the dusty path to the crematorium.

'So few people,' mutters her mum at her elbow. 'They've all abandoned her.'

Barbara wasn't evil, Sandra thinks. She was well known, even loved, in town, but word has got out and Sandra, like her mum, suspects many people who would have come to pay their respects have stayed away. Sandra and Barbara had been junior staff together at the local hospital. Barbara would often be up on the wards, meeting with patients and getting them into rehab and emergency housing. When their tea breaks coincided, she would fill Sandra in on her patients' progress on the outside; who had returned to violent husbands, who was back on the grog and living in the sand dunes south of town, who had started an apprenticeship and had secured a public housing flat. She was committed to the cause, always giving people the benefit of the doubt.

The arrival of their sons gave their relationship another dimension. Barbara already had Rebecca, a moppet with curly red hair who carried a Cabbage Patch doll and regarded the world with solemn, dark eyes, but Darren was Sandra's first and only child. Together, he and Colin would go on to share playgroup, primary school and junior high school classes, and give their mothers an unexpected friendship that bonded over car-pooling, team sports and sleepovers. They happily shared their grandparents as well, learning how to say granny and grumpy, nanna and pops. Sandra couldn't begin to count the number of times the boys had crossed the sandbar walking to each other's houses.

The cemetery board has planted lavender on either side of the path, and it has recently been pruned. The bushes are static and lifeless without their tall heads to wave in the breeze. Bottlebrushes drop flowers on the path but are too thin and far apart to shade mourners on the path. Sandra is glad she brought a hat. She waves flies away from her face and looks at the backs of the people in front of her. There are two children at the front, Jessica and Sam, walking with a woman who looks to be in her late thirties. She is wearing flat shoes and an ankle-length skirt and holds Jessica's hand.

'Colin's wife,' whispers her mum.

Jessica is walking on her toes, holding the hem of her skirt out to the side with her free hand, little chin pointed down, her eyes fixed on her white sandals. Sam is wearing ironed jeans and a button-down short-sleeved shirt. He is looking straight ahead, holding his face blank. Sandra can see the muscles working in his jaw. His hands are swinging by his sides and he puts them in his pockets, then takes them out again. Sandra swallows and feels the tension in her own jaw. Funerals are hard for children, and Sam has always seemed young for his age. He'd arrived early, she remembers, giving them all a fright. He won't know how to behave today. Colin hasn't had any kids yet, she remembers.

Sandra scans the group of people but can't make out anyone who might be Tim's parents. She didn't expect Tim to be here, but she had hoped to see Rochelle and Peter. Tim had surprised them all only three months after Darren died by announcing he had been accepted into the air force and would relocate to Canberra before the start of the next school year. Sandra had seen him only twice in the last ten years, when he had returned home to visit his mum and dad. She'd heard he had trained as an engineer and was now working on a joint defence forces project in the United States. She's not sure if she would recognise his parents anymore, even if they are here. They looked and dressed alike, she remembers, like people do when they have been married a long time. They were both public servants. Tim's mum worked part-time for the Port Authority and Tim's dad was a science teacher. They were nice people; she hopes their son stays in touch with them.

Sandra finds a seat at the back of the church and stands while the family enter with the coffin. Stuart is at the front, his eyes up, his back straight. What did he think when the police came to his house last week, she wonders? He had reported the gun missing ten years ago and now it would seem his wife might have had it all along. He would be trying to work out where she had kept it. Inside the fold-out bed. Under the linen no-one uses anymore. Sandra wonders where she would hide a gun if it were her. Inside the shed, of course, but the police have already searched there. She looks past the minister and through the windows behind the coffin and the speaker's podium. The windows look onto a dense native garden of gumtrees and grevilleas, blocking the view of the gravestones beyond, taller and thicker than they were ten years ago. Honeyeaters have discovered the sheltered spot and are bobbing in and out of the red blooms. The little black-and-yellow birds hop onto the rim of a birdbath, tilting their heads at the windows. Sandra wonders how much they can see inside or whether the glass confuses them with reflections. She doesn't remember much of Darren's funeral service. The same minister delivered it, but she has no recollection of what he said. She has a list of mourners. It was written in a burgundy book the funeral director gave her afterwards. She supposes it was compiled from the cards handed out as people arrived.

Sandra finds herself drifting away from the service from the moment the minister begins to speak. He is the minister from the Church of England near the primary school the boys attended. It is a pretty church, built from the same local sandstone as the nursing home and positioned at the top of a cliff overlooking the sea, but this minister is old-school and seemingly uninspired by the beauty of his surroundings. His teachings are Bible-based, taking the literal meaning of the words. Sandra finds them exclusionary and punitive and too hard to reconcile with the Christ of her Sunday school. What happened to the gentle man who searched for lost lambs, she thinks? It occurs to her Barbara was once a lost lamb, at least in the secular sense. As far as Sandra knows, Barbara died an agnostic. When she had finally confided in Sandra – they had known each other for five years by then – she was firmly of the view she had already been saved, just not by Christ. Her life, she said, had been mapped out as one of unemployment, social welfare, single parenthood and alcoholism. The system had its faults, there was no denying it, but it had rescued

Barbara from that destiny. It was only more recently her view changed, and she had begun to ask questions. They had been tough questions, sometimes angry, asked and argued over coffees and glasses of wine, and usually circling back to agreeing the past was the past and best left there. Sandra had promised not to share them with anyone and still didn't know how much Barbara had told her own family.

CHAPTER 16

Colin

Eleven days before Darren dies

Colin hadn't told Darren and Tim what he'd seen when they left the ruin. The walk had been flat but longer than they had bargained and, rattled by the gun shots in the gully, they'd trudged in silence, only speaking to ask for the water bottles and squabble over the remaining food. Tim had made a joke about being soldiers dropped behind enemy lines and no-one had laughed. They went their separate ways as soon as they'd got back to the bridge. They were tired and hungry, and needed to shower, eat and sleep. When Colin arrived home, his dad was tinkering in the shed, Rebecca was in her room, and his mum was baking. He'd dumped his bag on the floor and went to the fridge to make himself a Milo.

'How was the hike?' asked his mum.

'Good.'

'Hot?'

'Yeah.'

'There were a lot of boats out there today,' she observed, looking out the window as she cracked eggs into the flour.

'What?' Colin looked up, frowning.

'Off North Point. The yacht club must have had some sort of regatta on.'

'We weren't up at North Point.'

'I thought Tim's dad was dropping you at the point so you could hike back through the dunes.'

'No, Mum. Geez. I told you.'

'OK, keep your undies on.' She started the benchtop mixer and raised her voice above the noise. 'Where'd you go then?'

'Through the river gully up in the hills.'

She was watching the cake mixture so he couldn't see her face, but he did see her flinch. When she turned around, her eyes were dark and her voice low and deliberate.

'I never gave you permission to go up there.'

'Mum, I told you where we were going. You never said we couldn't.'

'Well I don't remember that.'

'Doesn't mean it didn't happen,' he muttered.

'I beg your pardon?' Her voice was darker, and he knew he'd gone too far.

'Sorry, Mum. It's just I did tell you and, really, you didn't say I couldn't. You know I wouldn't have gone if you'd said no.'

'No, you wouldn't,' she softened. 'You're a good kid even if you are a ratbag.' She ruffled his hair.

'Did you see anything interesting out there?' Her back was turned away again.

'Just the old ruin. There was no-one else around.'

'Hmm.'

'Can I have some bandaids to put on my feet?'

His mum pulled the medicine box off the top of the fridge.

'Sure, there are some in here.'

'These ones just rub between my toes and bunch up. Can I use the special ones you use? Please?'

She came around to the couch and inspected his feet.

'I suppose, yes.'

'Thanks, I'll get them.'

He took the bandaids out of the top drawer of his mum's dressing table. Her backpack was on the floor next to the bedroom door. Sitting on the floor, he pushed the door halfway closed, so he was hidden from the hallway and arranged the bandaid box next to his blistered toes. He reached across and pulled the backpack toward him. Inside, he found the black baseball cap and a bottle of water. There was no gun. She must have put it back in the safe. Without shifting position, he leaned over and slid the wardrobe open as far as he could reach. He got the combination to the safe right on the second go. Rebecca's birthday. The gun was not there either. He sat, his elbows on the points of his knees, thinking. From his position on the floor, he could see under his parent's bed and the row of suitcases they used each time they went away. On his mum's side, she kept a basket for spare pillows and rugs. Colin bum-shuffled across the floor and felt around inside the basket. His hand closed around the metal barrel of the handgun, nestled between the two top cushions. She'd be able to reach it from where she slept. His mum, he figured, was not so calm about the Weymouth rapist after all.

Three days after the gully and unusually for midweek, the boys had no homework, but a late season cold front had pushed up from the south, bringing their school jumpers back from their bottom drawers. It was too wet to go to the river. The rain rapped against the windows of the bus as they rode home from school and the sea foamed white. The ships on the horizon were solid and impervious against the blur of sea and sky. The boys had decided to hang out at Darren's house and the three of them walked together after getting off the bus. The wind whipped their faces and they kept their heads down and their hands in their pockets. It was too late in the season to be seen wearing long pants – the jumpers had already been a stretch – and they shivered as they walked. Goosebumps rose on their bare legs and raindrops trickled into their socks and down the backs of their collars.

Fittingly, the weather had all but passed by the time the boys reached Darren's house. Ignoring the front door, they walked down the driveway to the backyard. Mr Davies' Ford was parked at an angle, nose to the open shed, a thick black tarpaulin covering the tray back, red dust on the wheel arches streaked from the rain. Colin saw him look over his shoulder as the boys dumped their school bags at the back door. He wore board shorts and a t-shirt despite the cold, thongs on his feet.

'Hi, Mr Davies,' Colin called, raising his hand.

'Hi boys,' Darren's dad replied. He turned away from the workbench, hammer swinging by his side. He stood with a wide stance, broad-shouldered and narrow-hipped, as though he still stood on the deck of the fishing boat, and was still as he regarded them. The muscles in his arm gripping the hammer were tense and defined. Colin looked down at his feet, unsure if the banter from the boat still applied here on land.

'How was school?' Mr Davies asked, narrowing his eyes across the yard. Hard streaks of light were breaking through the clouds.

'Good.'

'Good.'

'Good.'

Colin and Tim shuffled their feet, not sure whether they were supposed to go to the shed or into the house.

'What's in the back of the truck, dad?' asked Darren, walking back across the wet grass and slapping the tarp with his hand.

'Never you mind. Leave that alone,' Mr Davies replied, his eyes still on Colin and Tim. He flicked his head toward the back door. 'Your mum's in the house. You can come out and help me with the pots when you've had something to eat.' He turned back to the workbench and swung a craypot onto the ground. Darren slid back the flyscreen door and they scuttled in out of the cold.

The back of Darren's house was open-plan, with a kitchen on the west side and windows looking out to the coast. Through them, Colin could see the next rain shower coming in across the water. A television stood on a jarrah entertainment unit on the opposite wall, faced by a circle of brown leather couches. Darren's mum had arranged photos of Darren across an internal wall, evidence of his progress from toddler to teenager. Colin and Tim were in some of them, invariably with wet hair and sandy feet and backgrounded by waves. Colin's favourite was the one of the three of them on the Christmas they all got foamies. They were still too little to take them into the surf, so they paddled them on the river. The photo had the three boys, Darren in the middle, in a line sitting astride the boards in the shallow river water, chins lifted and grins on their faces. In the background, the nursing home was just visible on the south bank, sitting high above the trees and the dull paddock. Colin looked closer at the photo. Lauren was right, Darren did look like an elf. The tops of his ears stuck out from his head, his face broad and flat across his eyes and nose.

Darren called out to his mum, announcing Colin and Tim were with him, and they filed into the kitchen where Darren pulled out bread, peanut butter and Milo. Mrs Davies came out of the laundry, still in her nursing uniform, as they made a sandwich production line.

'Hi boys,' she said. She eyed the line of bread. 'Make sure you leave enough for lunches tomorrow.'

Darren nodded through a mouthful of bread and peanut butter. He reached for a glass of milk to wash it down. 'How was work?'

'Busy.' She kissed the back of his head and flicked the kettle on. Darren's mum was the same age as Colin's mum, which in Colin's mind was a noteworthy coincidence, especially as they hadn't gone to school together. Colin's mum went to boarding school in Perth and Darren's mum went to the same high school Darren and Colin attended. Mrs Davies was skinny and exercised a lot and wore her hair in a blonde ponytail. She was a bit bony when she hugged him. Darren said she'd had cancer when she was a girl and she couldn't have kids.

'How's your granny after her adventure?' she asked Colin.

'She's OK, Mrs Davies,' he replied. 'Dad has given her some change to keep in her purse for when she goes to the dining room.'

'Poor Elsie.' She poured the boiling water into her cup, steam rising in front of her face. 'It's so hard when people get old.'

'Dad says if she wanders off again, they'll lock her up.' As he spoke, a lump formed in his throat and he swallowed, embarrassed, and blinked it away.

'Oh love, it's not like that.' Her face softened at his distress. 'She'll still be able to go out, just as long as it's with someone. I've been in the dementia ward. It's not as bad as all that.'

Colin managed a smile. 'Thanks, Mrs D.'

'Mr Stevens said there was an accident on the highway,' said Darren through a mouthful of bread and peanut butter.

'One of cray trucks from the co-op,' she confirmed, stirring her tea and pouring in the milk. 'It overturned south of town. They brought them in just before I left. They were lucky they were travelling in convoy; the guys in the second truck called the ambulance.'

'What will happen to the catch?'

'The co-op sent another truck to pick it up.' Mrs Davies looked at her watch. 'They should be all on their way to the depot now. Your dad went down to lend a hand.' She poured her tea and took the cup with the tea bag still in it to the couches and opened a magazine. 'Why don't you take Colin and Tim out to the shed and have a look at the car? Dad got a new fanbelt. You can help him put it in.'

The boys drained their glasses and trooped back outside, sandwiches in hand. Darren's dad was still bending over craypots, levering off a piece of rotten wood with the back of the claw hammer. He looked up at them and Colin could see a flicker of annoyance on his face as he took in Colin's and Tim's reappearance. He glanced at Tim, who turned away to look at the car.

'I hear the police were at your place the other day, Colin,' Mr Davies said as he tossed the rotten wood to the side. 'I hope you didn't let on your belly was full of undersize crays.'

'No, Mr Davies.' Colin felt himself flush. 'He was just there about Granny.'

'Dad, you should see this awesome cave we found at the river,' Darren interjected, putting himself into his dad's range of vision.

'Pass me the nails.' He pointed to an ice-cream container halfway down the bench.

'It's all covered by bushes and its right under our house. It's the best place for hiding stuff you don't want anyone to find.' Darren picked up the container and put it within his dad's reach.

'Is that right?'

Darren tipped out the nails on the bench and began arranging them in rows while his dad hammered.

'Mum said one of the co-op trucks overturned on the highway.'

His dad nodded.

'Mum said you had to go down there with the back-up truck and pick up some stuff.'

'Yeah, I did.'

'What happened? Was Geoff driving?'

'Don't know. Yes.'

'Is he alright?'

'Don't know.'

Colin thought he should join Tim at the car and leave father and son to it, but he didn't know if that would be rude. He rocked his weight from foot to foot, looking at the cobwebs overhead. Maybe he'd just ride it out. Maybe Tim would come back in a minute and say he had to go home. That would give Colin an excuse as well. Maybe they could all go to Tim's house and watch a video.

'You always said he drove too fast,' Darren persisted, adopting a knowing tone. He'd never been too good at reading people. 'You said he'd have an accident one day.'

'For crying out loud, Darren, put a sock in it. Just pass me the fucking nail.'

Colin jumped and Darren paled. Mr Davies shook his head. He hammered a loose piece of wood into the craypot in front of him and swung the pot onto the pile next to the workbench. It clattered into place. Tim appeared behind him.

'Hey, I have to go home for Mum. Mr Davies, is it alright if Darren comes over to watch a video?'

'Can I, Dad, can I?' Darren's face lit up.

'Go ask your mother.'

CHAPTER 17

Sandra

After the funeral, Sandra attended the wake at the community centre. Her mum had had enough for one day and Sandra dropped her back at the retirement village with promises of coffee on her next day off. People had been surprised to see Sandra there; she could see their expressions when she walked into the room. A few of them had frowned and turned their backs, unable to reconcile her presence with the rumours they were now hearing. At the tea urn, one woman hissed at her across her shoulder.

'What are you doing here?'

Already on guard from the tension in the room, Sandra felt herself stiffen but continued to eke some colour out of the home brand tea bag.

'Barbara was my best friend, I've come to pay my respects to the family,' she replied without looking up.

'She *killed your son*. Where is your loyalty?'

Sandra turned to face her, disinclined to participate in the whispering.

'Right where it should be,' she said out loud, 'with the family of a woman who I consider innocent.'

A group of people standing nearby turned to look at her, aghast. The conversation around them died. The woman – Sandra could place her now she could see her front on; she was a physiotherapist from the hospital – also raised her voice.

'Well I think you need to reconsider your priorities, lady.'

'Thanks for the advice,' Sandra muttered as the woman turned and stalked away, looking right and left for support. She watched her join a group at the opposite side of the room. They turned their heads to look at Sandra, incredulity on their faces.

She was saved from being stranded by Stuart, who took her cup from her hand and wrapped her in a hug. She breathed deep and let the woman go. His smell reminded her of Barbara, the washing powder she used, the woodiness of his aftershave that would sometimes linger on her.

'Thank you,' he said, holding her at arms' length, a sad smile on his face. 'It means a lot that you're here.'

'Where else would I be?' she reassured him. Sandra remembered how awkward people can be with you when you lose a family member too young. The way they offer inane words in their desperate search to explain the loss. *God wanted him back* was the worst. What rubbish. *He's in a better place. He's with his grandparents. He'll always be young.* None of these things, she knows, are a comfort. She wasn't going to say them to Barbara's family.

'I am so sorry for your loss, Stuart,' she said. 'I loved her. She was a good friend and a good colleague.' Stuart nodded, his long face drooping. She saw Colin behind his shoulder, awkwardly waiting his turn to be comforted. She smiled at him, said she hoped he was doing well in the city, and agreed they should catch up before he went back. Rebecca had hugged her, and so had Sam, and she'd carried Jessica on her hip while they explored the sandwiches and cakes the members of Barbara's choir had insisted on supplying. No-one mentioned the investigation. Before she left, and away from the rest of the family, Stuart promised to call her.

Now, walking up the steps to the front bar of the Town Beach Hotel, Sandra remembers that she still hasn't heard from Stuart. The bar is quiet midweek. Sandra gets herself a glass of sauvignon blanc, finds a table near the window and sits facing the door even though she won't be too hard to find. She crosses her legs and leans back, looking out at the sea. The beach here is protected from the southerly by the wharf and the water is flat and clear. Toddlers wearing sun hats and rashies stagger at the edge of the flat water and their mums look relaxed and unconcerned. Beyond them, people unconstrained by nine-to-five working hours are laid out on their backs on a floating pontoon. On the grass, three women in loose print dresses and oversized cardigans are watching children play on the new adventure equipment the council installed last year. A baby lies next to them, his chubby legs waving in the air as he tries to catch his mother's attention. She looks down at him and squeezes his fat cheeks between her finger and thumb. She must have said something funny because the other two women laugh and slap the ground. Sandra can just hear the sound through the window.

Sitting in the hotel, rocking her glass backwards and forwards on the table, Sandra wonders at her declaration to the physiotherapist. She hadn't, until the wake, confronted whether she believed Barbara could have done it. Barbara had abhorred violence. Like Sandra, she had seen too much of it and what it takes away from people and families and communities. They had often discussed – sometimes right here in this pub – what it takes for an ordinary person to snap. Most murders, they knew, were committed by ordinary people. Ready access to guns and alcohol are usually part of it. The husband and father who drinks too much and shoots his brother with his licenced rifle after an argument about inheritance. The tradie who has had too many beers at the pub and decks another man with one punch for looking at his girlfriend. Women, she knows, rarely use firearms on other people, although it does happen.

'How good is this?' Keith is standing next to the table, beer in hand, dragging her thoughts back into the pub.

Sandra looks up at him through her sunglasses and shifts gear. 'Close to perfect.'

'Only close?' He sits down and drains the top inch out of his glass. 'Damn I needed that.'

'Hard day?'

'There was a bit of aggro at the TAB earlier. Probably cousins of this mob.' He looks over at the three women on the grass.

'Excuse me?'

He blinks at her tone, missing a beat, then corrects himself. 'Yeah, you're right, that's not cool.'

'No, Keith, it isn't, especially coming from you.'

'Sorry.'

Sandra contemplates giving him a dressing down then decides against it. The point has been made. Instead she asks if anyone was hurt.

'Just some pride,' he replies, careful with his tone.

She nods, looking into her glass.

'You know, the whole station's been pretty shaken up about this,' he adds. 'We might've locked horns with Barbara from time to time ...'

Sandra raises her eyebrows.

'OK, a lot of the time,' he concedes, 'but we respected the way she always tried to get a second chance for her clients. She'd come into the station most weeks. You always knew when she was in, taking up the whole of the front desk with her big skirts, and files, and that voice.'

Sandra smiled despite herself. It was true Barbara had only one volume setting, and an accent that four years in a posh city university had not rubbed away. And she was a substantial woman. Sandra could easily imagine her leaning her alarming forearms on the reception desk at the police station and demanding to know why the police had brought in her client *this time*. Barbara was not what Sandra would describe as a quiet advocate.

'How's the investigation going?' she asks Keith. 'Have you been able to place Barbara at the scene?'

'No.' He looks out of the window. 'She was definitely in the area, but you knew that. The investigating team made it clear in the files. In her interview, she said she was with Arthur from three until quarter to four. Her own case notes tally with that and Arthur confirmed it in his interview. Although, being a suspect himself, that's kind of convenient.'

Sandra takes another sip of wine. She knows where he is going.

'After she saw Arthur, she sat with her mother-in-law, Elsie Russell, until five, when she went home. The receptionist at the front desk confirmed she was in Mrs Russell's room – she was doing the afternoon tea rounds because they were short-staffed – and that Barbara left at the same time she locked up reception for the night. Just after five.'

Keith pauses and drinks his beer. 'What time were you visiting Arthur?'

'I got there just before three.'

'So, you and Barbara were visiting him together.'

'Not together, no. Like I said in the interview, Barbara came in while I was there, I stayed a bit longer. Arthur loved a chat. He was lonely in there, poor man. I think the other residents were a bit scared of him. It's a shame, because he knew so much about the district and had no-one to share it with. Then I left so she could get on with her job.'

'And that was three fifteen pm.'

'That's right,' she confirms.

'The thing is, if the receptionist was doing the afternoon tea rounds, Barbara could have left after you. She could have got to the riverbank by three thirty.'

'But why would she do that?' Sandra has had this argument before. 'Why would she follow me down to the river? And why shoot Darren? There is no motive.'

'What about Stuart?'

'Stuart? What about Stuart?' She is confused and irritated by the abrupt switch in suspect. 'He was at home watching the test match.'

'The investigation says his thongs were found at the riverbank during the search for the gun.'

This is news to Sandra. She thought she knew everything about the investigation. She didn't know they had found Stuart's thongs and shakes her head.

'I don't know. Are you sure they were his?'

'His name was written on the sole, so yeah, they were his. There's nothing on record about him being asked about them.'

They sit in silence. The toddlers have been gathered up and taken home now but the people on the pontoon are soaking in the last of the afternoon sun while they can. The women with the baby have gone. Sandra thinks about Stuart. He'll be lost without Barbara now. There will only be him in that big house by the beach. She imagines Stuart at their breakfast table, dressed for work and eating cereal, the sea through the trees, the house quiet and breathing out the last of its Barbara smell. She thinks about him visiting the pharmacy, the bank, the supermarket. Will he be aware of the sideways looks? People will be awkward with him, but she hopes they will be kind.

She blinks as Keith breaks the silence to ask about her job. They swap emergency room stories. They had both worked on, or knew second-hand about, the more gruesome presentations at the hospital. Last month, a farmer had been shot in the stomach by a neighbouring landowner in a dispute over sheep. Sandra had been on shift and Keith was the first on the scene, keeping the aggrieved neighbour at bay with one hand while pressing on the wound with the other. He'd taken him to the station once the ambulance had been and gone and spent the rest of the day documenting twenty years of complaints about sheep, water, fencing, and firebreaks. At the hospital, Sandra had heard the same story from the injured man. He'd survived, and with no organ damage, although he wouldn't be slinging hay bales any time soon. Keith said a restraining order had been given and the shooter was due in court next week.

'Did Darren have a part-time job?' he asks when they exhausted the gossip.

'No, he helped his dad out in the shed, but nothing else.'

'Pocket money?'

'Same as the other kids. I used to check what the other mums were giving their sons and I gave him more or less the same.'

'More, or less?'

'The same.'

'Is there any chance his dad gave him a bit extra? For the stuff he did in the shed, or on the boat maybe?'

Sandra thinks. Of course, it's possible. Greg always carried cash. He preferred it to using credit cards, which he said he didn't trust. You never knew when some bastard was going to copy your details and sell it to a crime syndicate, he said. *Before you know it, your card will be paying for hookers in Thailand.* Sandra didn't monitor Darren's spending so she wouldn't know if he bought more than other kids. He never complained he didn't have enough, she knew that. The other mums often talked about their kids wanting them to increase their pocket money, but Darren never mentioned it. Maybe Greg did give him some extra cash here and there.

'It's possible,' she says. 'Why?'

'Jack Stevens said he saw him go into the bank on the corner of the main street a couple of times. Did he have a savings account there?'

Sandra shakes her head. 'Not that I know of, but the bank is next door to the pharmacy where Rebecca Russell works. He was probably going to see her. I think he was a bit besotted at one point.'

Keith chuckles. 'The best friend's older sister, hey? What would his mate have thought of that?'

Sandra pictures Colin Russell at fifteen, a smart, studious boy with skin too pale for the mid-west sun. He would have been perplexed, she thinks, at the idea that someone could be attracted to his sister. He would have ignored it, hoped it would go away.

Keith downs the rest of his beer and looks pointedly at Sandra's empty wine glass.

'Another?'

She checks her watch. 'No thanks, I'm expecting someone.' She is astonished as she looks back at him and sees his disappointment. Oh no, she thinks, not that. He's a nice guy and good at his job but she can't contemplate anything else.

'I'd better be off, then,' he says, looking out the window at a rental car trying to fit into a tight space across the road. His eyes widen and he looks back at her as Colin Russell climbs out.

CHAPTER 18

Colin

Eleven days before Darren dies

The video store was busy for a weeknight. The only shopfront alight in a row of electrical and second-hand stores on the highway, it's hard, fluorescent lights spilled out onto the carpark where high school students with no homework and ragged parents dashed in and out through the rain. The boys could see from the car window that there were already gaps on the shelves of new releases. They ran across the carpark through the squall, dodging potholes, and pushed open the door. Muddy footprints mottled the linoleum floor.

'Shut that door!'

The wind blew over a cardboard actor wearing a suit and poised with a handgun.

'Sorry.'

'Sorry.'

'Sorry.'

Colin bent down to pick up the statue. The prop at the back had folded after too many collapses and he couldn't make it stand up. The man at the counter, wearing a beanie over blond dreadlocks, leaned across the returns slot and made a face.

'Stupid piece of crap. You can have it if you want.'

'Cool.' Colin held the statue at arms'-length. 'Who is it?'

'James Bond? Pierce Brosnan? Where've you been, kid? It's on the shelves against the back wall if you want to watch it. I think we've got one left.'

Colin tucked the statue under his arm and made his way to the aisles.

'Hey, you can't take it in there. Leave it against the wall. You can get it when you go.'

Colin followed Darren and Tim to the new releases shelves, his thongs slapping on the wet floor. Darren's mum had said yes to going to Tim's house after grilling them about assignments and tests that were due in the next week. Colin and Tim had a maths test coming up, but it wasn't until Monday. Darren did vocational maths and his test was the week after. Otherwise, they were free. When they got to Tim's house, his mum said she'd treat them all to pizza if they wanted to stay for dinner and after they called and pleaded with their parents, she loaded them into the back of the station wagon and drove them into town.

Tim and Darren had taken *Star Trek First Contact* off the shelves and were reading the back cover. They passed it to Colin. The front cover had men in blue-and-orange skivvies gazing apprehensively into a black, star-filled sky. He looked at the shelves for *Tomorrow Never Dies*.

'The guy at the counter said this one is good,' he said, pulling it down and passing it to Tim. 'He said we could have the statue.'

'Definitely *Star Trek*,' said a girl's voice behind him. Colin knew who had pronounced the judgement before he turned around. The smell of chlorine followed her everywhere.

'Hi Amy.'

She was wearing her squad tracksuit and her hair was wet.

'How was training?'

She shrugged. 'Same old, same old.' She was eating her way through a family pack of salt and vinegar chips and held the packet out to them. They each dived their hands in.

'Aren't you supposed to pay for these before you start eating them?'

'No, it's OK. They know me in here. Wednesday night is pizza and a movie night. Mum doesn't have time to cook after being at the pool all afternoon.'

Amy's mum came up behind her and looked at the video cover. She looked just like Amy. Tracksuited, tanned, and blonde hair tied back in a ponytail.

'*Star Trek First Contact*. Excellent. We saw it last week. You'll enjoy that, boys.' She waved her own selection at Amy. 'Look what I found.'

Amy squealed. '*Mr Bean*!' She clapped her hands together like a five-year-old.

Colin felt his own face lifting. Cool and aloof was not Amy's style and her joy was infectious. She grabbed the video case from her mum and gave her a hug, scattering chips onto the floor. Tim jabbed him in the ribs.

'Earth to Colin. Which one is it: James Bond or aliens?'

'Aliens,' he replied, pulling himself together, 'definitely aliens.'

'How did I guess?' said Tim, rolling his eyes. 'Let's go find Mum.'

Amy and her mum had finished paying for the video and the chips when they got to the checkout, and Amy turned and waved as she dropped the finished packet in the bin near the door. Arthur Zelinski came in with the wind as they left and settled himself in a corner.

'Hey, Arthur,' Tim's mum called to him, 'not a good night to be out.'

'I've seen worse,' he replied. 'It'll blow over in a couple of hours.'

'Can I get you anything?'

'A Coke and some chips would be nice, Mrs Patten.'

'Salt and vinegar?'

'Just salt, thanks.'

Mrs Patten paid, and they trooped out behind her into the carpark, Colin grabbing Pierce Brosnan on the way. They put him across their knees in the back seat. As they pulled out, Colin looked back inside and saw the video store guy passing Arthur the key to the staff toilets. They were laughing and Colin turned his head to watch as Arthur gave him a thumbs up and headed back out the front door, bent forward anticipating the wind. Is that what it's like, he wondered, living rough with no home to go to each night? Using video store toilets and eating food from school mums. Mr Arthur had left his rucksack in the corner inside the shop, its canvas shell marked with dark stains and plastic shopping bags tied to the sides. It rested on a bed roll, itself muddied at the edges. The rucksack was heavy. Colin knew because he'd seen Mr Arthur lift it out of a shopping trolley once when the guy from the supermarket had made him give the trolley back. He'd struggled to get it over the side and the trolley guy had to help him.

'Where will Mr Arthur sleep tonight?' he asked Tim's mum.

'Brad will let him roll out his bed on the floor when he locks up,' she replied. 'It stops people breaking in.'

At Tim's house, Tim's mum let them sit on the floor in the games room to eat their pizza while they watched the movie, although they had to let Tim's parents and his sister take their slices first. They had three different pizzas: Super Supreme, Barbeque Chicken and Hawaiian. The Hawaiian was Tim's sister's choice and the boys registered their disgust.

'Only little kids have Hawaiian. She just takes off all the pineapple and feeds it to the dog anyway,' complained Tim to his mum.

'Don't have any then, if you don't like it,' she replied, not interested in his grievance.

Tim's mum let them have Coke as well – a banned substance in Colin's and Darren's houses – and they poured it into half litre glasses which they balanced on the open pizza lids on the floor, shooing the dog away. When the pizzas were done, Darren pulled out six Mars Bars he'd bought at the video store and they ate those too, taking turns to perform salty, chocolatey burps. James Bond aimed his gun at the ceiling from the carpet behind the couch.

Amy's mum was right about the movie. There were aliens, spaceships and guns. Patrick Stewart was in charge, and the Borg were defeated. When Data was captured, they hid behind cushions and when he betrayed the Borg queen, they cheered. Darren's mum arrived just as the movie finished.

'You lot look comfortable. I could probably just turn off the lights and leave you all here for the night.'

'Can we? Please, Mum?' Darren's face lit up, hopeful. She laughed.

'Not on a school night, but if Colin's and Tim's parents say yes, maybe they can sleep over our place on Friday.'

Tim's mum said yes too, provided he was home by nine am the next day and Colin said he would ask his mum later. Darren asked his mum if he could stay until Colin's mum arrived, but Mrs Davies said no, his dad needed him to help with a delivery when he got home, and she had an early shift the next day.

Colin's mum arrived as they walked out the door. She swept in, beaming and hugging people, black tunic and pants flowing, red curls shooting around her head. She asked the boys if the movie was any good, and what type of pizza they had, and if Mrs Patten made her famous chocolate cake. She put her face down into the dog's face and then asked why his breath smelled of pineapple. She told Mrs Davies she *would be delighted* if Colin slept over on Friday and did Sandra want him to bring anything. She would make a cake anyway, which of course wouldn't be anywhere near as nice as Tim's mum's, but she was sure they would eat it. Embarrassed, Colin ushered her out the door. For once, he wished his mum would accept that he did, in fact, have friends and they liked him and weren't going anywhere. He didn't need her to cosy up to them on his behalf. He also wished she would wear tracksuits like Mrs Davies and Mrs Patten.

As they reached the end of Tim's street, Mr Davies' big Ford passed in front of them and turned onto the highway and across the bridge. Darren was in the passenger's seat next to his dad.

'They're heading out late,' Colin's mum observed, frowning. 'I would have thought Greg would be in bed by now. Doesn't he get up at something ridiculous like three am to take the boat out?'

'Four, I think,' Colin replied, looking at his friend through the windscreen. Darren looked glum; all traces of his evening wiped off his face. He didn't see them, staring straight ahead, forearm resting against the window. They were so close Colin could see his fingers tapping. He lifted his arm to wave, and then brought it down again. They followed the Ford across the bridge and past the tennis courts. Colin watched it turn left in the distance, onto the road to the suburbs east of the highway, its tail-lights blurred in the rain.

CHAPTER 19

Sandra

Colin walks into the front bar with the same self-consciousness he had when he was fifteen. He looks like he'd hand over his credit card to become invisible, but in reality, he is dressed in the same anonymous uniform as every other person. Blue jeans, unremarkable sneakers, and a check, button-down, open-neck shirt. His red curls are cut close to his head and have faded since he was in high school. His face, Sandra notices, is still pale and she wonders if his wife makes him use sunscreen like his mum used to do when he was a kid. He glances at the solo drinkers, who ignore him, and then at the backpackers gathered ready to take photos of their beers in front of the sunset. They also pay him no attention, intent on capturing the light through the straw-coloured liquid. His eyes suddenly go wide and he flushes when he sees Keith sitting with Sandra, and she regrets agreeing to meet him here. For a minute she thinks he might turn and bolt. She reminds herself that he is still very young.

Keith stands as he walks over to their table and reaches out to shake Colin's hand.

'It's alright, mate, I'm just leaving.'

Keith is taller and heavier than Colin and he stands too close to him. Sandra watches Colin take a step backwards and wonders if Keith's action is deliberate or just clumsy. He lays his large, footballer's hand on Colin's shoulder and turns to Sandra.

'I'll be in touch soon.'

She decides it is deliberate. Greg could be like that too, keeping people in their place by reminding them of his physical size. It didn't take much. A step too close, a heavy hand on the shoulder, a grip on the wrist during a handshake. She'd seen him do it with employees and people he did business with. She'd seen them wince and their faces flush. Just like Colin's is doing right now.

Keith leaves, striding between the tables and raising his hand to the bartender. Sandra smiles at Colin and gestures for him to sit down. Instead, he asks her if she wants a drink and goes to the bar. He is only in his mid-twenties, Sandra thinks, but he could be ten years older. Working in finance in the city has given him an extra ten kilos and up close she can see his skin is not just pale but clammy with it. She guesses a lot of the extra weight is sitting as fat around his heart and lungs. She wonders what his blood pressure is. He's not too old to turn it around. If he cuts the alcohol and sugar and walks the dog each day, he could lose the weight and the hypertension in a year. She knew from Barbara that he and his wife are expecting their first baby after a miscarriage. They nearly separated when it happened, and Barbara said they are still having to work hard at keeping it together. Sandra is sympathetic. She and Greg only lasted another year after Darren died. Life can get the better of a marriage sometimes.

'How's your dad coping?' she asks him when he returns. 'It must have been hard, not knowing where your mum was.'

'He doesn't say much. You know Dad. He keeps it to himself.'

'Always the quiet one.'

'He kind of had to be with Mum around.' Colin catches himself by surprise with the unexpected joke and he looks at her with a guilty expression. Sandra smiles at him to show that it's alright, she understands.

'Do you know what happened; why your mum was up north?' she says. She wants to find out how much Colin knows. 'She was found a few kilometres out of town, wasn't she?'

'We don't know, to be honest. She said she was going to Perth for the week for a conference, but they said she registered and never turned up.'

'That was the reconciliation conference.'

Colin looks up at her, surprised. 'It was. How did you know?' Between his eyes, Sandra can see the same two lines that appeared when his mother was perplexed. The same two lines that were on his grandmother's face in the photo Barbara had shown Sandra two weeks ago. She will tell him about that one day, but now is not the time.

'She mentioned it the last time I saw her,' she says. 'She was looking forward to it, hoping to get some ideas for Sorry Day next year.'

He smiles down into his glass. 'She never stopped campaigning, did she?'

'No, she didn't. It was something that was especially important to her.'

'Why though?' he asks. 'Why did she have to do all that stuff? It's not like it was part of her job.'

'Your mum used to say to me that we are the lucky ones. We have an education, good jobs and a roof over our heads. The kids she would see every day, going to school with no breakfast and no lunch – they broke her heart. She knew they had no chance of doing well in class.'

'I remember her saying once she could walk into a classroom and tell you which kids she'd be visiting in jail in ten years' time.'

'She probably could,' Sandra agrees.

'Is that what would have happened to Darren?' he asks, then flushes. 'If, you know, you hadn't taken him in?'

'It's likely, Colin,' Sandra says. Her voice is kind. 'His mum was an alcoholic. So was his dad, although he wasn't around. He wasn't in a good way when he came to us. He was very underweight, crying all the time. He hated being touched.'

'I guess he was lucky.' He flushes again. 'For a while.'

'Yes, we gave him a good life,' she says, 'for a while.' She puts her hand on his. 'We all did, Colin. You played your part too.'

He gives her a grateful look. 'I tried to be a good friend.'

'How long are you in town?' she asks.

'I've got a week's leave. I'm going to stay here with Dad, sort out Mum's stuff, catch up with Rebecca.' He pauses, awkward. 'I just want to say, Mrs Davies, that I'm sorry about all this. I still don't know what to think and I can't imagine how you are feeling.'

'It's a shock to all of us, Colin. I don't know what to think either.' She looks at his downcast face. 'I think you can call me Sandra from now on, though. You're a bit too old for Mrs Davies, don't you think?'

He gives her a half smile. 'Do you think she could have done it?'

'No. No, I don't. I can't see how this latest information makes any difference. It still doesn't place your mum at the scene. Even if it did, why would she do it? It doesn't make sense.'

Colin flushes again, exactly like he used to do when he was a teenager, from the roots of his red hair to his throat at his collar.

'What if it was an accident?'

She stares at him.

'What if what was an accident? Your mum shooting Darren?' She can hear the horror in her own voice.

'Yeah,' he says, before adding, 'or someone else. What if they hadn't meant to hurt him?'

'You can't be serious, Colin. Why would she do something like that? Why would she even have a gun on her?'

Colin just shrugs and looks down into his beer. Sandra can see tears are not far away, and she feels a weight in her own chest as she contemplates the awful sadness and confusion that she imagines must be inside him. She wonders what Darren would have been like at this age; how he would have been if he thought his mum had killed his best friend. Probably just as fragile.

'Your mum did not shoot Darren, Colin,' she says, making her voice firm, 'not on purpose, not by accident. You know where she was when it happened. She wasn't there.'

He rubs his eyes and blows his nose and she looks away.

They talk some more about Colin's life. He tells her about his work, describing the *high net worth individuals* who are his clients and the outrageous amount of money they spend on booze, restaurants and toys. One guy, he says, a mining company director, has a yacht moored in Fremantle worth ninety million. The annual insurance alone costs him more than one million. He writes it off against his tax because he uses it to entertain clients. The boat only ever goes to Rottnest and back, Colin says, although it could easily sail up to Indonesia, even across to the Middle East. Sandra remembers when Colin wanted to be an engineer and build boats himself. She wonders what changed his mind but doesn't ask.

'Darren loved boats,' he says. 'Remember his little tinnie? He used to take us out in it. We'd go out behind the reef and then all the way to the point.'

'Hmm, I believe you weren't allowed to go that far. That reef is dangerous,' she says. Colin's mood has lightened with his memory.

'We were always safe, though.' He wants to reassure her. 'Darren was good on the water. Mr Davies taught him how to judge when the swell was highest to carry you across the rocks. We never got stuck. And he always made sure he had flares and lifejackets and he never went too far if he thought we might not have enough fuel.'

Sandra doubts it but goes along with Colin's memory. 'That's good to know.'

'He wanted to be a fisherman, like his dad. He said he couldn't think of anything better than to spend every day out on the water, catching crays.'

It's true, thinks Sandra. Darren loved fishing. He even loved doing shed work, helping his dad fix pots and paint floats. When his dad let him go out with the crew, they all went home early because Darren was happy to wash out the boat on his own. He'd surprised her once, telling her being a fisherman was *noble*, because it was all about catching food and feeding people. To her shame, she remembers thinking at the time that he was probably repeating what he'd heard someone else say.

'He wanted his own boat,' Colin is saying. 'He said he was going to do his skipper's ticket when he finished high school, in Perth like his dad, and then he'd give jobs to people like him who didn't have the marks to go to university. He was saving up for it. He already had twenty grand and figured he'd have saved half by the time he got his ticket, and then he'd ask his dad if he would buy it with him. They were going to be co-owners.'

CHAPTER 20

Colin

Ten days before Darren dies

At the bus stop the next morning, Darren was yawning and rubbing his eyes.

'Aw, did the big kids keep you up too late, little man?' Tim ruffled Darren's hair with his knuckles. 'Next time we'll remember to start the movie early, so it ends before your bedtime.'

Darren ducked away from him and grunted. He leaned against the fence, shoved his hands deep into his pockets, and closed his eyes.

'Wake me up when the bus gets here.'

Tim looked at Colin, who just shrugged. He was tired, so what? He wasn't going to spill Darren's secrets until Darren had a chance to tell them himself what he'd been up to with his dad last night.

On the ride into school, Darren really did fall asleep, his bag propped between his head and the window. Seated next to him, Tim slipped his fingers into Darren's shirt pocket and eased out a pair of sunglasses. He turned and looked at Colin, holding them out in front of him.

'Expensive,' he said under his breath.

'I think his dad pays him to help out in the shed,' said Colin, keeping his voice down.

'What does he do?'

'Fixes craypots, paints the floats, goes with his dad on deliveries, I don't know,' Colin shrugged. 'Fisherman stuff.'

'My mum says Mr Davies is reckless,' said Tim, holding the sunglasses up to his face and looking out the window. 'He has pots in the water off North Point, where that guy put his boat on the reef that time. My mum said no-one else is game to go up there because the swell is too big, and it pushes you too close to the rocks. She says she doesn't know why he bothers because his catch isn't better than anyone else's.'

'That's where Darren goes in the tinnie,' said Colin, thinking about the visit to the cray boat last weekend.

'It's alright for a small boat like that, but in a big boat you have to time it right, so you can get over the rocks. Mum said if you don't, you'll get smashed. Anyway, I wish my dad gave me that much money to help him out.' Tim slid the sunglasses back into Darren's pocket. 'I wouldn't be buying fancy sunglasses with it though.'

'Yeah? What would you buy?'

'A long board. *Endless Summer*, man.' He showed him the peace sign then flipped it.

Colin rolled his eyes. Tim was the best surfer of the three of them, but the hippy culture wasn't his thing. When everyone else was doing grunge and fighting their mums to let them grow their hair like Kurt Cobain, Tim was wearing polo shirts and going to the hairdresser once a month. Like Amy, he was a natural athlete. If he had money, his dad's shed would be full of surfboards, dirt bikes, cricket bats, tennis rackets, even golf bags. He didn't have money though. Neither did Colin's parents. Like Tim's family, they were ordinary people with ordinary jobs and enough money to raise their kids to become like them. No-one else seemed to mind, but Colin knew he wouldn't come back to Weymouth after he left for boarding school. Despite what Mr Davies had said on the boat, he wanted to use his brain to make money and hang out with people who did the same. He wanted to buy nice things. He wouldn't mind a pair of sunglasses like Darren's.

The boys went separate ways after form room. Colin had advanced maths in the main building and walked on his own across the quadrangle. Amy was going to the same class and met him halfway, walking over from the science block. He could smell the chlorine in her hair and see the circles from the swimming goggles around her eyes.

'Hey Colin, how was *Star Trek*?' she said as she got closer.

'Great, yeah,' he replied. 'That was a good call, thanks. How was *Mr*, ah ...?'

'*Bean*. Really funny. He put a raw turkey on his head. He had his face right up inside its guts.'

'Right. Slapstick then?' Colin couldn't see that being Amy's thing. He pictured her more of a Kate Winslet in *Titanic* kind of girl, weeping as Leonardo DiCaprio slid into the icy ocean, all blue from the cold.

'Yeah, kind of. He's got this great face.' She twisted her mouth and crossed her eyes. It was not a good look.

'Oh-kay.' He looked at her sideways and she punched him in the arm.

'Go get it out yourself if you don't believe me.'

'Nah, I think I'll pass,' he said, rubbing his shoulder. Girls needed to be taught how to punch without hurting people when they didn't mean it.

'Your loss.'

They walked up the red painted concrete steps into the building and followed the wide corridor around to the left. It was cool inside after the quadrangle. Voices and footsteps echoed as students made their way to class. At the far end, Colin could see a group of year nine boys walking four abreast toward them, leering as they forced other students to dodge out of their way. The public address system crackled open. *Students are reminded to respect their peers and kept left on school paths and in corridors.* The boys laughed and vaulted down the next set of stairs, heading away from the building and the school grounds.

A girl in their year came toward them, a little girl beside her, holding her hand and clutching a football to her chest.

'Hi Jaelyn,' said Amy. She squatted on her heels. 'Hi Ashleigh, give me five.' She held out her palm and the little girl handed the ball to her sister and tapped her own hand against Amy's, a delighted grin on her face.

'Are you going to high school now? Wow, you must be so smart.'

Ashleigh giggled and hid her face against Jaelyn's leg. She wore an oversized club jumper and yellow leggings, scuffed white sneakers on her feet.

'She came with me on the bus,' Jaelyn explained. 'Aunty Robyne's picking her up out the front.'

'Oh no, I was hoping you could help Colin with his maths.' Amy feigned dismay. She leaned closer and whispered in Ashleigh's ear. The little girl giggled and stole a look at Colin around her sister's legs.

'I have a football,' she said, suddenly remembering and reaching up to reclaim the ball, her eyes fixed on Colin.

'Oh wow.' Amy inspected the small, foam-filled oval. 'Did your brother give it to you?'

'Wesley plays for Railways. In the league.' Ashleigh's face was serious as she spoke.

'He must be good.'

'He is.' Ashleigh took her ball, clutching it to her chest, and looked up at her sister. 'He's going to be Fairest and Best.'

'He sure is, Ash.'

Amy and Colin waved them goodbye and ducked into the classroom as the second bell rang, the maths teacher giving them a look but saying nothing. They were both A students and Colin knew he had better things to do than give them a hard time for getting to class right on the bell. They settled into their seats and took out their workbooks.

Colin's last class before lunch was English with Darren and Tim and they met outside the classroom so they could walk to the canteen together. Darren fished the sunglasses out of his pocket.

'Since when did you start wearing shades?' asked Tim with a knowing glance at Colin.

'Since I became cooler than you.'

'Let me see,' Tim plucked the glasses off Darren's face. 'Ray-Bans. Nice.' He put them on and drew himself up tall, rolling his shoulders backwards, and thrusting his face at Darren.

'If you were any other man, I'd kill you where you stand.'

Darren just laughed. 'Yeah, except when did a Klingon need sunnies?' He crouched and blasted an air-machine gun at Tim. 'Resistance is futile!' Tim pretended to explode backwards, falling into the English block bins, and landing on his butt.

'Hey, careful with the shades, man.' Darren reclaimed his glasses and they picked Tim up, righted the bins and walked to the canteen, reciting quotes from the movie from the night before.

The school canteen had been added to the end of the main administration building on the opposite side of the quadrangle. The counter was locked up at night with roller doors and was wide enough to take six lines. Students queued on a concrete floor under a corrugated iron roof, each line separated by galvanised pipe railing. The lines already reached the outside of the covered area by the time they arrived, and the boys joined Amy in the sun at the end of the queue.

'How was English?' she asked as they walked up.

'Same old, same old,' Colin shrugged. 'Not my thing.'

'The new teacher's cute, though,' said Darren. 'Nice arse.'

'Ms Johnson? She's Mr Johnson's sister. You'd better not let him catch you saying that.'

'Do you know everyone?' asked Colin.

'She's in the masters' squad,' Amy replied, 'and she was in the state team for butterfly so, Darren, you'd better not let her hear you saying that sexist shit either.'

She turned her backs on them. Darren studied his shoes. Colin shuffled closer to Amy in the line.

'Hey, how do you know Jaelyn Worner?'

'I don't,' she answered, 'Darren does. We saw them at the playground near the civic centre one day after school. Darren's dad was talking to Mr Worner and I had to push Ashleigh, like, a hundred times on the swing.'

'Dad sells Mr Worner undersized crays for cash,' Darren explained, trying to recover lost ground. 'I sometimes go with him.'

'How does that work?' asked Tim. 'Don't fisheries inspect the catch?'

Darren gives him a look like he's just asked if the earth is flat. 'We don't bring them in through the wharf. What'd you think we're stupid or something?'

'Is that where you were going last night? To the Worners' place?' Colin asked.

Darren looked surprised. 'Yeah. Jaelyn was there but I thought she was already in bed. How did you know? Did she say something?'

'You passed us when we were leaving Tim's. I waved but you didn't see me.'

Darren shrugged. 'More important things to do, mate.' Colin batted him across the head.

'Isn't she friends with your sister?' Amy asked over her shoulder as she paid for her order.

'Who?'

'You've only got one sister, idiot.' Darren batted Colin back. 'Rebecca, remember? The red-headed chick who lives in your house?'

'The one Darren has a crush on,' said Tim, cutting in.

'As if,' Darren shot back, but his face turned red and they all laughed at him.

'I meant Jaelyn,' says Amy. 'She's friends with Rebecca. Don't they play netball together or something?'

'Maybe, yeah.' Colin frowned. Amy laughed at his puzzled expression.

'Obviously, you never go and watch your sister play. Jaelyn's brother Wesley goes every week. I see them in the carpark after training on Wednesdays. He's hot. I think he has a thing for Rebecca.'

Darren scowled.

'Who'd want to date a stupid footballer?' He put a fifty dollar note on the counter and ordered his lunch.

CHAPTER 21

Sandra

Sandra leaves the pub not long after Colin and walks to her car. She has had two drinks over two hours and thinks she should be good to drive. As she walks, she shifts her bag away from the road and balls her keys in her hand, the car key pointing out between her second and third knuckles. Orange floodlights have come on over the foreshore, making the now empty playground look sickly and strange. Further along, the marina is the same and the masts of closed-up sailing boats rock backwards and forwards under the orange glow. Seagulls sit on the rigging, unconcerned by the movement.

There is something about this part of town at night that Sandra has never liked. She remembers Keith's comments about the TAB and the group of boys she had seen two nights ago with their hidden grog. It's the street drinking that does it. People soaked in alcohol lose their inhibitions. They talk loudly to each other, swear, and walk past you on the street closer than they would if they were sober. They look at you openly, appraisingly, even when you make yourself small, keeping your eyes down and your steps steady and even. Sometimes they make comments. She knows the sense of threat is not just in her head. She has seen the results of late-night brawls and beatings that happen in the park across the road from here; she's locked the emergency department doors against drinkers who have wandered up to the hospital, smashing bottles and shouting in the floodlit carpark. This evening it is still quiet, but she is glad, nevertheless, when she reaches her car and has locked the doors.

She drives north along the bay, the same route the school bus takes each day. The ocean is dark and flat. Sandra can feel the reassuring weight of it beside her, its unhurried movement as it breathes in and out. Red-and-green shipping lights blink on and off out in the bay. She winds down the windows to hear the shush of the water on the beach, fills her lungs with salty air and feels her own breath come easier as she leaves the town centre behind. She shakes her head to herself, returning to Colin's revelation. It couldn't be true. Darren must have been shooting his mouth off. It wasn't possible he could have twenty thousand dollars stashed away somewhere. She thinks it is more likely his dad had told him he could earn a half share in a boat if he kept doing chores for him. Maybe he told him once he was twenty thousand dollars worth of the way there. That was the more likely explanation.

She feels tired. Her lungs deflate, pushing out the sea air, and with them her shoulders sink down and back into the car seat. She locks her elbows, pushing against the steering wheel. Does it matter if Darren had money? He has been gone ten years now. How much of a difference is it going to make? If it had anything to do with his death, it is long gone now, much like the Weymouth rapist and Mr Arthur and any other suspect from that time. Except Greg, of course; he is still here even if he is not part of her life anymore. And now Barbara is gone too. Sandra knows Barbara didn't kill Darren. She might have had sharp words with him from time to time, as they all did with each other's kids, but she loved him like her own children and would have defended him to her last breath. But even if she didn't feel that way, even if she had a motive, even if she was a protective mother, she couldn't have done it. There wasn't time that day for Barbara to get down to the river mouth. Digging it all up will not bring back Barbara or Darren. Sandra has nothing more to say or do that will help anyone.

Before the highway crosses the bridge, she pulls onto the gravel shoulder. It is dark here. Her headlights pick out the trees on the embankment and reflect off the water below. The other side of the river is black except for a single floodlight that illuminates the barbeque station. She gets out of the car and picks her way down to the riverside, thankful she chose to wear flat shoes. The rocks are dry, and she sits to contemplate the water. It is barely moving. The small channel at the river mouth where Jessica played, she guesses, will having stopped flowing by morning. There won't be any more water coming down the river until winter unless a cyclone in the north brings rain inland. When that happens, the flood can bring debris that chokes the trees on either side until the council comes to clear it away. The rocks can be four metres underwater at the peak. She remembers bringing the three boys down here when they were little, letting them throw leaves off the bridge into the rushing water and watching them float downstream, holding tight to their small bodies as they clambered onto the railing to get a better view. She has a sudden memory of their little-boy smell, of shampoo and soap and the deeper scents of sweat, socks and mud. The dark crescents of unwashed fingernails. The line-up of cuts, scrapes, bruises and bee stings. Only one broken bone between the three of them, she thinks, eyeing the handrail.

Sandra hears a branch crack on the path toward the beach and she tightens. She slides her car key back between her knuckles, ready to jump to her feet and run. There is a snuffling sound and she feels the back of her neck prickle. She strains into the darkness, unwilling to move until she knows what is out there. A dog barks on the other side of the river and a car comes around the corner and onto the bridge. Its headlights sweep across the water and she glimpses a figure walking toward her, twenty metres away. She rises silently and hurries back toward the embankment. A voice stops her.

'Sandra?'

She pauses and looks back.

'It's OK, Sandra, it's me, Stuart.'

Her breath catches as the figure resolves out of the darkness. She peers toward it, still ready to escape. It is not until he is within two metres and she can make out his face that she breathes out again.

'Oh,' he sees her distress, 'I've frightened you. I'm sorry.'

She gathers herself and he puts a hand on her arm. It is dry and weightless.

'Come on, sit down here with me,' he says.

They go back to the rocks and sit side by side, facing the water. Stuart opens his backpack and pulls out a bottle and a plastic cup. Sandra feels her heart slowing.

'I'm afraid I've been doing what we always thought our kids were up to.' She can smell the wine on his breath and hear the sheepishness in his voice.

'That seems perfectly reasonable under the circumstances.'

He pours wine into the cup and passes it to her.

'As it turns out, I've just had a drink with Colin,' she says, taking the cup from him.

He looks at her sharply and she registers the alarm on his face.

'That's good, I suppose,' he says, carefully. 'Good that he feels he can talk with you.'

'He seems to think his mum did it.'

'Does he? Do you?'

'No. But he thinks she could have been at the scene.'

Stuart doesn't say anything and stares out at the water.

'Keith Samson seems to think so too,' she adds. 'He's worked out that the receptionist wasn't at the desk when I left.'

'I see.' He inclines his head at the river. 'It still doesn't mean anything though, does it? The evidence is still circumstantial, and it doesn't give her a motive.'

'It doesn't explain the DNA under Darren's fingernails though.' She can hear impatience in her voice and isn't surprised when Stuart reacts.

'You said you thought she didn't do it.'

'No. Yes,' she backpedals, alarmed at his raised voice. 'I don't think she did it, but Keith will want to find an explanation for the DNA.'

'I don't give a fuck what Keith Samson wants. Who cares how the DNA got there? My wife wasn't on the riverbank when your son was shot.'

Sandra picks up her keys and gathers her cardigan around her, ready to leave for the second time.

'I'm sorry,' he says. He puts a hand on her arm. It is firmer this time. 'Please don't go.'

They sit in silence in the dark, staring across the water at the floodlight on the opposite bank. It makes the barbeque shelter look lonely, isolated, an ugly manufactured thing with sharp corners and hard shadows against the softer shapes of river and trees. Sandra loves the way native trees look at night. The scruffiness of their canopies is obscured in the moonlight and their slender trunks and branches become elegant and wistful. She looks up and sees that above them, the sky is clear and littered with stars. She remembers the night Darren called her into his bedroom, his child's voice full of wonder.

'Mum, look what I've found,' he'd exclaimed, pointing out the window. 'The sky is sparkling. It's so beautiful.'

She'd sat with him while he pointed out the stars that he'd decided were his favourites and wished she'd known their names so she could tell him.

The sky at night in the Pilbara is the same, she thinks. Deep black, and the cosmic lights shining through the clear, dry air brighter than they do anywhere else on earth. Barbara would have spent at least one or two nights under that sky. Sandra knew she was planning to sleep outside, wanting to immerse herself in the landscape. She wonders what she felt, if she experienced the same sense of wonder, or perhaps reconnection.

'Do you think she was happy to be there?' Stuart asks, as though reading her mind.

'I don't know. Yes, I guess,' she replies. 'She'd wanted to go for a long time.'

'I wish she'd had longer. To have gone that far ...'

'I know.' She lays a hand on his shoulder. 'That's hard.'

'I wish I knew what she was thinking. I hope she wasn't scared.'

Sandra thinks Barbara was scared. At least for a time until the confusion set in. She doesn't say anything, not wanting to lie but not wanting to hurt him either.

'Do you think she was comforted by being up there?' he asks.

'I don't know. I don't know if that's a real thing or something we just make up, so we feel better about stolen children rediscovering their own country. She never lived there. She was born in the city.'

'But isn't there a – you know – kind of genetic memory? Maybe she knew she was back where she belonged?' Sandra hears pleading in his voice.

'Maybe there is.' She gives in. What does it matter if it comforts him? Even if all Barbara saw in her last hours were unfamiliar rocks and dry sand, Sandra was sure she would have been happy she'd finally made the trip. It doesn't make it any better for Sandra, though. A life has still been lost and a wife and mother and best friend taken. It might be romantic to think Barbara had finally made her pilgrimage but there is now one less person in the world who loved and was loved back and still had so much to do. Sandra is sure if Barbara could choose, she would want to live long into old age, snuggle grandchildren, and die in her own bed in the town where she lived most of her life, content knowing she was respected for her contribution to her community. That's what Sandra wants.

'Did we do the right thing?' Stuart asks, his voice catching. 'Maybe we should tell the truth now she's not there anymore.'

'No Stuart, we shouldn't. It will only make everything worse.'

In the darkness, she can hear him working hard to control his breath and she knows he is crying. She reaches into her pocket and passes him a tissue.

'Thanks.'

Sandra waits while Stuart composes himself then stands to leave.

'Does Colin know you were at the river that day?' she asks, looking down at him.

He doesn't look up. 'Yes, he does.'

She looks out across the rocks and the water and the grass. The line of trees where the path disappears is black, opaque in its secrets. She wonders if it will ever reveal what happened in there ten years ago, who was lurking, and why they did what they did.

'Then you'd better talk to him before Keith does.'

CHAPTER 22

Colin

Ten days before Darren dies

Auntie Sandra was sitting at the kitchen table with his mum when Colin arrived home from school. They had two glasses of wine and a plate of cheese and crackers on the table between them. His mum put a piece of cheese in her mouth as he walked into the kitchen and she gestured wordlessly with the other hand for him to come to the table for a hug. He didn't mind hugging his mum in front of Darren's mum when he was on his own, but when Darren was there too, he found reasons to break away. He leaned into her, received an upward kiss, and stayed there with his arm draped over her shoulder, scoping out the cheese board.

'How come Jaelyn Worner's auntie picks her little sister up from school?' he asked as he reached for the knife. He cut a fat slice of hard cheese and put it in his mouth, wincing at the sharp taste.

'What do you mean?' his mum replied.

'Yesterday, Ashleigh came into school with Jaelyn on the bus and her auntie picked her up from out the front.'

'That's because Jaelyn lives east of the highway with her granddad and Auntie Robyne lives in town.'

'Why doesn't she just go out there and pick her up?'

'Because she doesn't have a licence, bub.'

'Why not?' He swallowed the cheese down and sliced the wedge of soft cheese. It oozed around the knife as he pushed down, and he scraped it off the board with the blade. He caught his mum giving Auntie Sandra a look.

'Auntie Robyne lost too many demerit points and had her licence suspended,' Auntie Sandra explained.

'Is that because she was caught driving under the influence?' He felt a stab of pleasure as his mum looked up at him in surprise.

'We learned it at school,' he explained. 'I like the soft cheese best. Is there any more?' He put another sloppy piece of cheese in his mouth and walked back to the fridge.

'What about Ashleigh's mum and dad?' he asked, with his head inside. There wasn't any more soft cheese, so he decided to make a Milo instead. He pulled a two-litre bottle of milk out of the fridge door.

'Her dad drives trucks for Smithson's and he's away a lot. Her mum lives in Perth.'

'That sucks.'

'Yes, it does, doesn't it?'

'What about Jaelyn's mum, why can't she look after her?' He put a glass on the kitchen benchtop and started filling it with Milo.

'Aw, bub, Jaelyn's mum took off years ago. We don't know where she is.'

Colin looked up as Auntie Sandra glanced at his mum and saw his mum shake her head and look away.

'What do you mean, *took off*?' he asked. He didn't like it when adults tried to be evasive. They weren't any good at it.

'Your mum means she's missing,' Auntie Sandra replied. 'No-one knows why.'

'But mums don't just leave their kids,' Colin protested. 'Why aren't they looking for her?'

'It's complicated, love.'

Colin stirred the milk into the Milo hard, making it slop over the edges. He knew some adults drank too much and lost their licences, or even went to prison and had their kids taken off them. But mums don't *take off* without their kids for no reason. He felt his throat go tight, thinking about the little girl with her foam football and yellow leggings. What if his mum just decided to up and leave one day? He looked back and forth between the two women at the kitchen table.

'Adults are full of shit sometimes,' he declared, and took his Milo to his room. He thought about shutting his door to show his disgust but left it open in case they said anything interesting.

Colin knew Ashleigh's dad, Randall, was really her stepdad, or maybe not even that because someone said he and Ashleigh's mum never got married. Ashleigh's dad was also Jaelyn's dad, but because he used to work in the city, Jaelyn had to live with her granddad. He only came back last year and that's when Ashleigh came with him. They live together in old Mr Worner's house – Ashleigh, Jaelyn, Wesley, their dad, and their granddad. There weren't any mums there. Colin heard the kids who live east of the highway walk the long way around to school to avoid going past the Worners' house because they're scared of the old man. It's the same as all the other houses – a blue fibro bungalow bleached by the sun and sitting up on wooden stumps. Colin drove past there once with his mum. Two dogs eyed the street from the shade underneath the house, too arrogant to cross the crispy lawn and bark at passing cars. The front door was open, and the screen door propped ajar with a brick. A bitumen driveway, ragged at the edges, disappeared around the side of the house, but there were no vehicles and no sign of any people, just a thin hibiscus with a single red flower next to the veranda steps.

Colin's mum had pulled up at the front of a house opposite, instructing him to stay in the car. He'd sat there looking at the empty Worner house, watching the heat shimmer off the roof. He'd heard Jaelyn's brother Wesley lived in a caravan in the backyard, even when he was at high school. Colin wished his mum had parked further along the street so he could see it. Living in a caravan was cool, even if it was east of the highway. Colin was working up the nerve to get out of the car and have a look when his mum came out, the screen door clattering behind her and setting off the Worners' dogs.

'Shut up, ya mongrels,' yelled a man's voice from across the street.

Colin jumped in fright and stared wild-eyed at the empty house, unable to find the person who spoke. He flicked his head from side to side until he locked on the doorway. Behind the partly open screen door, he could just make out the outline of a thin man standing very still. Colin willed his eyes to bring him into focus but the contrast between the dark doorway and the bright yard was too much. He thought he saw the man's head flick upwards in acknowledgement at him, but then his mum interrupted his view by climbing back in the car. He looked again as they pulled away, but the man was gone.

Still hungry after the cheese and the Milo, Colin remembered the half full packet of crackers on the kitchen bench and left his bedroom to retrieve them. His mum's voice got clearer as he walked down the hallway and he slowed down to listen to her.

'It's becoming more and more of a problem,' she was saying. 'Children of people like me are at risk, you know. They have a higher rate of truancy and poor health outcomes, even the ones that don't end up with a habit. They'll be forever stressed out about money. They won't do well when they grow up and they'll end up as my clients and your patients again with their own children.'

'Are you worried Rebecca and Colin might be at risk of those things too?' Auntie Sandra replied. Colin could hear a careful, gentle tone in her voice. He imagined that was what she sounded like when she was at the hospital.

'Don't you go doing the social worker thing with me, Sandra,' he heard his mum say. He could see her at the table, tilting her glass at Auntie Sandra, and heard the smile in her voice. 'I can outdo you on that score any day of the week.'

'What am I supposed to be stressed about?' he asked, emerging back into the kitchen and grabbing the crackers.

'Your grades, my son,' his mum replied.

He pulled a face. If she was going to lie, she'd have to do better than that.

'I don't need good grades,' he teased her, 'I could leave school now and earn more money than anyone by getting a job on the mines.'

'You still need a qualification to work on the mines,' she retorted, dismissing the taunt. She knew he was desperate to go to university.

'Cyril Worner doesn't have a university degree and he works on the mines.'

Colin's mum gave him a sharp look.

'What do you know about Cyril Worner?' she asks. Her voice had an edge to it.

'I saw him that day when you went to visit a client. And he was up at North Point when we went there with Mr Davies in the school holidays. Mr Davies said he's an unskilled labourer and he makes more than a schoolteacher. And he's really old and can still do it.'

'What was he doing up at North Point?'

'I dunno.' He wished he hadn't said anything now. His mum was determined to miss the point and be nosy. 'He probably took Jaelyn and Ashleigh up there to go sandboarding. You know. Just like us.'

'Don't speak to me in that tone of voice, young man,' she shot back at him.

'Whatever.'

'What was that?'

'Sorry, Mum.' He circled around the table and gave her a conciliatory kiss. She wrapped her arms around him and pulled him up against her chair.

'You're a good kid, really, aren't you, bub?' she said, looking at Sandra. Auntie Sandra beamed at them both.

Colin took the packet of crackers downstairs and started flicking through the television channels. What did Mum care what Jaelyn's granddad was doing up at North Point? Just because Jaelyn and Ashleigh were girls didn't mean they wouldn't want to go sandboarding. And who else was going to take them except their granddad? Their parents weren't around to do it. Maybe Wesley, but he was busy with his new girlfriend, according to Jaelyn. She'd given Colin a funny look when she said it and Colin had blushed and Darren turned away.

They'd had fun on the dunes that day. Mr Davies had driven Colin and Darren through the sand in his big Ford all the way to North Point. There was an old house up there, a weatherboard on stumps built when farmers put up shacks anywhere on the coast for holiday homes. This one was abandoned and the two rooms on the south side were half full of sand where the dunes were taking over. Mr Davies had said it would be buried in another ten years. The dune at the front of the shack was the highest at North Point and Mr Davies had brought some old cardboard boxes he said the boys could flatten and use to ride all the way down to the beach. He was going to lift the floorboards out of the back rooms before they were gone forever, he said. He'd taken the boards from the front rooms fifteen years ago and no-one had said anything.

The boys dragged the boxes off the back of the truck and knocked them flat with their feet. They took them to the top of the dune and sat, digging their heels into the sand as brakes. The dune was higher than it had looked from the boat last week. Below, the beach looked flat and far away. It was empty in both directions, up to the nearby point and stretching all the way back to the edge of town, a white strip along the bay. From the top of the dune, Colin could see the reef under the water and how it extended the line of the point out into the sea. The waves were choppy on the south side, the dark blue water tipped with white. On the leeside, there were no white caps and the water was light blue, almost green, with darker patches over reef and weed. Colin wondered if he would be able to see fish and sharks if they were in the water.

'Last one to the bottom carries both boxes back,' said Darren as he lifted his heels and pushed off with his hands. He was already two metres away when Colin pushed off himself.

It took some coaxing for the sandhill to let go of the cardboard. Colin slid a few centimetres and stuck. He needed to wriggle his bum to release it again. This time, he found a drop and felt the board leave the sand just for a fraction of time before touching again. It was enough to get him moving and gain ground on Darren, who was stuck on a shallow slope off to the right. Colin looked down the dune ahead of him and realised that the surface, which looked smooth from above, was contoured with ridges and hollows. He picked out a long straight run to the bottom and trailed his fingers through the sand to steer the board toward it. He picked up speed, adjusting direction to avoid slow spots and the odd pigface clinging to the slope. He worked out he could direct the board by rocking his hips to one side and he made some experimental zigzags, imagining himself on snow skis, zooming down a mountain. As he approached the bottom of the sandhill, he let his fingers drop deeper into the sand, feeling the coolness under the surface and enjoying the drag through his shoulders as his arms pulled backwards. Directly behind him, he heard Darren whoop and figured he had also found the straight run. He looked over his shoulder as he slowed. Darren was gaining on him fast, hands in the air. Colin used the last of his momentum to swerve left and he watched as Darren lost control and tumbled to the beach, the cardboard scooting out from underneath him, catching the breeze off the sea and lifting into the air.

The walk back to the top was harder than it looked, and the boys took a break at the bottom after the third go. This time, Colin went down on his stomach, his hands gripping the front of the board and using his hips and shoulders to steer, like on a boogie board. They'd pushed off, side by side, and he'd got his nose in front of Darren and cut in front of him, making Darren stack it sideways. He laughed at him as Darren spat sand out of his mouth and rubbed his face with his t-shirt. At the bottom, they walked across the sand to the water, where it rippled in over the reef.

'That was sick. We should come up here with our boogie boards,' said Colin.

'We can come up in the tinnie. I reckon I can get it through that channel there,' Darren pointed to a clear patch of water on the north side of the reef, 'and pull it up on the beach. Maybe Rebecca could come too. Get her away from those cows she hangs out with.'

'Moo,' said Colin, and Darren punched him in the arm.

The third walk back up the sandhill was harder again, and the boys were sweating and thirsty by the time they made it to the top. A second car was parked at the shack alongside Darren's dad's truck, both doors open and a forty-five-gallon drum tied to the rollbars behind the cab. Ashleigh Worner was standing on top of it on tiptoes, trying to see the sea. She waved and called out as they scrambled over the crest of the dune.

'They're here! Jaelee, they're here.'

Jaelyn walked around from the front of the cab, carrying a water cooler in one hand. She held the other hand up and waved.

'Well done, Ashleigh. I told you, you'd find them.'

Ashleigh bent down and half disappeared behind the sides of the tray-back. Her head rose back up again, her face concentrated and red.

'We've got boxes! Jaylee, I can't pick them up.'

'Hang on, bub, let me do it for you.'

'I'll get them,' said Colin. 'I'll swap you for a drink.'

He climbed onto the back wheel and reached into the tray, flinging two more cardboard boxes onto the sand. As he straightened up, something glittering on the drum caught his eye. A battery and a light were taped to the top, held fast to the lid with duct tape. He hoisted himself onto the tray to take a better look. The drum smelled of seawater and the bulb was glowing, but only just, and whoever put it there had made sure it wasn't going anywhere. He turned to point it out to Darren and was startled to find him at the wheel arch, arms hanging over the side of the tray, looking at him silently.

'Might be good to get down from there, Col,' he said, his voice quiet. He flicked his head to the side and frowned. *Now.* He pushed away from the tray and Colin climbed down. They both helped themselves from the water cooler.

'Is this your granddad's truck?' Colin asked Jaelyn as they drank.

'Yeah, he said he had some people to see north of town and we could go sandboarding while we were up here.'

Colin looked at the shack's empty doorway. He could see straight through to the sunlight and the scrub at the back, but now it seemed darker than before.

'Come on,' he said to Ashleigh, picking up two sheets of cardboard. 'I'll show you how to go fast.'

When they got back, the first thing Colin saw was Cyril Worner standing in the doorway of the house, smoking, his eyes fixed on the exact spot where they crested the sand dune, sweating and puffing. The drum was gone from the back of the truck, the beacon visible through the open passenger door of Darren's dad's cab where it had been placed on the front seat.

CHAPTER 23

Sandra

Sandra types *inactive bank accounts australia* into her search engine. The top two hits are advertisements for banks. *Find your perfect bank account* and *Apply online for a credit card in five minutes*. The third is *Find unclaimed money – ASIC's Moneysmart*. She clicks on the link and reads that there is 1.1 billion dollars in lost shares, bank accounts and life insurance managed by the federal government. Bank accounts, she learns, become inactive if there have been no transactions in seven years. Money from inactive bank accounts transferred to the government can be claimed at any time and paid back with interest. Intrigued, Sandra types in her own name. There are no results. She tries her maiden name. Again, no results. There are no missing millions for her. She types in Darren's name. Nothing. She leans back in her chair and drinks the rest of her tea, which is now lukewarm. She contemplates the screen. Leaning forward, she types in *Greg Davies*. Again, there is nothing. Her family, it seems, is good at keeping track of their money.

Sandra rakes her fingers through her hair and stretches her back. She hasn't been for a walk today and now it is dark and too late. She unhooks her bra, pulls it out through her sleeve, and tosses it onto the desk. It was foolish, she thinks, going down to the riverbank after the pub this week. She was lucky it was Stuart down there and not someone else. Anyone could be lurking when it was dark. The highway ran straight past, taking all sorts of people up and down the long, empty west coast. Who knew what people stopped for the night? Hitchhikers, drug runners, rapists, fugitives. Murderers. No-one would ever know. Arthur Zelinski said he never saw anyone local down there at night. Only kids during the day, poking sticks into the mud and swinging off the rope swing. The Aboriginal community didn't go there. Not to camp or fish or cook. It wasn't a good place, they said, especially for young men. Looking out of the window, everything between Sandra and the illuminated Virgin on the opposite bank is dark. No cars pass by on the street. To her left, she can see the streetlights on the bridge and on her right, she can see the phosphorescence on the waves. She opens the window so she can hear the water.

If Colin was right, and Darren had been saving for a cray boat and thought he would have enough for a fifty per cent share in three years, he must have put the money somewhere. Sandra hopes it wasn't in a plastic shopping bag under a mattress. If it was, it wasn't a mattress in her house unless it had been secretly taken in the search after Darren died. She remembers the apologetic look on the investigating officer's face when he'd handed Greg the warrant. *Sorry about this mate, we've got to do it. You understand?* Greg had clapped his heavy hand on the man's shoulder. *Sure, mate. Just make it quick, I've got my own work to do.* Police officers had worked through each of the rooms in the house while she waited outside on the lawn. She watched them file out through the back door, shaking their heads and turning to the shed, where most of them had stood only last Friday, stubbies in hand. They poked through the toolboxes, stacks of craypots and piles of nets, checked the glovebox, under the bonnet and in the boot of the Torana, and shaken tins of engine oil. By lunchtime they were done, with handshakes and promises of crayfish at the next barbeque.

Sandra goes downstairs and takes the remains of last night's pasta bake out of the fridge. She pops the vent on the plastic lid and puts the container in the microwave. She has chocolate in her handbag, too, she remembers, and while her meal is heating, she jogs back upstairs to fetch it. Headlights from an approaching car shine on the road and, conscious of the view into the house, she reaches up to close the curtains. She assumes the vehicle is going to go past her toward the beach, but the lights swing inward at the last minute and it pulls onto the verge, a big, red four-wheel drive. Keith climbs out of the driver's seat, empty-handed and alone.

She meets him at the front door. He's not in uniform and he looks uncertain about being here. He takes in Sandra's track pants and cardigan and shifts his weight from foot to foot. She remembers she is braless and pulls the cardigan across her breasts, feigning cold.

'Hi,' he says, and stops. She waits. 'I was up this way and ... do you have a minute?'

She stands aside and lets him in. As she follows him down the hallway, she remembers the pasta in the microwave.

'You'll have to watch me eat, I'm afraid. But I can offer you a cup of tea.'

'You don't have anything stronger by any chance?'

She raises her eyebrows but takes a bottle of white wine out of the fridge and puts it on the kitchen bench with two glasses.

Keith looks apologetic. 'I don't suppose you have a beer?'

She smiles in spite of herself and fetches a bottle from the fridge.

'Here, take these to the table.' She hands him the wine and the beer, collects her pasta and a fork and follows him, a tea towel protecting her hand from the hot container. She takes care not to touch the sides while she eats.

Keith pours her wine, comments on the weather and asks about her day at work. She takes part, allowing the preliminary conversation to resolve itself so he can get to the real reason for his unannounced visit. He doesn't get there until he's drained his beer and she's finished her pasta and taken the container back to the sink. She nods toward the empty bottle on the table and fetches him another from the fridge when he nods back.

'How was your meeting with Colin Russell this week?' he asks.

Of course, she thinks, I should have expected this. Keith was all eyes when Colin arrived at the pub and he'd probably been counting the minutes until he could ask her about it without appearing rude.

'I guess he's doing as well as he can,' she says, aware she is deflecting. 'He's confused and sad; not unexpected in the circumstances, I suppose.'

'No,' he says, tilting the bottle. 'I met with him today. He's doing alright for himself by the looks of things. Married, decent job in the city.'

'Yes, well he's worked hard for it.'

'Was that what he was like at school? Hard-working kid? Bit of a swot?' Sandra can hear the edge of a sneer. Christ, she thinks, what's got into you? The poor kid has just lost his mum.

'He was a nice boy,' she says, defending him. 'He was smart, worked hard, was good to his mum and a good friend to his mates.'

'Yeah, of course he was. What did you really think of him?'

She stares him down.

'I like him, Keith. You've probably worked out that Darren didn't have many friends. Colin and Tim stuck by him. I respect them for that.'

'Darren could be hard work, could he?' He doesn't look chastened and she wonders how some people have relationships at all if they can't read another person's body language.

'He tried hard, but like most kids like Darren, he sometimes couldn't read the play. He'd get the wrong signals, take things too far, and it pissed the other kids off. They thought he was weird.'

'What made Colin and Tim any different?'

'He'd known both of them, mostly Colin, since he was a toddler. He was best with people he knew well, and they were used to his quirks.'

'Did they ever blue? Any fisticuffs over girls? Jealousies?'

Sandra laughed.

'Not beyond the usual rough and tumble. They were more likely to come home half drowned from surfing the river when it was in flood than with bruises from punching each other.'

'Did they drink?'

'No.'

'Drugs?'

'No.'

'I guess they were still too young for all of that.'

Something inside of her stills. 'Yes, I guess they were,' she says softly. Darren would always be too young for all that.

'Sorry.' Keith, to give him credit, looks contrite. 'That was a bit insensitive.'

She waves it away. He changes tack.

'I asked Colin where his parents were that day while he was at the river. His answer was in line with the rest of the investigation. His mum was at work and his dad was at home.' He watches her. 'I told him his dad's thongs were found at the river during the search. Colin said he borrowed them without asking and then lost them at the river the day before. He said he got into trouble for it, had to buy his dad a new pair with his pocket money.'

Yes, thinks Sandra, that's exactly what Barbara would have made him do.

'He also said Darren always had a lot of pocket money. More than the other kids. Colin said he could afford to buy pies and soft drink at the tennis club every week, and sometimes he treated his friends at the school canteen. He was at pains to tell me Darren was quiet about it though, never flashed his cash when other people were around. Apparently, Darren said his dad told him that wasn't cool.'

Sandra nods. That sounds like Greg. Throughout their marriage they had never wanted for anything, but they didn't live big. He kept their spending unobtrusive, mindful of the jealousies flashes of cash can cause in a small town. They bought their clothes, their furniture and their cars from local businesses, eschewing the big city shopping trips made by other families. If they ate out, it was at the local pub and rarely outside of special occasions like birthdays or anniversaries. When they entertained, it was a barbeque in the backyard, the meat cooked on a slab of iron propped over an open fire and the drinks kept cold in an old bathtub filled with ice on the lawn.

Greg had insisted she keep the house, even though the set-up was perfect for his fishing business. It was her home, he said. Shortly after they separated, he also started sending her money. The courts didn't require that she get either the house or the money and Sandra didn't demand it; she didn't even need it. Greg didn't make a fuss. He just came over one day after work and told her that was what he was going to do. The house would be transferred into her name, unencumbered, and the money would be paid directly into her account every fortnight. If she needed more – money for a new car or to fix the washing machine – she should just ask. After that, she heard little of him, no telephone calls, not even any gossip around town. Occasionally she would pass him in the street, and they would stop and chat. He would ask her how she was doing, how things were at the hospital, and then they would go their separate ways.

Keith is determined to pursue the money angle. He is convinced the murder is somehow connected. He doesn't say anything about Barbara.

'I've checked at that bank next door to the pharmacy. The manager there said they don't have any accounts for a Darren Davies. None of the other banks do either.'

Sandra purses her lips and shakes her head.

'What about another account; something that wasn't in his name?'

he asks. 'Money held in trust, anything like that. Somewhere Darren might have deposited money?'

'No, nothing like that.' Sandra knew other families had trust accounts for their kids. Barbara had established one for Colin when he was born. She and Greg had never done it though. She doesn't mention her half-hearted online search or running into Stuart at the river.

Keith exhales, frustrated. She can see he believes he is on the right track but can't find a way to make it work. He's wasting his time. She sees him out and goes to bed, listening to the sea.

CHAPTER 24

Colin

Nine days before Darren dies

It was easy to start a fire at the front of the cave and the boys sat around the flames, poking the wood back into the circle of stones when it fell away. Shadows hovered on the bushes and the white cliff walls. The illuminated Virgin Mary shone between a gap in the trees on the other side of the river. Over her head, the lights from the wharf were a distant orange glow and below her feet the carpark was floodlit and still. The night shift had already arrived. The sea breeze had died. The boys took turns to drink from the bottle of Coke they brought with them from Darren's house. They'd also brought the remains of the pizza Darren's dad had ordered them for dinner, and they fed strips of the empty box into the fire.

Colin hadn't been camping since his parents took him and Rebecca on a road trip around the Pilbara. They'd free camped, pulling in at waterholes or by the sides of dry riverbeds, sleeping under the stars on blow-up mattresses, and waking up shivering with dew on their sleeping bags and animal footprints in the red dirt next to them. Rebecca had been good on that trip, he remembered. She consented to playing hangman in the car when they got bored and went exploring with him each day while Mum and Dad set up their camp sites. One time, they'd walked to the top of a breakaway and found a waterhole on the other side. Their parents let them go swimming there and even joined them for a while, the four of them splashing in the strangely chilly water, their shouts echoing off the rocks. It was too shallow for diving, but Colin and Rebecca took turns at being thrown out of the water by their dad. Even his mum had a go. It was late in the day, but they were dry by the time they got back to the camp, the rocks under their feet still warm from the sun. Colin's dad made a fire on the riverbed and cooked them sausages that they ate between slices of white bread with tomato sauce. There was nothing to do after they'd eaten, so Colin wriggled into his sleeping bag on the wobbly mattress and looked for shooting stars and satellites. Rebecca fell asleep straight away. He could hear her snoring between him and the car.

At the cave, Colin sat on his sleeping bag, but it was thin between his butt and the limestone floor. He wished they'd brought some mattresses, but they were not supposed to be there anyway, and it was hard enough sneaking out at all.

'What do we do now?' Tim asked Darren when they'd finished the pizza. It was Darren's idea to come down here. They'd waited until Mr and Mrs Davies turned out their bedroom light and Darren's dad started snoring, then let themselves out the back door. 'I'm not ready to go to sleep.'

Darren looked pleased with himself. He was waiting for this moment.

'I've got a plan.' He rummaged in the backpack he'd brought with him and pulled out three small bottles of red fluid. 'Shane told me about these guys at some posh school in the city. On their last day, they smeared oil on the windscreens of the teachers' cars and filled the wiper fluid bottles with red food dye. The teachers put the wipers on to clean the windscreens and thought they had blood spraying out of their cars.' Darren fell over himself laughing.

Colin and Tim looked at each other and smiled. It sounded made-up but it was still funny.

'So, what's the plan?'

Darren looked across the water at the glowing Virgin. 'We prank the nursing home cars.'

Half an hour later they were standing in the sheep paddock just outside the reach of the carpark lights. There were four cars in the carpark, three at the back with their bonnets facing the fence, away from the building and in darkness. Tim said they should do those ones first. Darren climbed through the wire and popped the bonnet on the first car, a white Commodore station wagon, and rested the backpack on the engine block. Leaning over, he unscrewed the lid of the wiper fluid reservoir, fished in the backpack for the food dye, and poured in half a bottle. Unable to see the result from the other side of the fence, Tim climbed through and leaned over the bonnet. He laughed.

'Cool. Now what?'

Darren closed the bonnet, taking care to secure it without making a noise, and pulled out a bottle of kerosene and a rag.

'I couldn't find any oil in the shed, but this will work. We wipe it across the windscreen, so the glass smears and they need to clean it in the morning.'

Tim did the honours, dousing the glass from end to end with the kerosene-soaked rag.

'Let's do the next one.'

The second and third cars were spaced out across the row in the same position as the Commodore and they repeated the procedure, keeping out of the light. The fourth car was parked closer to the building. Colin said they shouldn't walk through the floodlit carpark. There was nowhere to hide if someone came out. Tim pointed to the fence line.

'If we walk around the outside, we can come back through the fence next to the corner. We can hide there if someone comes out the front door. They won't see us.'

They climbed back through the fence and circled the carpark. Off to their right, the small flock of sheep made pale, still shapes against the grass. The two closest to them lifted their heads but made no effort to get up. The houses on the other side of the paddock were dark and silent. Beyond the paddock and the houses, the sea shone where it caught moonlight and then was dark as it filled the far reaches of the bay. Colin could hear waves breaking on the shore.

Headlights appeared on the road and the boys flattened themselves on the grass amongst the black pebbles of sheep poo. A patrol car rolled along the road at the end of the paddock. Tim swore. They watched it turn into the driveway of the nursing home and do a slow circuit of the carpark. Its headlights lit up the Commodore and swept across the paddock.

'What do we do?' yelped Darren.

'We shut up and stay where we are,' Tim hissed.

Colin turned his head to look at Darren, who was also flat on his stomach. His face was white, and the rims of his eyes were red.

'Darren, where's your backpack?'

'Oh fuck.' Darren patted the ground around himself with his hands, not daring to lift his head. 'I left it behind.'

Colin felt his stomach sink. The backpack was still at the third car. He couldn't remember where Darren had put it down and he prayed it was somewhere out of sight. He swivelled his head to the left, pressing his lips together against the dirt and the poo, and tried to locate it. The headlights caught the car. Colin could see the tyres and the exhaust pipe but no backpack. It was probably between the bonnet and the fence, he thought. Darren would have put it down to climb through the wire and then forgotten to pick it up again. The patrol car swung toward them. Colin turned his head back the other way and watched the headlights made a lazy arc over the sheep and the houses, reflecting off window glass. He heard voices as the car passed him.

'Look at that, windows wide open.'

'It doesn't matter how many times you tell people.'

'You know whose fault it will be when they get robbed. Or worse.'

'Ours.'

'Yep. Never their own stupid fucking fault, is it?'

The police finished their lap of the carpark and the boys watched the tail-lights as they receded down the road toward the highway and disappeared into the dark. Tim got up and retrieved the backpack.

They turned to the fourth car, a dark blue BMW. It was parked in the closest bay to the entrance, nosed up against a *Reserved* sign.

'Must be the boss,' observed Tim.

They filled the wiper fluid bottle with dye and this time it was Colin's turn to wipe the windscreen. He took the kerosene bottle and the filthy rag and looked over his shoulder into the sliding glass doors of the nursing home. The lobby was fully lit, and he had a clear view of the portrait of the Virgin and the row of lights that led down the corridor to his granny's room. The Virgin looked out at him from above the broad, bare reception desk with her knowing eyes and blue-and-white robes. Colin knew there was a more modern painting in the residents' dining room where the artist had made her pale cheeks darker and her robes less fancy. That was his mum's doing. She'd hassled the nuns about it after Granny moved in and eventually they'd given up and let her have her way.

'Hey Colon, you constipated again?' said Tim, 'Get moving, we don't have all night.'

Colin leaned over the bonnet and wiped the rag back and forward across the windscreen, pushing it into the corners. For good measure, he tipped the rest of the bottle over the windscreen as well. He got a nose full of the fumes and he stepped back, looking at the oily smears shimmering under the carpark lights.

'Done.'

'I'm hungry,' said Tim. 'Will the fish and chip shop still be open?'

They agreed to find out, and Tim lead them back through the fence and across the dark paddock toward the highway.

'How will we know if it works?' asked Colin.

Darren shrugged. He hadn't thought of that.

'We have to get up early anyway to go back to Darren's before his mum wakes up,' said Tim. 'We can come here at the shift change tomorrow morning and watch the fun.'

Behind them, the front doors of the nursing home slid open and they bolted to the tree line. When they turned to look back, panting, they could see a nurse standing at the edge of the portico. She lit a cigarette and wandered into the carpark, eyeing the BMW in the reserved bay and blowing smoke out of the side of her mouth. They watched as she reached into her pocket and, checking first over her shoulder, squatted next to the car and scraped her key along the wheel arch, the teeth-aching sound cutting across the paddock. The boys looked at each other, eyes wide, and slunk off, following the direction of the patrol car.

CHAPTER 25

Sandra

Sandra has the day off and she's booked a hair appointment. She's known her hairdresser since they were in primary school and sees her every eight weeks for a cut and colour. It takes two hours and during that time Sandra drinks tea, eats biscuits, and catches up on the town gossip she hasn't already heard at the hospital. Teresa will want to know all about Barbara today, of course. Teresa and Barbara didn't socialise together, but Teresa also did Barbara's hair and knew Barbara and Sandra had been close since the kids were born. She will be able to tell her what people are saying about the DNA results. Sandra assumes it is common knowledge.

Teresa's own daughter, Sophie, is the same age as Rebecca but attended the Catholic girls' school next to the cathedral in the centre of town. When she graduated, Sophie went to university in the city and now works in the bank on the main street next door to the pharmacy. Like her mother, she wears bright colours and has an open-mouthed laugh that can be heard from halfway down the main street.

As she turns into the carpark, Sandra wonders what Darren would have done if he'd lived to finish high school, if he'd have found work in town like Sophie and Rebecca or gone away like Colin and Tim. He wouldn't have attended university. He wouldn't have got the grades or known what to do when he got there. Perhaps he could have completed a course at the local technical college, maybe even worked toward a trade qualification. Greg knew plenty of tradies in town who could afford to take on an apprentice. One of them would have had the patience to work with Darren, she's sure. Sandra imagines Darren at nineteen with work boots and a high-vis vest, travelling around town in the passenger seat of a white trade ute. She pictures a man in his thirties at the wheel. He would be taking on the family business, apprenticed to his father back in the day, and was now doing his bit for the industry by training up another willing young lad. A plumber, perhaps, with kids of his own who aren't interested in joining the family business. He'd learn Darren's quirks and let Darren learn from his mistakes. His mum would still be doing the books and she'd call Sandra if the boys were working late. Darren would come home each night exhausted but exhilarated and full of stories. Sandra sits in the car, staring out the windscreen, then blinks her eyes, gathers up her purse and steps out into the heat.

The doors to the salon slide open and she enters the cool, muted black-and-grey space. The moody decor is helped along by the dark scent of amber and background music that hums tones instead of melodies. Teresa sees her in the mirror and turns to greet her, shimmying across the floor in a sparkling red-and-green kaftan that makes her stand out against the background.

'There you are. I thought you were never going to get out of the car.' Teresa takes her into her arms, jingling at her ears and hips. 'I was so sorry to hear about Barbara.'

She holds Sandra at arms'-length and scrutinises her face. Sandra watches as Teresa's face adopts her own expression and she sees she must look tired, worried and old. Against her sparkly friend she is suddenly self-conscious in her mum jeans and white t-shirt.

'You need this today,' Teresa declares, and propels her across the room, settles her into a chair and calls for an assistant to bring tea, biscuits and magazines. *The good ones, not the rubbish ones.* The assistant is wearing black and grey and fades into the decor. The teacup is deep red.

'What are we doing with this?' Teresa asks, running her fingers through Sandra's hair. Her touch is gentle, and Sandra leans back into it. This is what she misses most about being single. She'd pay to have her hair done just for the feeling of another person's hands touching her. Teresa's long fingernails rake her scalp, making it tingle. She replies that she just wants the usual cut and colour.

'I'll leave myself in your hands.'

'Excellent. I'll get the colour mixed up and be back in a minute.'

They had always planned to get their hair done together, she and Barbara, but had never found the right time. Shift work made it difficult for Sandra to plan in advance and Barbara wasn't free on weekdays. Teresa had promised them champagne for when they finally got around to it. She would give them new 'do's, something different, a surprise. That wouldn't happen now.

'So, what do you make of this DNA business?' Teresa asks when she returns with her trolley full of hair dye and brushes. 'I think it's bullshit.'

'It is a bit strange,' Sandra admits, 'but it doesn't mean she was there when it happened.'

'Of course not,' Teresa says. 'Not in a million years would someone like Barbara do a thing like that. Keith's out of his mind.'

She pauses while she brushes the colour into Sandra's hair. 'Between you and me, he should take a break from police work and go visit his son. He never stops working.' She dips the brush back into the pot. 'Joe used to see him in the surf all the time, with his big old dog waiting on the beach. You remember Fred?'

Sandra did remember. Keith and Fred would drive past the house in Keith's old red Hilux whenever the swell was up at the river mouth. Fred was famous for being distracted by nothing as he watched his master paddle out to the reef break, sitting stoically on his towel until Keith came back in. He was even in the local newspaper one day. *Faithful Fred* and his big, shaggy head, staring out to sea.

'Well Joe says he's never out there anymore. He says ever since Adrian moved to the city, Keith goes to work, comes home from work, looks after his dad and that's it. If you ask me, he needs to take his long service leave, go and see his son, go up to Bali for week, maybe on one of those surfing safaris. Live a little.'

Sandra purses her lips. She's been on the end of similar advice herself, but she never considered that Keith would also be the subject of town gossip. Suddenly, she feels bad for him, and then feels guilty that it never occurred to her to feel bad before. Keith's wife died from a meningococcal infection after a visit to a local swimming hole one Boxing Day about four years ago. The swimming hole was thirty kilometres out of town and spring-fed, but the top layers of water could heat up after a long hot spell and there were signs in the carpark warning people of the risk. Two other people had also been hospitalised that week, Sandra remembers, but Michelle was the only one that died. Adrian had finished high school the following year, then joined the exodus of bright young people to the city, leaving Keith alone in the house.

'Well I guess he's got an investigation to conduct now, so that'll keep him occupied for a while,' she replies.

'It's weird, though, don't you think?'

Sandra is momentarily confused until she realises Teresa has switched back to the DNA evidence.

'It could have come from anywhere,' says Sandra with a sigh. She will be having this conversation over and over. She might as well get used to it and learn how to keep her story straight. 'Darren was at Barbara's house all the time. She even washed his clothes.'

'You still think it was the Weymouth rapist, don't you.' It is a statement, not a question, and she doesn't wait for an answer. 'I agree with you. They never got that bastard. I bet he's long gone. Did you know that one of his victims wasn't actually raped?' She leans in. 'Apparently the girl said he came in the window and tried to tie her up, but she struggled so much that he gave up and left.'

Sandra raises her eyebrows in response but says nothing. Teresa finishes her colour and sets the timer.

'Twenty minutes and then we'll take you to the basin.'

'What do you know about this assault at the high school the other day?' Teresa asks when Sandra is finished having her hair washed. She combs out her hair and finds her part. 'I heard she was brought into the hospital afterwards.'

'The girl that was beaten up by her dad at the bus stop?'

'That's the one; it was in the paper. They said she is only fifteen, poor lamb. Did you treat her? Apparently, he did a good job on her, smashed up her face.'

'I didn't see, but Nat said she'll be alright.' Sandra shuffles in her seat, hoping Teresa will take the hint and not dig further about a patient.

'Bastard. He came in here once, looking for his wife.' Teresa's eyebrows fold in on themselves and her eyes darken. 'He acted like he owned the place. And her.'

'How do you know who it was? Those things are supposed to be confidential.'

Teresa waves her confidentiality into the air.

'Everyone knows. Craig Boyle. We went to school with him, don't you remember? He was an arsehole then too. Mathilda is from his second marriage. She left him too.'

Sandra does remember him. He played football with Keith and was an ugly player, always getting pulled up for high tackles. She never saw much of him at school. They didn't do any classes together and he hung out at the basketball courts next to the bottom oval. She has a vague impression of dirty blond hair and a tan and that she avoided him.

'He got suspended once for biting a kid's ear in a school footy final,' she says, the memory coming to her of a dark-haired boy being escorted up to the nurse's office, his hand clamped to the side of his head and blood dripping through his fingers.

'That sounds about right. He was mean on the field.' Teresa stops to take a drink of water from a pink water bottle with a ring of crystals around its neck. 'His kids went to school with our kids. Darren would have known them. Jason and Shane. They were the ones who everyone thought were responsible for the shenanigans behind the science building.'

Sandra swallows. 'I only found out about that this week.'

'Seriously? Well, I suppose under the circumstances, you probably wouldn't have known.'

'How many times did it happen?'

'No idea. At least four that I know of. It was pretty tough as a mother of girls having that going on at school and the Weymouth rapist running around at night.'

'I can imagine.' Sandra has a horrible thought. 'Sophie was never involved though, was she?'

'No, but she knows the girls who were.'

They discuss Teresa's daughter while Teresa snips. Sophie's been seeing a boy. Teresa likes him. He works on the mines, fly-in fly-out, as a mechanic and has bought a house on five acres south of town. Sophie says his parents gave him the deposit out of a trust fund they'd set up when he was born. His dad runs the industrial equipment supplies store on the highway and Sophie goes to their house for dinner on Friday nights before they go out. His mum, she says, makes great laksa.

'Not Catholic then?' asks Sandra.

'No, but does it matter anymore?'

'I suppose not.'

It is almost lunchtime when Sandra leaves. She walks across the carpark to the supermarket, feeling the wind catch her hair. It is soft against her skin from the chemicals and the blow-dry. She buys milk and some soft, fresh bread for her lunch. She hesitates, then picks up half a barbequed chicken from the warmer. It will have too much salt but will be delicious between slices of the bread with some mayonnaise. She starts to salivate at the thought and smiles at herself. Maybe she should put some lettuce and tomato in there too; make a token effort to be healthy.

As she pulls into her driveway, she comes bumper to bumper with a patrol car. Between the car and the shed, two officers are setting up a line of police tape. Keith walks across the front of the house, where it seems he was knocking on the front door. He is in uniform and gives her an apologetic smile.

'Sandra, we have a warrant to search the shed.' He passes her an envelope, which she puts in her handbag without opening it. 'We'll need the keys to the Torana.'

'Knock yourself out. I'll be in the house if you need anything. I've got no beers left though.'

To her satisfaction, the two officers in her backyard look up at this last comment. She goes into the house to get them the keys.

CHAPTER 26

Colin

Eight days before Darren dies

A police car was parked outside Colin's house for the second time when he walked back from Darren's the next morning. He was late getting home. After Darren saw the intruder, they'd been too spooked to sleep at the cave and had crept back into Darren's house and didn't wake up until nine. They'd agreed not to tell anyone about it. They weren't supposed to be out and if anyone knew they were on that side of the river, that person might put two and two together and work out they'd put the food dye in the nursing home cars. They hadn't woken up in time to go back for the shift change and Colin didn't want to take responsibility for a practical joke that he didn't even get to enjoy. Darren's mum cooked them bacon and eggs, which they ate after finishing all her breakfast cereal, and then sent them home. She had to work that afternoon, she said, and Darren had to do chores for his dad.

The police officer was inside the front door with Colin's dad. Colin's mum was sitting on the couch with a cup of tea. Her hands were shaking, and her eyes were red. All the lights were on. She put the cup down and opened her arms to him.

'There you are. Come here.' Her hug was engulfing, tight, and long. Alarmed, Colin submitted to it, waiting for her to decide when to release him. Over her shoulder, he could see through the window to the ocean. The clouds had thinned, and the sky was clear on the horizon. There won't be any rain, he thought. They had no tennis today and he wondered what Darren was up to later, then remembered he was working for his dad. Maybe he'd call Tim and they could go hang out at the river in the afternoon. His mum relaxed her grip and held his face in her hands. Her eyes welled up again. He realised he'd been planning his day while she'd been sitting here crying. He took one of her hands and held it in his lap, the way he'd seen her do when other people cried.

'Someone broke into the house last night, bub,' she said to him, dabbing at her eyes with the tissue in her free hand.

Colin's chest tightened and he remembered Darren's face as he'd come running down the dark street. They'd been eating chips in the park next to the tennis courts – they had made it to the fish and chip shop before closing after they'd left the nursing home carpark, and even scored a free box of chips that would have been thrown in the bins – and then walked back through the streets. Colin and Tim had gone for a piss in a vacant block when Darren ran toward them, his face wild.

'He's here, he's fucking right here,' he'd gasped as he passed them, heading for the bridge and the north side of the river. Not waiting for an explanation, Colin and Tim ran after him, Darren's fear catching them and driving their legs. Darren pulled up when he reached the bridge lights, his hands on his knees, sucking in air.

'What the hell, Darren?' gasped Colin as he reached him. He braced himself against the railing, thinking he wasn't as fast as he thought he was. 'Who's here? What did you see?'

'The fucking Weymouth rapist.' Darren was walking in circles now, with his fingers interlaced behind his head. He tilted his head backwards to the sky. 'He was right there, climbing in the window of that house. Swear to God.'

'Bullshit, you were seeing things,' said Tim, who had slowed to a walk when the others had reached the lights and now strolled up to them as though nothing had just happened. 'It was probably a cat.'

'Cats don't open windows with their hands, dumb arse,' Darren spat back at him. 'I know what I saw. And he dropped this.'

Darren fished in his back pocket and pulled out a bright, multicoloured square of fabric. He waved it at Tim.

'Believe me now?'

Colin and Tim looked in horror at the scarf.

'Oh shit.' Colin's scalp prickled. 'It's not the same as the others is it?'

'How would I know?'

'We've got to hand it in to the cops.'

'Fuck.' Tim looked taken aback. 'What'd he look like?'

'I don't know, it was dark. Same height as you.'

'I guess we have to report it,' said Colin.

'Oh no, no fucking way,' said Darren, his hands in front of him. 'I'm not having some violent criminal hunting me down because I caught him in the act.'

Colin and Tim looked at each other, eyebrows raised.

'But he might be the Weymouth rapist. There might be evidence at the scene. What if he does it again? And you can't keep that thing anyway.'

'Why not? I found it.' Darren backed away, holding the scarf at arm's-length like a racing flag.

'Because it's withholding evidence – or something – that's why not.'

'Come on, Daz, it's the right thing to do,' Colin pleaded, as Tim's hand whipped out and snatched the scarf away.

'Do what you want, Darren, but you're not keeping this. I'm reporting it to the police tomorrow. I'll say it was me who found it if you're too chicken.'

Colin's mum was talking. He realised he was looking over her shoulder at the sea again.

'Was anything taken?' he asked, bringing himself back to the story of the break-in at his own house. 'How'd they get in? Where's Rebecca? Is she OK?'

'He climbed in through the window in the spare room. I must have forgotten to lock it.' She patted his hand. 'Rebecca is in her bedroom, she's not well. We're taking her to the doctor this morning when the police have finished.'

'Why do you both have to go?'

'Because we do.'

'Did he get into the safe? What did he take?' Colin looked at his dad, who caught Colin's eye and turned away from him, shaking his head, looking down at the floor. The officer was making notes.

'No, no-one else uses it,' his dad was saying. 'Barbara and I are the only ones who know the combination.'

Colin felt his mum's hand tug at his, reclaiming his attention.

'Some money is missing, that's all.' She stood up and brushed down her dress. 'I have to get Rebecca ready.'

'What about me?' His voice came out high and thin, like a girl's.

'You'll be fine. Make yourself some breakfast. The test match will be starting soon. You can watch that while we're out. I'll get something nice for lunch in town.'

'How...?' He went to ask his mum, but she was already disappearing down the hallway.

Colin looked at his dad and the police officer, who was copying down numbers from documents his dad had spread out on the kitchen bench.

'Busy night at your end of town last night,' the officer commented. 'We usually spend all our time east of the highway.'

'Why? Anything I need to know about?'

'A car caught fire in the nursing home carpark around eleven o'clock. One of the night staff saw it go up. She was out there for a smoke. She said one minute everything was fine and the next the car was on fire.'

Colin's dad frowned.

'Do you believe her?'

The officer chuckled.

'She admitted her cigarette might have hit the windscreen when she flicked it away.'

'Deliberate?'

'From what I gather, there's no love lost between some of the staff up there, so yeah, I'd say it was deliberate. But a cigarette doesn't start a car fire, does it?'

Left alone in the house, Colin found himself a pasta bowl and filled it with Coco Pops. It was still a while until lunchtime. He poured in milk until he had a crunchy, chocolate soup slopping over the sides. He used all the milk and left the empty carton on the kitchen bench. No-one had asked him how his night had been, whether they'd seen or heard anything unusual at Darren's house. No-one had asked him anything. The police officer talked to his dad, made some notes and drove away. Rebecca had finally come out of her room, dressed in her pink track pants and a long, baggy jumper. She'd scowled at him from under her hair and said nothing, leaving the house with their parents trailing behind her. His dad put his arm across his mum's shoulders, and he heard him check the lock after shutting the door.

Colin skimmed the floating Coco Pops off the top of the bowl, then put his head down to bench height and slurped off the top centimetre of oversweet chocolate milk. He wondered if he should call Darren and Tim about the fire. They'd really be in the shit now if anyone found out they'd been up there. He trudged downstairs to the games room, flicked on the television to the morning music videos, and folded his feet over the coffee table, resting his breakfast on his chest. On the television screen, a man in an orange shirt danced on a salt pan under a hard, blue sky. Colin knew he was singing about Wittenoom, the town up north in the Pilbara where people got cancer from the asbestos mine. He seen the town's name on the road signs when they'd gone camping that time. The song was an old one but had been played three times at the last school disco. He wondered where the gun was now. He knew his mum had kept it in the basket with the spare pillows because he'd checked every day since they went to the gully. He figured she didn't confess to the police when his dad reported it missing because she was scared of getting in trouble. He got up to check the basket again. Inside his parents' room, the bed was still unmade, and pyjamas left on the floor. He reached under the bed; the basket held only pillows and rugs. He reached further to check inside the suitcases, thinking she'd want to keep it close at night. It wasn't there either. Twenty minutes later, he'd searched through his mum's drawers and wardrobe, shoeboxes, and behind the folded towels in the ensuite, his second breakfast forgotten. It occurred to him she might have hidden it further away while the police were here in case they searched the house.

Outside the bedroom window, Colin heard his dad's car slow down to turn into the driveway and backed out of the room, checking to make sure he'd left everything the way he'd found it. Rebecca's bedroom was open as he went back down the hallway, and he took the opportunity to glance in. It was the usual mess of pastel-coloured girl rubbish. Torn-up balls of pink and blue notepaper, fluffy animals with big eyes, patterned doona and curtains. Colin didn't have curtains, just a solid dark blue blind, and he'd reluctantly given in to having a dark blue check on his doona cover. He looked again at the curtains. Something was off. The flyscreen, he realised, had been removed and placed upright against the side fence. He frowned: he thought his mum said the intruder came in through the spare room window. Maybe Rebecca had just forgotten her house key again. Typical that she hadn't got into trouble for that, he thought. He heard the front door open and went back to his own room to catch up on sleep from the night before.

CHAPTER 27

Sandra

Sandra makes her chicken and mayonnaise sandwich and a cup of tea, and stands at the back window, watching the three police officers do their thing. They have gone straight for the Torana, she sees. They have the boot and the bonnet open and the third man is tapping the interior door panels. She guesses they are looking for the money or the gun or both. They're not there, she thinks, although she acknowledges it would be a good hiding place. Darren wasn't allowed to touch the Torana without his dad. They would work on it together, Greg had said, so Darren could learn. They never seemed to make much progress, despite the hours in the shed and out on the road sourcing parts. It didn't matter. Sandra was just pleased Darren got to spend time with his dad. He worshipped him. Every boy does that, she thinks, but Greg made for a good idol with his working man's physique and distant look. He was sparing with his attention, passing out praise or invitations into his company as though they were currency that was rarely printed. Sandra had no doubt he understood its worth. Like his son, his crew would never grow rich on the coins he threw them, but they hung off his words and jumped on command at the chance of a *well done* and a nod in their direction. An invitation to join him at the pub after work, casually called out of the car window as he drove off, was cash in the bank.

Greg had been the same at school. He wasn't the best looking or a great athlete, but he held himself apart, confident people would come to him. He never chased. If he wanted to go surfing and no-one else would go, he shrugged and went alone. If there was a party on Saturday night but he didn't want to go, he stayed home, casually withdrawing his presence without apology or excuse. It ensured he was picked first for sports teams, had seats reserved for him at the back of the class, and knew where to hang out on weekends. When he asked Sandra out, saying no wasn't an option that occurred to either of them. Staying together through high school and getting married, though, surprised them both, as well as their parents, teachers, and all their friends. When she is asked – and she is often asked – how that happened, when everyone else was flirting at parties and flitting between relationships, she says they just didn't feel the need to change the way things were. They were in love, the sex was amazing (although she had nothing to compare it with), they had someone to travel with, and they were both content to live in Weymouth for the rest of their lives.

She wonders what it says about her that she couldn't keep the marriage together after Darren died. Maybe people were right when they said she didn't look after Greg enough, didn't pay attention to what he needed while they were both grieving. Maybe she could have kept them going if she hadn't focussed so much on her own needs, encouraged him to talk. They'd been to counselling together. The police victim support officer said that serious crime could have a negative impact on relationships and made the referral. The counsellor had talked to them both about the stages of grieving and explained that everyone progresses through them at different rates. She taught them how to recognise the stages in themselves and each other. They needed to allow the other person room to grieve in their own way, she said, and not be judgemental when one of them was feeling angry and the other moving into acceptance. That wasn't the problem, though. Neither she nor Greg, even in their grieving over their murdered son, were inclined to judge each other. She had quietly observed Greg as he passed through denial and then slipped back and forth between anger and depression. He had raged, throwing tools around the shed, even putting a spanner through the window of his car one night, then coming to bed, sobbing with exhaustion. He would spend the following days encircled by a fog through which nothing passed, no sound, no touch, no eye contact, sometimes it seemed not even food. Sandra didn't try to clear it. She went to work, bought groceries, cooked dinner, washed his clothes, and waited until he was ready. Maybe she should have tried harder to break through.

Sandra has no idea how her own grieving had appeared to Greg at that time. He'd never said anything. Did he think she was cold, unresponsive – they certainly didn't have sex – or did he think of her as a rock, holding everything stable? She can't remember her own emotions. It all feels blank when she tries to resurrect them, as though anything she felt at that time was only on the surface; sand that would blow away in the lightest sea breeze. She wonders if she harboured her own rage that she has now forgotten and what it looked like to Greg. Did she slam dinner plates down on the table? Did she snap at cashiers in the supermarket? Did he understand her grieving and forgive her, or did he silently resent the way she behaved?

Sandra watches as the police officers lever the first of the internal panels off the car doors. Figuring they will be there for a while, she fetches her handbag and locks the house.

'I have to go into town,' she says to one of the officers as he retrieves a toolbox from the boot of the patrol car. He nods and she turns her own car back toward the bridge.

The police are wasting their time pulling the Torana apart, she thinks. It was impossible to come up with any scenario that led to someone hiding the gun in the car and, as for the money, Darren wouldn't even think about touching the Torana without his dad, let alone hide anything in it. If Darren had money – if he had money – he'd have put it somewhere that someone else would have told him was a good hiding place. He wouldn't have thought of it himself.

Sandra parks on the main street. School is out and a group of girls in uniform huddle at the front entrance of the pharmacy, whispering and looking over their shoulders. Their shirts are untucked, and they have rolled the waist bands of their skirts, so they reach mid-thigh. Sandra wishes she could tell them they look ridiculous, but she knows they will only giggle and smirk. She would have done the same. An older woman at the front counter is watching them and she rolls her eyes at Sandra as she walks through the doors.

'First-timers?' Sandra asks.

'Wannabes,' she replies with an amused smile. 'I'm keeping an eye on them, though. Maybe they'll work out it's not a clever idea.'

'It worked on me.'

'You were always easy to intimidate, Sandra.'

Sandra walks through to the prescription desk, the aisles smelling floral and then astringent as she passes the perfumes and then the toothpaste shelves. Rebecca looks up and reaches out for the prescription.

'It'll be about ten minutes.'

'I'll go to the bank while I'm waiting.' She has an insurance rebate to deposit.

Next door, Greg is in line for the tellers and he turns and sees her when the doors open. She raises her hand and he leaves his place to join her at the back of the queue. They are both still using the same bank. It made it easier when they closed the joint account and opened their own. They'd done it together, coming into the branch and confusing the teller who seemed to think they were warring parties who he had to put in separate rooms. They are also still using the same insurer and they wave the blue-and-white branded cheques at each other. Her rebate is eight dollars fifty more than Greg's.

'You can afford to buy me a beer the next time I see you at the pub then,' he laughs. He smells of salt with a funky, smoky undertone.

They discuss the investigation. The police have contacted him, of course. They've asked him to go over his recollection of where he was at the time of the shooting, what he knew about Barbara's whereabouts, what she did and what she said the first time he saw her afterwards.

'The thing is,' he tells her, 'I just can't remember all of that stuff anymore. Not the details. People think you've got it burned in the back of your brain because you're traumatised or some rubbish like that, but I don't. It was ten years ago, for Chrissake.'

'I know.' Sandra sympathises with his frustration. Not everyone has a good memory and Greg's is worse than most. Sandra herself has had to keep careful track of what she has told people she saw and heard that day.

'I don't believe it was Barbara, by the way,' he says. 'The DNA doesn't make her the person who shot the gun. It might suggest a motive, I guess, but it doesn't put her at the scene.'

Sandra grimaces. 'What possible motive could she have for shooting her son's best friend?'

'Beats me. That's the cops' job to work out.' Greg squints out of the window into the sun. 'I just wish I knew where Stuart's damn gun got to.'

Sandra remembers Keith's questions. 'Do you know if Darren had any secret hiding places? Places where he might have stashed stuff he didn't want anyone to find? Maybe even away from the house?'

'Why?' Greg looks at her, misunderstanding and incredulous. 'So, his ghost could put the gun there?'

'No, for goodness sake,' she shakes her head at him. 'Not the gun. The police think he might have had some money.'

'Nah,' he dismisses it instantly. 'He had pocket money like the other kids. He kept it in a wallet in his room. The police would have found it when they did the search.'

'Keith thinks he had more than that. Quite a lot more.'

'How much more?'

'Maybe as much as twenty thousand dollars.'

He laughs. 'Where does Keith get that idea?'

Sandra shrugs. 'I don't know, but he seems pretty serious about it.'

'If he did, I don't know where he got it from.' Greg looks at the floor and rubs at a spot in the carpet with the toe of his work boot. She waits. When he looks up at her, his eyes are opaque. Like the sea with the sun on it, she thinks.

'I know he used to hide cigarettes under the tinnie at the beach, taped underneath the seat,' he offers. 'If he was hiding anything away from the house, that's where he'd put it. But Keith's dreaming; fifteen-year-old boys don't get their hands on twenty grand.'

'I didn't know he smoked.' It is Sandra's turn to look surprised. Greg shrugs.

'Boys. We can be good at hiding things from our mums. Especially things they don't want to see.'

They get to the front of the line and Greg turns to the teller to deposit his cheque. The tinnie is long gone, sold, or just given away to a recreational fisherman. Sandra doesn't remember. If there had ever been anything hidden in it, it would have been found years ago. The money, if there was any, is gone.

'Are you still happy with just one account statement or would you both like one?' The teller is addressing her, and she looks up at him, confused.

'No, just the one thanks,' Greg is saying.

'You are entitled to one each, as joint account holders.' The teller smiles at her.

'No, I don't need one,' she smiles back at him. 'Mr Davies and I are no longer married.'

'My mistake.' The teller folds the statement into an envelope and hands it to Greg. Sandra passes over her cheque.

CHAPTER 28

Colin

Five days before Darren dies

The sea breeze was pumping as Colin trudged across the sandbar, his schoolbag over his shoulder. He'd walked home with Darren, but Darren's dad had work for him to do in the shed, so Colin hadn't stayed. He was hot and hungry and the sand in his shoes was rubbing against his heel. He'd get a blister if he didn't stop to take them off, but he just wanted to get home and walked on. The wind gusted, driving sand across the beach and he turned his head away from the sea to keep it out of his eyes. He looked up at the sandstone arches and red clay tiles of the nursing home. He was ashamed of what they did there last week. How were they to know that stupid nurse would come outside and flick her cigarette on the boss's car? His mum would be livid if she found out. No, not livid. It would be that special, sad disappointment that made her go quiet and not speak to him for days. Colin felt a flush of anger. Why should she make him feel guilty? She's the one who took his dad's gun. And she said nothing to the police, letting them think it had been stolen.

Colin reached his street and was finally away from the sand. He walked the last hundred metres to his front door, unhooked the key from the side of his school bag and let himself inside. In the kitchen, he half filled a glass with spoonfuls of Milo, then topped it up with milk. He stirred it with a spoon as he walked to the window and looked out at the water, eating the undissolved crumbs off the top. Sheltered inside from the wind and the sand, he watched the windsurfers. Most of them were just racing backwards and forwards, into the shore and out again, but one guy was doing tricks. He pushed off the waves into the air, floating in the wind until he dropped down again. Before he got to the beach, he dropped the sail, flipped it around, and twisted his hips to turn the board. The back end dipped down into the water and it looked like he was going to sink, but then the wind caught the sail again and he was off, speeding out to the shipping lights.

Colin drained his glass and scraped the rest of the Milo off the side and into his mouth. He went back to the kitchen, found the peanut butter, pasted it on four slices of bread and checked the clock on the oven. No-one would be home for another hour. Last night, he'd checked under his parent's bed again for the gun, but it was still gone. Rebecca had sprung him in their parents' room, and he'd made up an excuse about looking for bandaids for his feet. She hadn't believed him but at least she hadn't threatened to tell their mum. She just scowled and went back to her room. Colin took his peanut butter sandwiches downstairs and stood in the middle of the games room, eating and wondering where he would hide a gun if he was his mum.

Rebecca had been a cow to him since the break-in. She'd come home that day and gone straight to her bedroom, where she stayed with the kitten Dad had bought her *to help her feel better*. It turned out they'd taken her to the hospital instead of the family doctor; Colin had only found out when he saw the outpatient forms on the kitchen bench. She was *not to be disturbed*, Colin was instructed, and he'd heard more *leave your sister alone* in the past three days than he'd heard in his whole life. When he pressed his mum, she said Rebecca wasn't well. The cause, apparently, was none of his business. He figured it was a girl thing. They'd learned all about it in school and, to be fair, being a girl sounded like a raw deal. He didn't see why she was such a bitch about it though. On the odd occasion he did see his sister, she just pulled her hair across her face or grimaced at him like he was something nasty she'd found on her shoe. She ate in her room. No friends came over, which was one good thing as it meant Colin didn't have to put up with Melissa or Lauren and their snarky comments about his hair or his friends.

The storeroom at the far end of the games room was locked, but Colin knew where his mum hid the spare key and he took it from under the base of his dad's club champion trophy. The trophy had a silver plastic man in a wide stance, looking down the barrel of a rifle. Colin thinks this is hilarious because his dad only shoots handguns. Rebecca didn't get the joke when he told her. She just rolled her eyes and turned the volume up on the television. The shooter was mounted on a black plastic plinth with an engraved plaque. *Stuart Russell, Club Champion, 1996.* The plinth was hollow, of course, and Colin's mum had fixed the storeroom key to the inside with Blu Tack. He guessed she would have hidden the gun on the top shelf behind the old camping gear. They hadn't been camping since Colin was nine, when they did the grand family Pilbara tour, and no-one had taken it out since then. Colin unfolded the stepladder and placed it in front of the shelves. The single, bare globe was too bright for the room and he squinted against it, searching for the camping gear behind the plastic buckets and eskies. A cockroach scampered away when he slid the rolled-up mattresses across to get at the tent. He figured it would be in the peg bag. He was right. His mum had emptied the bag of tent pegs and ropes and stuffed the gun in its soft suede cloth in the bottom before putting everything back in on top. Colin climbed back down the stepladder and unfolded the cloth on his lap.

CHAPTER 29

Sandra

By the time Sandra returns to the pharmacy it is almost closing time. A line has formed, and she waits her turn. She is thrown by Greg's comment. Does he really think there were things about Darren that she didn't want to see? That she turned a blind eye? Darren was hard work, like she told Keith, especially when things didn't happen the way he expected. He could lash out then, screaming wordlessly and pummelling her with tiny fists, over peanut butter spread too thin on his toast or a smear of dirt on a toy. The people around him – her and Greg, her mum, the Russells – learned to give him time to adjust to new places, to give him space to fidget, to stick to the plan, to avoid the explosions. They understood that none of it was deliberate, that he wanted to be good and didn't mean to cause trouble.

She watches Rebecca serve a teenage girl. She shows her the box of prescription medication and takes out a blister pack, pointing to one of the pills and then tracing her finger around the circle. The girl keeps her eyes down as Rebecca explains. Rebecca dips her head to catch the girl's eye and Sandra can see kindness in her face. It is the same kindness as her mother and the same kindness her family had shown to Darren when he was little. For a moment Sandra is blinking back the welling in her own eyes.

She feels someone move up close to her, an elbow brushing the top of her arm and she jerks her head up, startled. It is Colin.

'Hi Sandra,' he says, looking down at her.

He was always taller than Darren, Sandra thinks, but skinny with it. Not that Darren was heavy; he was lean as well, but unexpectedly hard-muscled and strong for a fifteen-year-old. Beside him, Colin had looked like a string boy, barely there. Now that Colin has gained weight, and is standing so close, she feels his presence more acutely. She wrinkles her nose. He doesn't smell so great either. It is the raw, stale smell of a person who hasn't been sleeping through the night or drinking enough water. She hadn't noticed it at the pub. He waves a prescription at her.

'Dad's doctor thinks I need a bit of help sleeping,' he says. He doesn't look happy about it. 'Apparently I also need to get a proper check-up when I get back to the city.'

'Do you have a regular GP?' she asks.

'Nah,' he replies, dismissive. 'I haven't seen a doctor for years.'

'Maybe it wouldn't hurt, then.'

Another voice greets them from the back of the queue.

'I didn't think I was going to make it before they closed. Hi, Sandra. Hi Colin, I was wondering if you were in town. Sorry to hear about your mum.'

It is Amy Jenkins. She hugs Colin and then withdraws, studying his face.

'You look terrible. Have you seen a doctor?'

He holds up the blue-and-white slip of paper, which she takes off him and studies.

'Temazepam. Fair enough. Make sure you see your GP when you get home, though.'

'Yes Mum,' he says, and all three of them wince. Sandra wades into the silence.

'Did you kids have any hiding places when you were younger? Any place you'd use if you wanted to stash stuff?'

'What sort of stuff?' Amy asks. She has the same open, interested face she had when she was fifteen. Guileless, Sandra thinks with nostalgia, and she still smells of chlorine. Amy works FIFO on a mine up north somewhere. She must be on break.

'You know, the usual stuff that kids hide from their parents. Booze, cigarettes.'

'Do you mean before Darren died?' asked Colin. 'We couldn't get our hands on any alcohol when we were that age. The bottle shops were too strict, and we were too scared of getting caught to pinch it from home. I don't think any of us have ever smoked.'

'I wish I could say the same for the guys on site,' says Amy, frowning. 'Walking timebombs, all of them. You wouldn't believe their cholesterol levels, Sandra, even in the younger ones.' She turns to Colin. 'What about that cave you told me about?'

'What cave?'

'The spooky one that you all slept in that night. You know, in the cliff under Darren's house.'

'Nah, we never slept there.' Colin is dismissive. Off-hand. 'Who told you that?'

'You did. You said you found a dead cat there once and there was a big crack in the limestone at the back where you could hide stuff, and no-one would ever find it.'

'I was full of shit. Probably trying to impress you.' He turns to Sandra. 'I wouldn't bother.'

Amy turns to Sandra as well. 'It might be worth a look though. Some other kids might have been through it by now, but you never know. What are you looking for?'

Sandra explains Keith's theory about the money.

'So, in short, he thinks Darren had become involved in something bigger than he could handle ...' She looks around but Colin is at the counter, passing the prescription to his sister. He raises his hand to them as he heads back down the toothpaste and shampoo aisle, and they watch as the glass doors slide open and release him onto the main street.

CHAPTER 30

Colin
Two days before Darren dies

After he found the gun in the storeroom, Colin shifted it between hiding places. He put it in his sports bag at the back of his wardrobe on the first day, but he got spooked when his mum went looking for tennis clothes to wash. He moved it to the cavity behind his desk drawer, but it rattled when he shut the drawer too hard, so he took a leaf out of his mum's book and slid it between the folds of the spare doona under his bed. The next day, he put it inside a tennis racket cover and moved it with his rackets to his locker at the tennis club. Two days after that and sweating on the possibility of a break-in at the tennis club, he decided to bring it home again. He stopped at the club on his way to school and let himself in to the grounds through the gate in the chain link fence at the side of the building.

The tennis club had been built in the 1960s and was a plain, single-storey blond brick building with an office, change rooms, and a canteen that served sandwiches and soft drinks through a roll-door hatch. Before that, it had been a white weatherboard cottage that was repurposed as clubrooms. Termites and a grant from the Department of Sport and Recreation had seen it demolished and replaced. Instead of sitting on the old veranda, members watched games from benches on a covered patch of lawn between the club building and the courts, the shade sail printed with the name of the Holden dealership on the highway. The younger kids climbed on play equipment off to one side. The older kids took themselves out of the gate and gathered under the trees in the carpark, out of sight.

Colin unlocked the door for the men's change rooms and walked across the cool concrete floor to his locker on the far side. At this time of day, the club was quiet and all he could hear were the crows in the trees outside and the traffic on the highway on the other side of the courts. Old people would start arriving soon, grandmas and granddads with thermoses and Tupperware containers. He would see them from the bus sometimes, warming up their skinny, wrinkly thighs and adjusting their sun visors. He opened his locker and put the racket in his school bag, working the extra bulk of the gun around his books. His shorts and socks from last weekend were still in the locker and he picked them up, considering taking them home to be washed. Underneath them, he found two muesli bars. He put the muesli bars in his bag and the clothes back in the locker, fitted the lock and hoisted the bag over his shoulders, the handle sticking up above his head.

The lock for the outside door of the change rooms was stiff from exposure and less easy to fit back into place. As he struggled with it, he heard a noise from the end of the building and flinched. Looking over his shoulder, he could see nothing except the forty-five-gallon drum they used as a bin outside the canteen hatch and two chairs left out on the grass. He turned his attention back to the lock, his heart hammering now, and swore under his breath as he finally got the angle right and slid it into place. As it clicked, he heard the sound again and he checked back over his shoulder as he straightened up. On the other side of the bin, two feet in dusty work boots stuck out from the edge of the building. One of them twitched. Colin breathed out. The feet belonged to Mr Arthur, bedded down for the night out of the wind. Colin walked to the end of the building and looked around the corner. Mr Arthur lay on his side, face turned into the wall, his rucksack still strapped to his back and a smaller bag held close against his stomach. He had laid his coat out on the concrete and pulled his hoodie up over his head. He grunted in his sleep. The early morning sun was pushing the shadow of the trees along the wall away from him, but Colin figured he still had an hour before he'd be in sun. He took one of the muesli bars out of his bag and cautiously placed it on top of the smaller bag. Mr Arthur would find it when he woke and one of the grandparents could give him a cup of tea to go with it.

The side trip to the club had taken longer than Colin had planned, and he had to run to the bus stop. The school bus was pulling in as he arrived. Darren and Tim cheered him on as he ran up to it and swung himself inside.

'You took your time,' Darren said as they took their seats at the back of the bus.

'I slept in.'

Darren curled his lip. 'Bullshit, you never sleep in.'

'I was up late, finishing that English assignment.'

'The one due today? Since when do you do assignments at the last minute? I reckon I know the real story, morning glory.' He smirked and grabbed his own crotch.

'Christ, Darren,' Tim pulled a face and glanced down at Colin's bag. 'What's with the tennis racket?' He jabbed his foot at the handle. 'We're doing cricket today in PE.'

'Dad said it needs restringing.' Colin put his own foot on the bag. 'I'm taking it in after school.'

'Mate, you've got to get better at lying.' Darren kicked Colin's foot off and reached down. 'Why's it so fucking heavy? Are you using it to smuggle shit into school?'

Darren zipped open the racket cover, fending Colin off with his other hand. Tim reached across both of them and snatched the bag away.

'Just leave it alone, Darren,' he snapped. He put the bag on the seat on the other side next to the window. Glancing down into the open racket cover, his eyes widened. His mouth snapped shut and he stared back at Colin.

'Yeah, that racket's fucked. Best you get it seen to.'

He re-zipped the cover and they sat in silence for the rest of the trip to school.

CHAPTER 31

Sandra

Sandra had never expected to be a mother. She had known she wouldn't be for a long time, long before she and her friends began to contemplate motherhood and children. Her condition was rare but not unknown in women who have never been sexually active, and she'd had no symptoms, the rogue cells quietly dividing and colonising her cervix for two years until she began to complain of abdominal pain to her mother. Her family doctor, a gentle man with a bow tie and a jar of jellybeans on his desk, had talked to her about the curse of female fertility and what women had to bear to have children. It was not fair, he said, but a fact of life. He told Sandra's mother to buy some over-the-counter paracetamol and codeine and come back in six months if the symptoms persisted. He was confident it would settle down in time. It didn't, of course. They knew that now. The cells continued their unseen multiplication, moving up the left side of her tiny teenage uterus. Not a baby, but another type of new life, unwelcome and destructive. When their genial general practitioner referred her to a specialist six months later, it was too late. Sandra had a total hysterectomy at fifteen. She was too young to feel a sense of loss and her mother was only glad her daughter was still alive.

When she and Greg got married, he already knew she was unable to have children. They were young, with other priorities like finishing their studies and travelling. They partied with their friends, drank too much, smoked too much weed, and parenthood seemed like a far-off thing that real grown-ups did, ones who were tied down by jobs and mortgages. When Greg wasn't on the boat, he was surfing, driving a battered 4x4 up and down the coast, sometimes staying overnight at the remote, secret breaks that the local surfers prized. He was an okay fisherman, not great. The weed made his head woolly, made him forget where he'd put the pots, and lose concentration when he was at the wheel. But he made enough to pay the deckhands and for the fuel, and with her income as well they had enough to live a good life as a young couple with no kids. It wasn't until later, when their friends started bringing babies to backyard barbeques, that they felt a pull for one of their own. They'd both heard stories about the terrible anxiety and heartbreak of would-be parents being assessed and languishing on the waitlist, so they were delighted and a little alarmed when they got the call after only six months. They became a settled family of three, Greg made an effort to cut down on his after-work joints, and by the time Darren was ten, he'd got his act together and was making good money.

Sandra wonders how people see her now. Before Darren died, she was a wife, mother and nurse. All respected roles for a woman in her community. People felt safe with her when they came into the emergency department with their fevers and football injuries. They talked to her at the pharmacy about their kids when she stood in line with them in her hospital uniform, familiar with her face from school assemblies and cake stalls. Or they knew her husband, that he fished alongside their own families, was happy to shout a round or pitch in at the tennis club busy bee. When those people look at her now, what do they see? She knows she is ten years older and a bit heavier around the hips and calves. She has gone up a dress size in those years, but so has everyone else. She wonders if her face reminds them that they have an unsolved murder in their town, if her presence makes them feel unsettled. They probably wonder why she hasn't found a new partner, remarried, gone on a honeymoon in Bali, moved to the city, moved to New Zealand, at least moved house. She wonders why she hasn't. She wonders if they still think she is a good nurse. She wonders if they think she has been a misguided friend for all these years. If, like Greg, they think she has been blind. Wilfully. Or a fool. Perhaps she is a fool. Some who needs to *reconsider her priorities*. Maybe she shouldn't have agreed not to tell. Maybe there are things, signs, she has deliberately overlooked so she could justify the omission to herself.

But there hadn't been signs. Barbara was everything she'd never had in a best friend. When she learned Sandra and Greg were adopting, she'd offered support and insight into the adoption process. She was the one who filled Sandra's arms with professional and academic papers on foetal alcohol spectrum disorder, arranged for her to meet other carers, talked her through the complications and challenges ahead if they chose to proceed. In Sandra's mind, there was never any option. Darren was a child needing safe parents and they were a husband and wife wanting to care for a child. It didn't matter if he had special needs. They would provide them, she and Greg together, as stable and committed members of their community. Barbara had been beside her for the next thirteen years of Darren's life, opening her arms and her home. She had been one of his safe people. Sandra had seen him huddle inside the swathes of black-and-red fabric after falling in the playground and bubbling in delight as he told his Auntie Barbara about some childish joy, a ride in the fire truck or a new action figure. No, there were no signs.

Immediately after it happened, Sandra had no sense of sifting through what she had seen. All she knew was the outcome. That her son was dead. Her mind, flooded with stress hormones, could process only that one fact. Her body, it seemed, went to autopilot – eating, sleeping, dressing, walking, without any guiding thoughts or decisions. She was grateful for that. It was only later she began to reconstruct what she had witnessed.

There were five people at the river mouth that day: Darren, Colin Russell, Timothy Patten, Amy Jenkins, and her, Sandra. Six, if you count Barbara, who was on the cliffs above, but they'd agreed to tell the police she was still at the nursing home. The kids had gone to the river for a swim after the tennis finals. After it happened, each of them was interviewed and Sandra has handwritten notes of what they all said, what they saw, what they were doing at the river, and what they did after it happened. Sandra remembers nothing of her own interview and her notes are based entirely on the transcript she was given afterwards. Even now, she reads through them as though she is reading words said by another person in another place.

She remembers the events that day well enough to know the words on the page are what she saw. She remembers why she was at the river, the sun overhead, the still, early-afternoon air, the sea breeze unusually late for the time of year. She remembers the sound of the kids screaming as they splashed in the water, the gunshot, and the horrible way the screams changed. She remembers running through the muddy south bank toward them, protective rage powering her legs and deadening the slashes to her face and arms that she later learned she received from branches of the she-oaks as she pushed her way through. She remembers arriving at the riverbank and seeing the broad shoulders of a girl in a blue swimsuit as she hauled her son out of the water. That girl – it was Amy Jenkins – spent twenty minutes working on Darren's chest until the ambulance arrived, and received a bravery award in the national honours list the following year.

Sandra knows from her notes that Colin Russell said he ran to the bridge and stood in the middle of the highway, flagging down traffic. He was almost hit by a road train travelling north. Tim Patten remembered hearing its horn blasting as he stood on the riverbank below. It was Jack Stevens who'd eventually stopped. He knew Colin from the school bus run and took him to the fish and chip shop five hundred metres down the road, where the manager called triple zero. Sandra remembers hearing the ambulance as it approached up the highway and seeing the officers, two men who had brought her a hundred gasping, bleeding and broken bodies over the years, scramble their way down from the road and take over the CPR. She remembers the exhausted girl sobbing and Tim, who had never made much of an impression on Sandra, standing tall and holding her in his arms.

Sandra knows from a separate set of notes that Darren died in the ambulance on the ten-minute trip to the hospital while she was following behind in Jack Stevens' car. She'd waited another ten minutes in the emergency department before someone came out to tell her. She doesn't remember who it was, only that she must have known the person and they took her to the staffroom and stayed with her until her husband arrived.

CHAPTER 32

Colin

Two days before Darren dies

The gun had weighed heavy in Colin's bag all day. After the incident on the bus, he'd avoided Tim, making excuses to go to the library at lunchtime and walking between classes with Amy. It had pissed Tim off, he knew, and he was expecting it when he cornered him in the boys' change rooms before the last class.

'So?' Tim was waiting for him, leaning against the basins when Colin came out of the cubicle.

'Like a sausage, with cracks on the surface,' he replied, washing his hands.

'I'm not asking about your stinking poo. What's with the hardware you've got in your bag?'

'Oh that.' Colin shrugged. 'I'm looking after it for a friend.'

'Bullshit you are. That's the gun your dad reported stolen, isn't it? The night you were robbed.'

'Christ, Tim, tell the world why don't you?' Colin hissed, looking at the door to the change rooms.

'What are you doing with it, you idiot? The police think the Weymouth rapist has it.'

'Mum had it. Dad didn't know. I don't know why she didn't put it back in the safe. It was hidden in the storeroom and I took it.' He slumped against the basin next to Tim, the bravado leaking out of him.

'Fuck Colin, what d'you think you're going to do with it? You can't just carry it around in your bag. Christ, you've just brought a fucking gun to school.'

'Yeah, I know,' he mustered up half a grin. 'That's bad-ass.'

'What's bad-ass?' Darren walked in the door. He looked from one to the other as they both tightened their lips. 'Jeez, you don't think I didn't hear you?' He looked at Colin, then Tim. 'Where is it?'

Tim ignored him.

'It's stupid-ass, that's what it is,' he said to Colin. 'Look, we'll go to the river mouth and stick it in the rocks at the back of the cave. Darren can take it out in the tinnie on the weekend and toss it at the back of the reef. We can all go with him.'

Pleased he was in on the plan, Darren straightened and shifted his bag on his shoulder. 'Let's meet at the river this afternoon. We can stash it after school.'

'I can't,' said Colin, 'I've got that exchange student thing.'

'Just find me down there afterwards.' Darren turned to Tim. 'And you can give me back that scarf.'

'No way. We're giving that to the police.'

'Bullshit we are. Give it back, it's mine, I found it.'

'Nuh.' Tim shook his head and shoved his hands in his pockets. 'No way.'

'Or I'll tell the office Colin has a gun in his bag.'

Colin paled.

'That's low, Daz,' Tim sneered, unmoved, 'dobbing in a mate.'

'Let's just dump it at the back of the reef with the gun,' said Colin. He was sweating, he could feel it running down his back. Dobbing in Colin was just the kind of lunatic thing Darren would do if he wasn't getting his own way. Never mind the consequences.

'Fine,' agreed Darren. 'Give it to me and we'll stash it in the cave.'

'Not until we get in the tinnie.' Tim stared him down until Darren swore and stormed out of the toilet block, slamming the door behind him.

Now, walking home alone along the river, Colin was having second thoughts. After the exchange student information session, he'd had to take the town bus instead of riding home with Darren and Tim. He wanted to go to America for twelve months between year eleven and year twelve. Four kids from his high school were applying and only one of the other three wanted to go to the US. She was freakishly tall and played basketball in the Weymouth A-league. The other two, both girls, wanted Japan and France. The woman who'd flown up from the city to talk to them said they expected to have six places available, but she couldn't guarantee where. This year, she had four students in the US, in New York, Seattle, Portland, and on a cattle ranch in Montana. The photos of Montana looked pretty, Colin thought, with all the mountains and snow and big rivers. The girl who'd gone there was from a dairy farm down south and they were shown photos of her on horses and canoeing on a dark lake, the snow-capped mountains behind her reflected in the water. The girls all gasped and Colin could see the French girl changing her mind, but he didn't want to get stuck for a year herding cows and going to another country-town high school, even if it did mean there were snow-capped mountains on the horizon. Colin wanted to be in a city. A big city, like New York or San Francisco. He wanted to go to movies and concerts, not barn dances. He wanted cool kids in his classes.

Colin didn't understand why his parents had moved to the country when they'd left university. His dad was an industrial chemist; they could have lived anywhere. Why they chose to come to a small town with nothing going for it other than a wharf, crayfish and a drug problem was beyond him. At least his mum was kept busy. There were enough teenage pregnancies, homeless people and kids with parents in prison to occupy her and an army until she retired. Then she'd probably set up her own soup kitchen. When he'd asked them about it, they'd said the country was *a better place to raise kids* than the city, and *we wanted you to feel part of a real community*. He'd like to ask his mum now what she thought about that community. Whether she feels safe. Why she needs to practise shooting his dad's gun out in the hills and then hide it under her bed. Why she lied to the police about it.

The cave had seemed like a good idea three hours ago, but the gap in the rock face wasn't that deep and they didn't know who else went there. What if some kid found it and shot himself? He was thinking maybe he should back out of the plan when he heard voices ahead on the other side of the trees.

'Hey Arthur, what's for dinner?'

'Got a tin of beans in there to heat up?'

'How about some cold chips from the bins at the fish and chip shop?'

'Nah mate, he's just going to have goon tonight.'

'Get wasted and pass out on the nuns' veranda hey, Arthur?'

Colin picked up his pace to a slow jog but hesitated when the trees thinned out. Ahead of him by the riverbank, a group of boys from school had formed a circle around Mr Arthur who was standing resigned but not, it seemed, alarmed by the taunts. Colin figured he was used to it. Darren stood on the edge of the group, at Arthur's back, eyes dark and uncertain.

'I bet you like them nuns, hey?' The boy standing in front of Arthur had a smirk on his face. Colin recognised him from school. His name was Shane Boyle and the last time he'd seen him, he was sitting inside the nurse's office with a bloodstained swab over his eye. He'd smirked then, too, and winked at Colin. *You should have seen the other guy.* Colin avoided him when he saw him at school. He was younger and smaller than Colin, but he had an older, taller brother who also had a reputation for being quick with his fists.

'Nah mate, they're all dried out,' said another of the boys. 'Arthur likes the young juicy ones.'

'Is that right?' asked Shane, 'young ones who are still in their beds?'

'I bet it's him who's been climbing through windows.'

Shane took a step forward, chest out. 'Was it you, Arthur? Are you the one who raped those girls?' He looked past Arthur at Darren, who was on the balls of his feet, tense.

Darren bent down and picked up a river stone. He drew his arm back and the stone flew, passing by Arthur's shoulder and landing in the river, startling the ducks and creating ripples across the surface. Colin saw Arthur flinch and look back up the track toward the trees where Colin stood. The circle tightened. Two boys on either side of Darren bent to pick up their own stones.

'The cops haven't worked it out yet, have they Arthur?' said Shane. 'Typical. They're fucken useless. They couldn't work out who set fire to your house either could they?' He nodded and another stone flew, closer this time and connecting with a tree trunk before it dropped onto the riverbank with a soft thud. The boys exchanged glances, nervous and excited. Shane rocked from side to side on the balls of his feet, his arms loose at his sides.

'Was it deliberate? I bet it was. You're a stupid drunk but I reckon you know what you're doing. I reckon you've got a wad of insurance money in the bottom of that bag. That's what everyone says. You're a fucken millionaire but you're too tight to buy a place to live. I suppose being homeless gives you a good excuse for hanging around outside girls' houses.'

Shane nodded a second time and this stone hit Arthur between his shoulder blades, making him arch his back and grunt. Colin squatted and opened his bag.

'You're a dirty old fuck, aren't you?' said Shane. The rest of the boys were picking up their own stones now. 'Someone should teach you a lesson.'

When the gun sounded, it was louder than Colin expected but it didn't echo like it had in the gully. The boys ducked and then scattered, leaving Arthur to hoist his bag and trudge back up the track with the same air of resignation that had met the taunts. Afterwards, Colin wondered at how quickly and soundlessly they all disappeared. No-one had seen him. Darren was gone. As he stood looking at the empty space where the circle had been, he caught another movement at the next tree line and looked up to see a short, silver-headed figure in green turn and hurry back down the path. He threw the gun into his bag and chased after her.

CHAPTER 33

Sandra

The wind is blowing from the sea and bringing with it spits of rain. It is not enough to get truly wet, but it carries the threat of something more drenching later in the afternoon if she isn't quick. Sandra walks purposefully toward the bridge along the road and then takes the path that veers down to the riverbank, crossing the picnic reserve. When she passes the barbeque, she turns back along the riverside path under the trees. It should face her back into the wind, but down here it is calm, the south-westerly passing over the tops of the cliffs. The path climbs and the bush becomes dense. A short, thick variety of melaleuca grows here, and the lower branches intrude into the path, their fragrant leaves brushing her thighs as she walks. Occasionally, she pushes with her legs to move small branches aside and they flick back into place behind her as she passes. She is not familiar with this route. Her usual walking circuit begins and ends at her house and follows the road along the clifftop, only coming down to the riverbank on the south side. She is surprised at how protected it is from the wind and the rain here below the cliffs, the bend in the river deflecting the weather and the traffic noise. Even the rumble of trucks on the highway has disappeared. Limestone rocks poke out from the topsoil below the shrubs. They glow in the low light. She kicks one with her toe and stumbles, knocking her knee painfully as she hits the ground. She rubs it and can feel the swelling start immediately, her body working on-cue to cushion the damage. It will be stiff tomorrow even if she ices it. As she stands, she sees a second path to the right, the fork marked by a rusted tin can sprouting winter grass. Walking unevenly and favouring the knocked knee, she goes right and upwards.

Sandra is still shaken from yesterday and it adds to her unease on the unfamiliar path. Rebecca had called her from the pharmacy when she got home. She wanted to meet. It was urgent. Could Sandra come when Rebecca finished work before it got dark? Sandra had picked up her handbag from where she had just dropped it on the kitchen bench and went back out the door. The police were gone for the day, but the security tape was still up, marking off the no-go zone around the shed. She doubted it would deter anyone who came looking while she was out. She reversed the car out of the driveway and drove back into town to the new cafe on the waterfront. Rebecca was already there, a half finished coffee in front of her. Sandra ordered one for herself. Through the open window, she could see early evening walkers slowing down to watch the sunset.

'What's up, love?' She took in Rebecca's tight face and her hand gripping the mobile phone as it lay face-up on the table. She placed her own hand over it. 'Hey. Are you OK?'

'Yes, I'm fine,' Rebecca met her eyes with an apologetic smile. 'It's just that, there are things I haven't told you. About Darren. I thought it was about time to get everything out. You know, with Mum.'

'I think I might have already guessed.' Sandra smiled and squeezed the young woman's hand under hers. 'And it's alright, it really is.'

Rebecca blushed and looked down at her lap.

'How did you know?'

The screen of Rebecca's phone lit up and they both looked down. She had a picture of Sam as her screensaver. She glanced at the text, turned the phone over and covered it with her hand.

'It was Darren who came into your room that night, wasn't it?' Sandra said, trying to be gentle. She already knew the intruder was not a would-be rapist. Rebecca had confessed to her parents and the police years ago after they began to question her story. She'd refused to give up the boy's name and, of course, when the pregnancy began to show, her reasons became clear.

The identity of Sam's father was one of the few things Sandra and Barbara had never discussed, even though Barbara had remained convinced that someone had forced their way into Rebecca's room that night. Rebecca was too distressed, she had told Sandra, to have been faking it. Sandra wasn't so sure. She'd seen teenagers in the emergency room, sobbing into their parents' arms, looking as though their world had ended. As soon as the mum and dad left to buy consoling magazines and chocolates, they turned into dry-eyed tyrants, unable to lift a finger except to type furiously into their mobile phones. As much as Sandra adored Rebecca, she guessed she wasn't above putting on a show in order to misdirect her parents from the real identity of her baby's father. Motherhood, Sandra figured, blinded Barbara to what she would have seen through immediately in her professional life.

When Sam was born, Sandra had searched his face for Darren, looking for signs in the shape of his brow, the colour of his eyes. But Sam's eyes are like his mother's and grandmother's, and no-one has Darren's features. As Sam got older, he would startle her sometimes. The lilt in his sentences or the way he set his face in defiance would drag Darren to the surface and Sandra would have to turn her own face away. She wishes now she'd asked Barbara if she saw it too.

'Sam is his son, isn't he?' she asked Rebecca.

'It only ever happened once,' Rebecca replied, looking out the window. The sun had almost touched the water. She flipped the phone and checked the screen, frowning. 'Not that night though. He came over to talk about it. We had a fight. Darren wanted to quit school and work as a deckhand. It was my idea to make up the story about the Weymouth rapist.'

'It would have been OK, you know,' Sandra said with another squeeze. 'We would have supported you, whatever you wanted to do.' She didn't know if this was true, but it doesn't matter now.

'The thing is, he told me about the money.' Rebecca looked Sandra in the eye and saw her confusion. 'From the drugs? He said he was cashed up and could support me and I wouldn't have to work.'

Sandra didn't respond. She sat, wordless, looking at the girl's face, scrunched in anxiety.

'I didn't want to be involved in anything like that,' Rebecca said, her voice pleading, wanting Sandra to understand. 'And when he died, I thought if people knew about the baby, someone might think I had the money and come after me.'

'Who would come after you, Rebecca?' Sandra asks, quietly. Her mind is turning circles.

'The Worners. Darren was mixed up with them, he went out there all the time. I'm scared of them. The girls hang out on the lawn in front of the civic centre, swearing and drinking. After it happened, they yelled at me across the street. They said I was a skinny little slut and that Darren had it coming. They still come into the pharmacy and laugh at me.'

'Did they say who did it?'

'No, but it was one of them, probably the old man. I know it was.'

Sandra sighed and rubbed her face with her hands. It seemed Keith was right about the money after all.

'Did Darren say where the money was?'

'He said he put most of it in the bank. He said he had thirty thousand in his account and twenty thousand in cash.'

Sandra shook her head. She wouldn't put it past Darren to be mixed up in passing around the odd foil and bag, but she couldn't see him selling enough pot to amass fifty thousand dollars. He didn't even know how to open a bank account. Unless Greg did it for him.

'What do you want to do now, Rebecca?' she asked. 'Do you want to tell the police? I can come with you if you like.'

'I don't want people thinking my mum's a murderer,' she replied, shaking her head. 'But I'm still scared of them.' Her phone pinged again, and she snapped her head down to the screen. 'Anyway, I've got to go, Dad says dinner's ready.' She pushed her chair back and stood up. 'I've always wondered what happened to that money after Darren died, but I guess you and Greg would have sorted it out. It wasn't my place to ask, especially when you've been so generous with Sam's allowance.' She bent down to kiss Sandra on the cheek and scurried out the door.

The path rises steeply but it is not far to the cave. Sandra's swollen knee is still up to the short climb and she reaches the limestone ledge and stops to catch her breath, hands on hips and looking across the river at the swamp and the nursing home. Sometime during the winter, rain has washed away the loose soil below the ledge, taking bushes and rocks with it, and she can see straight to the riverbank below. She is still stunned at Rebecca's sudden departure from the cafe yesterday. She'd been fidgety, anxious, preoccupied with her phone, but wanting to unburden herself. Once she'd done that, it seemed she couldn't get away quick enough. Sandra wonders if her dad had said more than just *dinner's ready* in the text she'd received. She hopes there isn't tension between them now Barbara is gone. Sandra has never had a sense of the father–daughter relationship in the Russell family, she realises now, and wonders if the cracks are showing. Barbara was their centre, their glue. Their calm in a crisis. Except, Sandra remembers, in that week between the break-in and Darren's death. Sandra had barely seen her except once in the carpark at work. Rebecca had been with her then, trailing behind, presumably getting a lift home. She'd called out to her mum to slow down and Barbara had turned on her heel so fast she was a blur. *Walk faster and get your butt into the car*, she'd snapped, before whipping the door open and thumping down into the driver's seat. Rebecca had caught Sandra's eye as she opened her own door, then ducked inside. They all believed at that point, of course, that Rebecca had been assaulted but perhaps, Sandra thinks, there was more to it even then. Mothers can read daughters like they can read themselves.

She looks down past her feet. She thinks she must be four metres above the water. The cliff face at her back is indented about two metres. It is not a real cave, she realises, just an overhang, and would only give shelter if the weather came from the north-west. The back wall is cracked and eroded, creating a vertical groove that dips to the right. It looks like the entrance to a passageway, but it is deceptive and closes in after half a metre. The small space smells of damp and soil. She slips her hand into the narrowing crease and realises it would be here that a person could wedge a parcel out of sight and out of reach. She takes a camping torch out of her pocket and shines it up and down. There are nooks and crannies but nothing there except snails and geckos.

Sandra backs away from the wall, scanning the rest of the cliff face for other possible nooks and gaps in the rock. Spits of rain hit her jacket as she emerges from the shelter and her heel is uncertain on the wet rock. Winter grass and capeweed cling to the loose soil at the edge of the overhang above her head. On either side, melaleuca bushes screen the approach of the path. She can see no other obvious hiding places. Disappointed, she turns her back on the cliff face, placing her foot awkwardly. It slides away from her, scraping the edge of the rock and bringing her down, hard, onto her hip. She braces the fall with her hands and feels the jarring up through her wrists and elbows. As she lands, the branches of the bushes on the seaward side of the cave rustle and push forward and a woman in a red jacket emerges from the path. It is the same woman Sandra saw last week. Seeing Sandra on the ground, she exclaims and rushes forward to help her up.

'We're a couple of silly women, walking out in this weather, aren't we?' she says, when Sandra is back on her feet. 'You might want to get some antiseptic on those grazes when you get home.'

Sandra winces as she brushes the dirt off her torn skin. 'Thanks. I think you might be right.'

'I like the wilder weather though. I like to feel the wind and see the ocean getting worked up.' She looks closer into Sandra's face.

'Oh, you're Sandra Davies, from the hospital, aren't you?' she says. 'You were a friend of Barbara's. I work at the day centre near the wharf. We met once when the new hostel opened. I'm Joanne.'

Sandra makes the connection. The woman is also a nurse, she remembers now. She moved to Weymouth five years ago to start a new medical service for people living rough.

'Of course, I remember you,' she says. The day centre gives homeless people a place to shower, wash their clothes, have medical checks and store their medication. 'I hear you're doing some good work there.'

'I was so sad to hear about Barbara. It is such a loss. She worked hard for people in this town.'

Sandra murmurs her agreement.

'I saw her son down here just yesterday, poor thing, right here in front of the cave. It was almost dark. He said he wanted to get away from everything for the day. He'd just finished a hike along the river. He said he'd come all the way from the hills.'

'Really?' Sandra frowns. 'I was talking to him at the pharmacy just before five. Are you sure it was late?'

'Yes, sure I'm sure. The sun was just going down. Beautiful sunset. But you know the family much better than me,' she shrugs, gracious. 'Maybe I mistook him for someone else.'

'Maybe you did,' said Sandra.

CHAPTER 34

Colin

Two days before Darren dies

Colin caught up with his grandmother as he cleared the trees. She was moving fast down the path, head down, taking short, quick steps and clutching her bag to her side. There was no sign of Darren or any of the other boys. He hoped none of them had seen him. He wouldn't put it past Darren to put two and two together though. What were the chances of there being two guns at the riverbank this afternoon? He slowed as he reached her. The path wasn't wide enough to walk alongside.

'Granny? Granny,' he called. 'it's me, Colin. Wait up.' He put out his hand and tugged on her arm.

'Granny, it's OK.'

Elsie stopped but didn't turn around. She was panting. Colin walked around the side of the path and squatted down to look into her face. She was pale and there were fine beads of sweat around her hairline and her upper lip.

'Are you OK, Granny?' he asked. 'Shall I take you home?'

Elsie lifted her head and met his eyes. Her own were blue, like his father's, and her gaze was hard. It was not the look of fear and confusion he had been expecting. He stood up.

'Those boys were going to hurt that man, Colin.' Her voice was firm. Disgusted.

'Yes, Granny, they were.'

'If I was younger, I would have thrashed them.'

Colin smiled. He had heard his granny was fearless back in the day.

'I can't do that anymore, but you stopped them, didn't you?' She eyeballed him, eyes narrowed and certain, as though she had expected nothing less. Colin wondered how much she'd seen.

'I did Granny, I told them to go home.'

'You're a good man, just like your father.' She turned to continue along the path, her pace slower. She said nothing about the gunshot. Colin walked beside in the grass. 'He was a godsend to your mum. Do you know how they met?'

Colin did. His parents had met at university where his dad was doing a chemistry degree and his mum was studying social work. They'd been to a Friday afternoon concert on the library lawn. The band was an all-girl group who sang songs about girl-power and had spiral perms. Cyndi Lauper with an Aussie twist, his mum had said. A good gig for meeting girls, his dad told him. Colin's dad saw Colin's mum dancing at one side of the stage with a group of girlfriends and when she went to the bar, he'd downed his beer and followed her. They didn't hit it off. Apparently, she'd taken one look at him and had him pegged for an accounting major, a Liberal Party member, and the essence of all that is wrong with neo-liberal economics. He'd gone from being smitten with her gypsy-grunge neckline and wild hair to sneering at her naive socialism. He took his beer back to his friends on the grass and watched her dance with her friends. When the concert finished, he got in his car – *bought by his parents*, Colin's mum always interjected – and went home to his bedroom in his parents' riverside house.

'And the next semester, they were in the same class,' his granny was saying. 'And they did that assignment together and that was that.'

It was true. The legend of his parents falling in love over a case study on how not-for-profit organisations balance mission and financial sustainability. They'd found themselves in the same elective unit and obliged to join the same group assignment. A crossing-the-tracks love story for the modern age. They fell in love as they solved the problems of serving the poor while keeping the company afloat. He saved her from a life of solitary, mission-driven servitude, and she saved his soul. Colin and Rebecca used to adore the story, would beg their parents to tell it over and over. *You forgot the part about driving to the city to get milkshakes at midnight*, they'd remind them. Colin scowled to himself. Lying to the police about stealing your husband's gun is not so cute.

They arrived back at the nursing home and Colin walked his grandmother to her room, where he poured her a glass of water and helped her take off her shoes. Her feet were swollen from the walk.

'I think I'll have my nanna nap now, bub,' she said, using Colin's mum's name for him.

'OK, Granny.' He turned down the sheets on her bed and hovered while she eased herself down. 'Shall I shut the door?'

'Just a little.' She rolled over to face the wall, the pink soles of her feet turned toward him.

Colin trudged back home along the south bank of the river, his school bag over his shoulder, pushing into the wind. Sand blew across the water and into his face and he kept his head down. He'd stayed until he heard his grandmother's breathing ease into sleep, then stashed the gun in the bottom drawer of the bedside table. The only things she kept there were two old handbags that she never used, and the thin key hung permanently from the lock. He'd put the gun in the white bag at the back, taking care to keep it wrapped in the suede cloth, and left the key hanging in its usual place, figuring its absence might cause a fuss. When he next saw Darren and Tim, he'd tell them what happened – Darren had some explaining to do – and they'd make a plan to take the tinnie out and dump it at the back of the reef.

He didn't know what to do about the scene at the river. Darren shouldn't be hanging out with those boys. They were bad news. A year below Colin and his friends at school, they'd caused trouble since they started high school, travelling in a pack and taking up room in corridors and doorways. Shoulder bumps and sideways remarks became face-to-face confrontations which became promises to finish it at the basketball courts after school. Shane was the one who always moved first, calling out to his targets on the quadrangle and echoed by his followers. Colin had heard that Shane had the year nine maths teacher in tears and refused to submit any English assignments this semester. Rumour was he would be held back next year, like his brother. So far, Colin and his friends had flown under the radar and hadn't been targeted by either Boyle brother. That would change if Colin told anyone what he saw. Maybe he'd keep it to himself.

Colin lifted his eyes as he approached the end of his street. Tim was standing on the front verge talking to Colin's mum, in the same place the police officer had been when Colin's granny last went for a walk without telling anyone. It made sense: Tim would have gone to Colin's house when he didn't show up at the river. Colin wondered if he'd seen

Darren and any of the others. He was about to raise his arm and call out when he saw Tim stiffen and then his mum step forward. The way she was standing, her chin up and her hands on her hips, made him pause. As he watched, Tim backed away, shuffling toward the footpath, shaking his head. Colin's mum stepped forward, following him. Colin was too far way to hear them, but he could see she was shouting. Tim put both hands in front of his chest, palms forward, and then turned to walk away down the street, head down. Colin stepped under the trees, out of sight. He knew Tim would have to come this way to get home. He sat down on his haunches to wait.

Tim came past a minute later, walking fast. He jumped and swore when Colin stood up.

'Fuck, Colin, where have you been? I've been trying to find you.' Tim had been running his hands through his hair and tufts stuck up at odd angles.

'I had to take Granny home; she got out again. Have you seen Darren?'

'Darren? No, he took off with those morons in year nine when we got off the bus.'

'Where'd they go?'

'How would I know? The river I guess.'

Colin eyed him. Tim didn't rattle easily.

'I've fucked up mate,' Tim said. 'Your mum knows we weren't at Darren's that night.'

'But we were,' Colin protested, 'well for most of the night anyway.'

'Yeah but we were out until after midnight.'

'But, technically, we slept at Darren's, even if we planned to sleep at the cave.'

'Yeah, whatever,' Tim dismissed the argument 'but she knows we were out and thinks we had something to do with that car fire.'

Colin felt his guts drop. He'd get a grilling when he got home and there'd be no way of explaining his way out of it. His mum could see him lying from across the street. 'So, what do you mean you fucked up?' he asked Tim.

'It wasn't my fault. I was looking for you after Darren fucked off and your mum said I could wait, and she made me a Milo and we were talking.'

'What about?'

'Stuff.'

'What stuff, Tim?'

'The cave.' Tim looked away, squinting across the water. Colin could see sweat beading around his hairline.

'You told her about the cave?'

'Not that we slept there.' Tim kept his eyes on the water. 'I told her that we found it and that Darren said he'd slept there sometimes. And then she said *when exactly*, and I said I thought he went there after we got back on Friday night.'

'*After we got back*? When we weren't supposed to be out?' Colin felt his lungs squeeze and his throat tighten. He'd never be allowed out of the house again. That was it. Grounded until he went away to college.

'I know, I know, I'm sorry.' Tim dragged his eyes away from the water and looked at Colin. They were huge. Miserable. Colin could see his jaw working. He wanted to punch him. 'You know what your mum's like, she gets you all comfortable, like you're mates, and you end up telling her stuff.'

Colin looked out at the horizon, where a bulk carrier sat in the afternoon blur of wind and water. The salt spray stung his eyes and he could feel tears collecting at the corners. He sniffed and swallowed. It wasn't his mum's fault that Tim couldn't keep his mouth shut. She'd dragged the truth out of all of them at some point and he should have known better.

'So where the fuck did Darren go after we got back to his place anyway?' Tim said.

'I don't know, I thought he went for a piss.'

'He was gone for hours.'

'Maybe he slept in his own room,' Colin shrugged. 'Maybe you snore.'

'Fuck you. And he wasn't. I checked.'

Colin thought about the time he saw Darren and his dad heading out in the truck late that night after the movie at Tim's house.

'I don't know, mate,' he said. 'He couldn't have gone far. Maybe he was out in the shed.'

They walked together back up the path along the riverbank. As they passed the point where Colin had fired the gun into the air, Colin figured Tim probably hadn't seen the incident with Mr Arthur. He wondered if he'd heard the gun go off. He wondered who else might have heard it. They probably would have thought it was a car. Cars and trucks backfired on the highway all the time. From what Tim said, he was in trouble anyway. He would get a bollocking when he got home, he was sure, and he was already late. He figured his mum could wait a bit longer. It wouldn't make things any different.

'Let's go get some chips,' he said to Tim.

CHAPTER 35

Sandra

After her meeting with Rebecca, Sandra had driven home, poured herself a wine and eaten a cheese toastie while she considered what Rebecca had said. If Darren had a bank account, like he had claimed to Rebecca and Colin, Greg must have helped him set it up. Remembering Teresa's comment at the salon about her prospective son-in-law, she'd rung her and asked about trust funds. The next day she went back to the bank.

She'd hung at the back of the queue until Sophie became free. Sophie is her mother's daughter and, like Teresa, has not yet adopted the muted speaking voice of her bank colleagues. She was gossiping with her customer, her laugh deep-throated and turning the heads of the other people in the queue. Above her blue-and-white uniform, her black curly hair teetered on top of her head, held in place by sparkling blue-and-silver clips – the colour scheme, Sandra supposed, a nod to the bank's corporate colours, although somewhat less restrained. She leaned across the wide counter when it was Sandra's turn, arms stretched as far as they could reach to pat Sandra on the back and offer her cheeks in turn.

'Auntie Sandra, it is so good to see you. Mum said you'd been to the salon. Your hair looks great. I love how you style it. What products do you use?'

'Two-in-one from the supermarket and the sea breeze,' Sandra replied. Sophie batted the air between them.

'You keep your secrets then, darls. I don't mind. We all have to have some mystery, hey? What can I do for you today?'

'I came in to ask you about the money Greg – Greg and I – give to Sam Russell. Did we set that up as a trust fund?'

'Oh, don't you know how that works? I know the one you mean, just give me a moment to bring it up.'

Sandra didn't know how the payments were set up because she didn't know about them at all until two days ago. She watches Sophie peer into the screen, pressing her lips together in concentration. Dark curls dangle at her temples.

'Here we are,' she says. 'The account is in the name of the Russell Trust; the trustees are you and Greg. It was opened on the ninth of June nineteen ninety-eight.'

'How does that work?'

'It is the same as the account you had for Darren. Greg pays money into the account and then every fortnight a set amount is dispersed to the beneficiary. In this case, it goes to Rebecca on Sam's behalf.' She swung the screen around so Sandra could see the list of transactions. 'I shouldn't do this, but you're an account holder and I know you. You can also see this on your monthly statements, except that – she pauses as she checks the screen – you've opted out of receiving them. They only go to Greg, but I can change that if you like. It's a very generous arrangement. I wish I had a benefactor like you.'

Sandra ran her eyes down the screen. It was indeed a generous arrangement. The fishing business must be doing well.

'So, what happened to the money in Darren's trust account?' She's taking a guess. 'He didn't have his own bank account so how did we give it to him?'

'You didn't, of course,' Sophie cocked her head to one side like a surprised chicken. 'You would have been putting it aside to help him out when he turned twenty-one.'

She shut down the screen and opened another. The Davies Trust: something else Sandra had never seen. She'd guessed right.

'You and Greg were the authorised signatories as trustees of the fund,' she pointed to the top left-hand corner where Sandra could see her own name. 'It's closed now, but you can see the transaction listing for the final six months here.' Sophie peered into the screen.

'The payments look like they were a bit different to the set-up for Sam,' she observes. 'They're not regular, they come in bigger lump sums every now and then and are cash payments. Maybe that's because your financial circumstances were different then. More uneven cashflow from the boat? But there were no payments out of the account for this period. As you can see, the closing balance was substantial.'

It was substantial all right, thought Sandra. Much more than Darren had told Colin or Rebecca.

'What happened to the money when Darren died?'

'I can't see that here, I'm afraid,' said Sophie, shaking her head, 'but it will have been dispersed under the terms of the trust deed. Do you still have a copy?'

'No, I don't.' She never had one. 'But I'm sure Greg put it back into our personal account when he closed this one.'

Sophie gave her a sympathetic smile. It was the kind Sandra hates, bordering on condescending, and suddenly she felt the need to leave the bank and the talk about money. When Sophie asked her if she could do anything else for her, she shook her head and turned to leave, unable to speak.

'And Sandra?' She hears uncertainty in Sophie's voice as she calls her back. 'I don't want to presume, but would you like one of these brochures for our Personal Finance for Women course? It's important that we know how our money is managed. We shouldn't leave it to the men, you know.'

Sandra accepted the brochure and squeezed out a smile.

'Thanks Sophie, you've been a great help.'

Now she sits on a pink-and-green striped armchair under a cafe window and gathers her cardigan around her shoulders. Most cafes in Weymouth spread themselves open to the sun. They have wide street frontages, big windows and alfresco tables under patio umbrellas. There are few days in a year that their doors are not flung open to the coastal air. The cafe in the old post office building on the main street, though, is tucked into a back corner, behind an art gallery. The thick limestone walls enclose the space, which is filled with mismatched sofas and tables sourced from a mix of design periods, price ranges, local op shops and city furniture stores. The deep, barred windowsills, which would be ideal for resting coffee cups, are too high for seated diners, who have to be content with looking at each other instead of the view. In any case, the windows overlook a laneway used by delivery trucks and the only thing to see is the side wall of the butcher's shop next door. It is always cool in here, even on the hottest days.

Sandra has placed a napkin wedge under one curly leg of the round table in front of her to keep it stable. Another napkin, soaked in coffee, is balled up inside an empty water glass. Keith sits across from her in a cane tub chair of a type she hasn't seen since the 1970s. It is too small for him and his thighs spill over the seat, his elbows braced on his knees. He is not in uniform and is explaining what has happened in the investigation in the past three days since Sandra called.

Keith drains the last of his coffee and puts the mug back on the wobbly table. Like the furniture, the crockery is an eclectic mix of second-hand shop finds. Keith's mug is from a 1980s public health campaign. A faded cartoon fat man in a blue shirt and oddly pink hair strides around the side, his thumb up. The words *Life. Be in it* are printed on the opposite side. Sandra had called Keith after she'd been to the bank. If Darren had that much money and someone found out, they might have been leaning on him for it. And if Darren had put the cash into a trust fund that he couldn't access without asking her or Greg, that someone could have become pissed off. Possibly enough to shoot him. Keith is saying they have questioned the Worner patriarch at the remand centre where he is awaiting trial for the rape of his step-granddaughter.

'I heard you got a DNA match,' Sandra says. 'But I thought you said at the hospital the perpetrator had climbed in through the bedroom window?'

'That's the old bastard's MO,' Keith says, his mouth turning downwards. 'He gets his kicks from leaving the house and then coming back in through the window.'

'Isn't he getting a bit old for that?'

'You'd think, wouldn't you? But he keeps a stepladder around the side of the house.'

Sandra stares into her coffee, contemplating the horror of a child being molested in her own bedroom. She wonders what she'd do if she ever came across him. Physical violence would not be out of the question, she thinks. But of course, she wouldn't. She'd look the other way and keep walking.

'I don't suppose his DNA matches the Weymouth rapist cases?' she says, thinking this might be too much to hope for.

Keith gives her a funny look. 'Nah, but we might have a new lead there too, incidentally,' he replies. 'I can't say anything at this point, but we could be making an arrest soon.' He looks down at his hands, clasped together over his knees. 'He denies having anything to do with Darren's death. Of course, he can't say where he was at the time. He reckons he knew Greg; claims he used to buy undersize crays from him. He said he knew Darren too. Apparently, Darren used to go on deliveries with his dad and he'd watch television with the Worner kids – Jaelyn and Wesley – while he and Greg had a beer. He reckons Darren was a bit sweet on Jaelyn.'

Sandra shrugs. Most teenage boys were a bit sweet on any girl who would talk to them, and Jaelyn had been a friendly kid who was on good terms with everyone. She got a scholarship to a posh school in the city in the same year as Colin, Sandra remembers. Now she is working as a judge's associate. People are saying she might come home and become the town's first female magistrate.

'If Darren was selling drugs, or involved in some way, the Worners would have been useful people to know,' Keith says.

'Did the old man say anything about that?'

'Yeah, something along the lines of *kids these days, who knows what they get up to*,' Keith replies with a worn look. 'He's been fined twice for possession, and he did three years on a minor supply conviction fifteen years ago. I've applied for a search warrant for the property; it should happen today or tomorrow.'

'What if Greg was just giving Darren money to help out with the crays?' mused Sandra.

'Then he was the best paid offsider in town,' Keith laughed. 'Anyway, that's where I'm up to. I've got to go; I've got a video-conference link-up with Canberra in half an hour and need to make sure the computer is set up properly. You know what technology is like; it knows when you're working to a deadline.'

Sandra wants to ask him about the Weymouth rapist lead, but he is already out the door. She checks the time on her phone. She has to go as well. She's working nightshift tonight and needs to rest up before she goes in.

CHAPTER 36

Colin

The day before Darren dies

Colin sat on the flat rocks next to the river. He'd kicked off his shoes and socks and put his feet in the cool water. Now he was pressing his wet soles into the dry rock, making patterns. One footprint was a slightly different shape to the other, he noticed. The left seemed narrower and shorter than the right. Or maybe it just looked that way because he was putting it down at a different angle. He experimented with different positions, swivelling on his butt across the rock to find new dry surfaces to imprint.

A shadow fell across the rocks and Colin startled. He hadn't heard anyone approach. He squinted upward at a bulky, shapeless figure that stood too close and was indistinguishable against the sun and the blue sky. It loomed over him and he felt his arms and legs prickle. He leaned backwards on his hand to make out the face.

'Geez, Arthur, why're you creeping around like that?' He let out a heavy breath that he hadn't known he'd been holding and looked down again, blinking the sun out of his eyes.

'Sorry Col, didn't mean to scare you.' Arthur sat down next to him with a soft thump. 'Oof. Standing up and sitting down isn't getting any easier. Thanks for the muesli bar yesterday. I like the nutty ones. No sultanas or chocolate. Not too sweet.'

'How did you know it was me?'

'Eyes in the back of my head.' Arthur elbows him and Colin catches a whiff of body odour underneath his clothes. 'Nah, I woke up and saw you running to catch the bus. And you didn't shut your locker properly. It was hanging open.'

Colin felt the blood drain from his face and beads of sweat form across his hairline. The gun was already in his bag when he left but leaving the locker open was careless.

'Don't worry, I shut it for you. The oldies let me in to take a shower on Thursdays.' Arthur turned his head and looked at him closely. Colin could see large, dark pores on his nose and the age spots that had formed on his temples and cheekbones. There were bruises on his face from the rain of rocks Shane Boyle and his mates had thrown in a last assault before they scattered, but there was something else, a pallor he hadn't noticed before and wouldn't have thought to associate with Arthur after his years of living and sleeping outside.

'Thanks for yesterday afternoon, too,' Arthur said, keeping his voice low. 'I hope you know what you're doing with that thing. Make sure you keep the safety on.'

'What thing?'

'You know what I mean,' Mr Arthur's eyes turned steely. 'Guns don't sound like cars backfiring, kid, doesn't matter how hard you try to convince yourself.'

He broke into a coughing fit. Like Colin, sweat shone along his forehead.

'Are you OK?' Colin said, alarmed.

'Nah I'm not, son.' He pulled his coat up his arm to reveal a PICC line in the back of his hand. 'This will be my last time down here. I'm with the nuns now, but your mum probably told you that. She's a good woman, your mum, you look after her.'

Colin scowled.

'Nah, don't be like that. We all have arguments with our mums. All of our women. We just see things differently, that's all. You've got to learn to work that out, son. Best if you do it sooner rather than later.'

Colin scraped at the rock with a stick and didn't answer. Arthur sighed.

'You know, I had a row with my missus on the day she left. That was the day I lost the house. Strictly speaking, she wasn't my missus, she was someone else's, but it was a silly thing and I wished I'd let it go. You never know when you're not going to get the chance to say sorry.'

Colin didn't reply and stared at the scratches he'd made in the rock. They weren't really scratches. The rock was harder than the stick and all he'd done was draw a few lines. They'd wash off as soon as it rained. He didn't care about some argument Arthur had with someone else's wife. He couldn't see how it had anything to do with him and his mum. She'd done the wrong thing, as far as he was concerned. She'd betrayed his dad and then lied about it to the police. There was no argument here, just some owning up that needed to happen.

'How's your sister?' Arthur asked.

Colin looked up in surprise.

'Rebecca?'

'Unless you've got another one.'

'She's fine. I guess.'

'She's a nice girl. Looks after my medicines at the pharmacy. She needs to keep better company, though. She's got a thing for boys from the wrong side of the tracks, if you know what I mean. Maybe you can introduce her to one of your friends.'

'Rebecca won't even talk to me right now,' he snorts, 'never mind my friends.'

'Are you fighting with your sister as well as your mum? You need to sort things out in your life, Colin.'

'Nah, it's just that she's been weird since the break-in.' He sees Mr Arthur's eyebrows go up and explains. 'Someone broke in last week while I was at Darren's house, and then Rebecca had to go to hospital, and they all lied to me about it and said she was just going to the doctor, and now she doesn't speak to me at all. She just mopes about the house and scowls all the time.'

'I didn't know about that.' Arthur frowns at the unexpected gap in his knowledge of local affairs. 'Did they catch the guy?'

'Nah.'

'Hmm. Well.' Arthur looks doubtful. 'That's hard for you, son, but I reckon your sister might be going through something and needs some support from her brother.'

'Yeah, well why don't they tell me what's wrong then?'

He heard voices and they both turned their heads toward the trees, where Amy was emerging with Tim and Jaelyn Worner. Ashleigh was on Jaelyn's hip and when she put her down, she ran to Colin and Mr Arthur. Colin readied himself for full body contact and was taken aback when she ploughed into Mr Arthur's lap, her little-girl arms around his neck.

'I was a friend of their mum,' Arthur said to him in apology. 'She's known me all her life, haven't you, bub?'

'We heard you were in the nursing home and came to see you,' said Jaelyn. 'What are you doing down here?'

'I came to get some fresh air,' he said, winking at Colin. 'Sleeping inside can make your lungs go foggy.'

'How's your dad?' he asked Jaelyn. She turned her face away toward the water.

'Don't know. We haven't seen him for two weeks.'

'Really? I'd heard Randall was back. He hit the road again?'

She frowns at the river.

'Yeah. Maybe. Granddad says he's not coming back at all this time.'

'Why's that?'

Jaelyn shrugged. Colin could see she didn't want to talk about it. He looked at Tim, who'd sat down next to him, but Tim just kept his head down, drawing circles with his finger in a wet patch on the rock. Amy had put her back to them and was playing on the rocks a few metres upriver with Ashleigh.

'They blued before he left,' Jaelyn said, still facing the water. 'Granddad said Dad needed to *keep things in the family* and Dad got mad and said Granddad was *no saint himself*. Then Granddad told him to piss off or he'd teach him a lesson like he did to you.'

Mr Arthur huffed.

'I'm not a fan of old Cyril, but I'm guessing your dad might've needed a talking to. You're best keeping your distance from both of them, if you ask me.'

'I sorted Granddad out, don't you worry.'

'Baseball bat under the bed?'

She nodded.

'Good girl.' He looked at Ashleigh. 'You keep an eye on that one too.'

'I will.' She looked across at the little girl and Colin followed her gaze. Ashleigh was balancing on Amy's knees. Their hands were clasped, and they grinned at each other as she wobbled, struggling to stay upright. Colin watched as Ashleigh tilted her body forward and slid down Amy's thighs and into her lap, arms wide for a cuddle.

'And you boys,' Arthur turned to Colin and Tim, 'you need to make sure anyone who hurts women and little girls get what they deserve.'

Mr Arthur made to get to his feet, struggling to get leverage to push himself up. He rocked to one side and fell back heavily. Colin and Tim jumped up and took his weight until he was steady. Underneath his coat, the arm was thin, and there was no more weight to hold than if he'd been Rebecca when she was twelve. The bulk that had startled Colin earlier was all clothes.

'Thanks, son. I owe you three times now.' He waved to them as he headed back down the path. 'Don't tell the nuns you saw me down here. They might not give me dessert and I don't have too many of those left.'

CHAPTER 37

Sandra

The emergency department is empty except for an eleven-year-old girl with asthma and her mother. They came in at nine thirty pm and triage sent them straight through. The mum told Sandra they'd had a quiet evening and her daughter ate dinner, then went to her room to work on a school project due at the end of the week. She'd turned her light out at eight thirty. Half an hour later she woke up short of breath and called out for her mother. The mum said she was wheezing – something she'd seen many times before – so she gave her the usual puffs of Ventolin. It hadn't relieved the symptoms and the girl had become panicky, so she thought it best to come in. This last was delivered with a note of apology.

'You did the right thing,' Sandra reassured her, 'and it's not like we're busy tonight anyway.'

Sandra does her routine assessment. The girl is breathing fast with an audible wheeze and is dusky around her mouth and nose. Sandra hooks her up to an oxygen saturation monitor, checks her respiratory rate and heart rate, and listens to her chest.

'How have you been in the last few days?' she asks the girl. Her eyes are fearful, as she struggles to pull air into her lungs. The girl shakes her head and Sandra looks to the mum, who is sitting on the bed facing her daughter, holding her free hand. The pair have locked eyes. The girl, Sandra realises, is trying to slow her breathing in time with her mother. 'Has she had a cough, runny nose, fever? Anyone else in the family sick?'

The mum shakes her head, her eyes not leaving her daughter.

'And has she been taking her preventative medication?'

'Yes, she's very disciplined about all that.' She leans in and kisses her daughter on the head.

'Good girl,' she says, as the girl's chest starts to rise and fall evenly. Sandra can see it is an effort she won't be able to sustain.

'We might need to give her a bit more help tonight,' she says. 'I'm going to contact the on-call doctor and see what she thinks. You'll have to stay in for another couple of hours so we can keep an eye on her though, I'm afraid.'

'That's OK,' the mum gives her a tired smile, 'we know the drill, don't we, love?'

Sandra returns to the nurses' station with her notes and calls Dr Kaur. Katie picks up on the first ring. Sandra knows she spends her on-call evenings on a leather recliner with her phone at her elbow and two golden retrievers at her feet. She will be reading aloud from a crime novel and feeding them liver treats. Over the phone, Katie says she is familiar with the patient and agrees she needs a bronchodilator to relieve the immediate symptoms. She'll come up to the hospital in an hour, she says, to see if the girl has stabilised enough to go home. Sandra has already checked with the after-hours nurse manager and confirmed that a bed is available on the ward if Katie wants the patient admitted. Back at the girl's bed, mother and daughter are quiet, mum reading a novel and the girl leaning back with her eyes closed, her breath still ragged but slowing and less panicked. Sandra administers a Ventolin nebuliser and Prednisolone and tells them she'll be back in fifteen minutes.

As she walks back to the nurses' station, the ambulance alarm sounds and, seeing no-one else at the desk, she jogs to the two-way and picks it up. The dispatch centre tells her there has been a motor vehicle accident on the highway south of town. Two ambulances have been sent out and will be at the hospital in fifteen minutes. A man in his thirties has had his leg amputated below the knee and a suspected spinal cord injury. The driver, a woman, has taken the impact of the steering wheel and has multiple injuries to her chest and abdomen. She has already been defibrillated once in the ambulance.

Sandra puts the emergency department on code blue and calls Dr Kaur again. She'll be here in ten minutes. The shift manager is already preparing two resuscitation bays and she asks Sandra to call up to the wards for extra nursing staff. When she hangs up, she hears the sirens approaching and goes to the ambulance doors to wait. Outside, across the empty, floodlit carpark, she sees the red-and-blue lights flicker against the leaves of the gumtrees then abruptly stop as the first vehicle pulls into the hospital grounds. It drives past the doors, then reverses, backing into the ambulance bay. The doors swing open and the ambos slide the gurney onto the ramp and up into the hospital. It is the male passenger. Sandra smells the tang of blood and alcohol as he is pushed past her to the first resus team.

The second ambulance pulls in and the nurse manager joins Sandra on the apron. They watch together as it slows and drives past the emergency and around the back of the building.

'She died in the ambulance, I'm afraid,' the manager says. 'I'll go there to admit her into the mortuary. Can you ask Katie to come around to sign the paperwork when she's ready?'

Sandra returns to her patient. The girl's heart rate is normal, but her oxygen saturation is still low and her lips blue. Dr Kaur has slipped in with the ambulance and disappeared into the resus bay with the motor vehicle accident patient. They will have to wait, Sandra explains, to the mum. She looks at her watch. There is too much happening to go on break but if she's quick she can bring a cup of tea back to the nurses' station.

She's only just put the cup down, teabag still inside, when the phone rings. It is the remand centre. They are bringing in a prisoner who is having trouble breathing. Seventy years old, diabetic, suspected congestive cardiac failure, says the prison nurse. Sandra goes cold. This will be Cyril Worner, on remand waiting trial for the rape of his step-granddaughter who Sandra treated only weeks ago. The police would have been at his house today, searching for clues to her son's murder. She glances at the resus bay: everyone else is in there with the car accident patient so it will have to be her. She gulps down half of her tea and goes to the bathroom to steel herself.

Five minutes later, Worner limps into the emergency department flanked by two corrections officers, and the triage desk waves him through. He is small and at first glance looks wiry, but a pot belly bulges against the baggy green prison tracksuit and Sandra can see his feet have been put in socks and thongs instead of the usual prison sneakers. She realises they will be swollen and tight from the damage diabetes has wrecked on his body. As they approach, she also sees he is handcuffed to one of the corrections officers and smells cigarette smoke and something else deeper and more rotten. She directs them to bay six and he gives her a wink. As he shuffles on his swollen feet, he looks pointedly at Sandra's asthma patient and the mum stands up, making her chair clatter to the floor, and pulls the curtain across. He chuckles as she does it.

'Pretty kid.'

The corrections officers transfer the handcuffs to the bedrail and stand either side of the bed. Sandra confirms his identity – *you know it already, love* – and takes a patient history. Like her asthma patient, he woke up struggling to breathe. He kept needing to get up to pee, he says, and his heart feels like it is doing somersaults in his chest. Sandra can see his lips are blue, and the tips of his fingers are purple. His breath rasps and, as he talks, he starts to cough. She hands him a tissue and he spits white phlegm.

'Have you been unwell – any coughs or colds? Chest pain?' she asks.

'Nah, just the same cough I always have,' he replies. He passes the tissue to one of the corrections officers, who ignores him. He smirks and another coughing fit starts. Sandra tells him he must sit upright to help with his breathing. He makes a show of getting onto his elbow then looks at the officers for assistance.

'Come on mate, help an old bloke.'

They are stoic in their silent refusal and Sandra elbows past them to do it herself. He is surprisingly heavy, and she has to tell him how to help himself upright. As she leans in, she blinks back the smell, which she realises now is coming from his legs. When she has him in a sitting position, she asks if she can remove his socks and roll up his pants as part of the assessment. She reaches across to the box of disposable gloves behind the bed. As she expected, underneath the socks, Cyril Worner's feet are swollen, the purple scaly skin as tight as a balloon. The toenails are thick and hardened and dig into the flesh. Two toes have been amputated already. She guesses they won't be the last.

Sandra rolls up the pant legs and finds the source of the smell. Worner has a five-centimetre diabetic ulcer on his right shin. It reaches to his ankle joint and when she removes the bandage, she can see it is deep enough to expose tendons and bone. The wound is full of pus and sloughy debris. Around the edges it is angry and inflamed. The stench is enough to make the impassive officers look sideways and flinch at what they see. Even though she is adept at hiding her reactions from patients, Sandra looks up and sees that Worner is staring at her face, smirking at her disgust.

'She's a beauty, isn't she?' he says. 'I knocked it when I tripped on a road verge. I could sue the council for that.'

Sandra doesn't respond. The wound will never heal. She will clean it up to prevent any immediate further infection, but she's seen ulcers like these before and knows that without ongoing care it is likely she will see him back in the hospital for a below-the-knee amputation within a year. No more climbing through bedroom windows for you, she thinks.

Sandra hooks Worner up to an oxygen saturation monitor and collects a kit to clean out the wound. She will ask Dr Kaur to look at him when she is finished with her other patients. Sandra guesses she will want to order blood tests and an ECG. Worner watches her work while she swabs and cleans out the wound with saline and gauze.

'You're that boy's mum, aren't you?' he says. 'The one who was killed down by the river.'

She ignores him.

'They say your best friend was the one who did it.' His voice takes a sly tone. 'He was a nice kid, your boy. I saw a bit of him and his dad back in the day, you know. Real nice kid. I reckon he might've given me another great-grandson if he'd stayed alive. I guess I'll have to be happy with the one I've already got.'

Sandra fills the wound with hydrogel and dresses it.

'You're done, Mr Worner,' she says. 'You'll still need to see the doctor for your breathing, and she'll want to hear from pathology about the swabs. You'll be here for three hours at least.'

'Come to think of it, I do have some chest pain,' he says, 'right here.' He grips his chest under his left arm and winces dramatically.

'I'll let the doctor know. Press the emergency button if it gets worse.'

As she bends to pick the emergency call handset and place it on the bed, he leans forward, unexpectedly agile, planting his face next to her ear.

'She didn't do it, you know.'

She turns her face into his, and feels the smoky, rotten breath travel into her nostrils and down the back of her throat.

'I know,' she says.

CHAPTER 38

Colin

The morning before Darren dies

On the morning of the tennis finals, Colin's mum drove all the boys to the club. She picked up Darren first, then Tim. Darren's parents had already left for work, his dad to the wharf and his mum to the hospital. Colin's mum was grumpy that morning, complaining she also had work to do that day. On the way to Tim's and then the tennis club, she spoke to them only once, to check what time Colin would be home. She only nodded when he said he would walk back from the club and didn't need a lift. Fine, he thought, be in a shitty mood if that's what you want. Don't expect me to cry about it.

At the clubhouse, the boys took their gear to their lockers and sat in the change rooms, their feet bare against the cool of the polished concrete floor.

'That house was just over the back there,' said Tim, nodding toward the street behind the tennis club. He'd kept quiet in the car, sitting as far from Colin's mum as he could. 'It's creepy thinking he was prowling around here just last week.'

'It might not have even been him,' said Colin, 'just some dude looking for cash.'

Tim looked at Darren, who was still rummaging through his bag, looking for his socks.

'Do you think he recognised you?' he asked him.

Darren shrugged without looking up.

'Nah. Maybe.' He straightened up and a square of bright fabric fell from his bag. He eyeballed them triumphantly. Colin and Tim looked in disbelief at the scarf.

'How the fuck ...' said Tim, his face flushing a deep, angry, red.

'Because you're rubbish at hiding stuff. Mate.' Darren returned, stuffing the scarf deep into his bag and out of reach.

'Did you break into my locker?' Tim's voice was dark with fury.

'Of course, I broke into your fucking locker. How else was I going to get back what's mine?'

'When are you going to get it through your head that it isn't yours?' Tim snapped at him. 'Do you have any idea in that stunted brain of yours how much trouble you'd be in if you get caught? You've got to get rid of it or hand it to the cops.'

'You don't get to tell me what to do, Tim. I found it. I'm keeping it. End of story.' Darren shoved his bag into his locker and swung the door shut with a clang. He hung the key around his neck. 'I'm going to practice.'

Tim and Colin looked at each other.

'The paper said it was just a break and enter,' said Colin. 'Nothing to do with the Weymouth rapist.'

'They might think differently if they knew about the scarf.'

'Maybe someone dropped it there as a prank. It's got Shane Boyle written all over it if you ask me.' Colin sat up straight and rolled his shoulders, stretching them out. He knew he was clutching at straws, but he didn't want to think they'd come so close to a real-life criminal. Breaking and entering was one thing, but coming face to face with a rapist was something else that he didn't want in his world, let alone the next street over.

'Shane's not smart enough to think that up,' Tim scoffed.

'Yeah, maybe,' he conceded. 'But the scarf's still evidence, isn't it? It's against the law to keep it. We should talk to Darren.'

Tim was putting on his shoes and looked at him over his shoulder. 'Maybe just let him stew on it for a bit. Talk to him later down at the river.' He stood and swung his racket – a smooth, controlled forehand despite his anger – and poked his fingers through the strings. 'Come on, let's get some practice hits in before we start.'

Tim won his first two games and then got knocked out before the final. Colin and Darren only made it through one round. Amy got in to the final and they cheered her on while they ate sausage rolls from the canteen. She lost in straight sets and came off the courts more disappointed than they expected. They consoled her with a pie and a Coke. In the mixed doubles, Tim and Amy made it through each round and were set to play the final against a boy and a girl from the two Catholic high schools.

Colin walked around the clubhouse to the carpark to find Darren and let him know that Amy's and Tim's game was starting. He paused while his eyes adjusted to the glare coming off the bonnets and squinted across the rows of cars. The heat radiated and shimmered. Through it, he could see Darren on the other side. He was facing him, hands in his pockets, a smirk on his face at the person who was waving her arms at him and shouting. Colin realised with alarm that it was his own mum. He thought she was at work. He shuffled closer to the trunk of the nearest gumtree and watched. She was turned away from him and he could only make out snatches of words, but he knew the tone well enough. Darren was the one getting a bollocking now. Colin had seen her yell at other kids before, including Tim two days ago, and knew the look that would be on her face. His mum and Darren's mum never had a problem with letting him and his friends know when they were out of line. He wondered what Darren had done this time, if it was the same thing she'd been shouting at Tim about. She thought they'd set fire to that car. She hadn't mentioned it to Colin yet, although he knew it was coming. She'd been shitty for days. He wondered when it would happen and what the consequences would be. He guessed he'd be grounded.

Colin shuffled between the cars, hoping to catch Darren's eye. He heard *roaming around* and *know better* and *take responsibility*. He saw Darren shrug, a smug, dismissive move that Colin had seen him use when he was toughing something out and didn't know what to say. It pushed teachers right to the edge and did the same to Colin's mum. She reached out with both hands and shoved Darren in the chest. Darren staggered backwards and screamed at her. Colin caught the words *black bitch* and saw spittle fly out of his mouth. His mum pushed him again, hard, and this time Darren grabbed at her shirt at the base of her neck to stop himself from falling backwards. Colin's mum was bigger than Darren and she reached her hand behind his head, grabbing a fistful of hair and pulling him toward her. She thrust her face at his. Colin strained to hear her, but she'd dropped her voice. They stayed that way until she jerked Darren's head back and pushed him away. Darren stood limp as she turned and stormed off, her hand to her throat where he'd grabbed her blouse.

CHAPTER 39

Sandra

Sandra had finished her shift early that day. It had been quiet at work, and after her lunch break their only patients were two elderly men who were waiting to go upstairs to the wards. On her way home, she had stopped at the supermarket then veered toward the beach instead of crossing the bridge. At the nursing home, she asked for the number of Arthur Zelinski's room and was directed to the first door on the main corridor. The receptionist on duty looked at her watch in surprise. 'I thought you were at work today.'

'It's been a slow day. I got off an hour early.'

'I suppose that's a good thing. A slow day in emergency means all is well out there in the world?'

'Yes, I guess it does.'

Sandra tapped on the door to Arthur's room and waited for his reply. She'd read his admission notes at the hospital but was still shocked at the state of his face. A purple-and-yellow bruise covered the side of his jaw and there were deep purple rings under both eyes. A cut above his right eye was held together with tape. He was out of bed and sitting in a chair, a gossip magazine across his knees.

'I'm a bit of a sight, aren't I?' he said in response to the expression on her face.

She pulled an extra chair over so she could sit next to him and studied the wounds.

'They did a good job on you, but you're healing well.'

'Yeah, well I'm a tough old bugger. It will take more than that to get rid of me.'

They both looked down at their laps. Barbara had found Arthur by the highway and brought him to the hospital, but the assault wasn't the reason he was at the nursing home.

'I heard about the diagnosis,' said Sandra. 'I'm so sorry.'

Arthur looked out of the window into the building's courtyard. Sandra remembers it was sunlit and bordered with geraniums in pots and the deep shade of the covered verandas.

'You've got to die of something,' he said. 'At least Barbara got me into this place.'

'She's a good woman, Barbara.'

'Yeah, she is. The nuns have been good to me too. You know they've been letting me sleep out there over the years? And they let me use the showers.' He paused and looked about the room. There were none of the usual photos and trinkets residents and their families use to personalise a room. 'I like sleeping inside, though. And I'm allowed to watch TV in the lounge room.'

They shared funny stories about daytime television. Arthur had discovered Oprah since being admitted and had become a fan. He didn't care for the soap operas, though. The pace was too slow. He figured he would only need to watch one episode each week to keep up with the story. He was describing the interweaving affairs of a Californian newspaper mogul and his family when Barbara put her head through the door. She was red-faced and puffing.

'Thank goodness you're here. Can you help? Elsie has wandered off again.'

'Of course.' Sandra turned to Arthur, who waved her away.

'Go and find her,' he said. 'She won't be far. She usually goes to the river. You'll probably find her down near the rope swing.'

'Thanks Arthur.' She bent to hug him goodbye. 'I'll pop in to see you next week.'

Sandra hurried out to reception where she found Barbara pacing in front of the door, sunglasses twirling in her hand and overstuffed bag hanging askew over her shoulder, papers threatening to tumble out. She had pulled her collar upright against the sun. Sandra grabbed her own glasses and dropped her bag behind the reception desk. The receptionist was nowhere to be seen.

'I've phoned Stuart,' Barbara said, the words falling out in a rush. 'He's at home and will start searching from the house back up toward the river. Can you take the track down to the riverbank and up toward the bridge? I'll follow the footpath along the road and come back along to track toward you.'

'Leave your bag at reception, it will get in the way. Put it next to mine behind the desk. And breathe. She'll be fine.' Sandra looked closer at her. Barbara had a long red scratch on her collarbone, disappearing below the popped collar of her shirt. The scab was fresh and the skin on either side was raised. 'What's that?'

Barbara touched her skin gingerly, wincing. 'That bloody kitten Stuart bought Rebecca. It scratched me when I tried to shut it in the laundry this morning.'

'It looks infected.'

'Priorities. Let's find Elsie first. Don't wait for me.' Barbara hurried back inside.

Sandra started down the track toward the river. It wasn't a proper track, just bare dirt, the result of years of people taking the most direct path to the water, but it was visible from the front door as it cut across the paddock toward the bush and would have been a logical path for Elsie to follow. A handful of sheep ignored her as she walked past. At the fence, an iron gate hung open. Sandra closed it behind her and stepped into the bush. Here, the track closed in with coastal shrubs and the limestone rocks showed through the sand. Sandra slowed and removed her sunglasses, squinting through the bushes. She didn't think Elsie would leave the track, but she couldn't be sure. The track dropped abruptly toward the river, and Sandra's left step was painfully heavy as it landed lower than she expected. It wouldn't have been kind on old legs. She kept her eyes down as she negotiated the slope, the bush becoming quiet as she descended toward the riverbank and the trees closed overhead.

Barbara said Elsie was wearing a green-and-white floral dress with a green cardigan. That's not helpful, Sandra thought. She entertained a brief mental image of the nursing home requiring all residents to wear fluorescent vests. She'd share that thought with Barbara later when they'd found Elsie. Barbara would get a good laugh out of it. Sandra frowned. It wasn't like Barbara to be so flustered; she was usually the calm one in a crisis. Sandra suspected the break-in had rattled her more than she admitted. She had been reluctant to talk about it when Sandra had asked and had been preoccupied and distant in the last week. Perhaps that was something they could talk about afterwards as well.

She reached the point where the track flattened out and divided, heading toward the beach in one direction and the bridge in the other. Knowing Stuart would be coming up the beachside track, Sandra turned toward the bridge, the water visible between the trees on her left-hand side, a short drop down from her feet. She leaned over to check the water's edge. It would be easy for a person unsteady on their feet to slip here and be unable to climb back up. The track dropped again, sloping downwards to become level with the water. Here, the bush opened out into a marshy area and the track became damp and littered with footprints. Other, narrower paths branched off and wound through the swamp grass. Sandra wondered how deep the water was in there and whether she would be able to see a person who had fallen. She took the next branch and followed its zigzags and loops. She had to be careful where she put her feet. At one point, although she was careful to step one foot in front of the other, her left ankle rolled outwards and she stumbled, arms windmilling as she stopped herself from falling into the mud. She realised Elsie couldn't have come this way.

As she turned back, she caught the sound of kids playing at the rope swing. The sea breeze was blowing the sound away from her, and their high-pitched voices and the sound of splashing water came in snatches. She remembers now she'd also heard the underlying tones of conflict. The kids were arguing. She wonders what it was about. Probably whose turn it was on the swing. One of the voices sounded like Darren and she realised he'd come down to the river with Colin and Tim after tennis. She'd reached the next line of trees when she heard the gun.

Sandra stands on the bridge looking down at the flat rocks that hang out across the river. They are dry and the water level is low. The sea breeze ruffles the surface and the tops of the trees. It is gentler on her face than it was that day. She inhales it, allowing the oxygen and the salt to brush away the stink of Cyril Worner's rotten breath and the revolting suggestion that they might one day have shared a grandchild. Well the joke was on him, she thought. She did have a grandchild, and he was a beautiful, kind boy and not related in any way to Cyril Worner.

Clearly, Greg had also believed Sam was Darren's son, if the trust account was anything to go by. Sandra wonders why he had never discussed it with her. She assumes she must have signed the trust deed at some point, consenting to becoming a trustee, but she doesn't remember it. That doesn't worry her. It would have been in one of the piles of papers Greg asked her to sign from time to time. Early in their marriage she had tried to show an interest, but after Darren arrived, she left those sorts of things in Greg's hands. She supposes it was an old-fashioned thing to do, but she couldn't have been less interested in legal documents and bank statements and was grateful he was happy to take care of it all. Even now, the existence of the trust fund and the eye-watering amount of money that has passed through it does not trouble her. She is pleased Greg saw to setting it up. Pleased her name is on the deed.

She looks down at the rope swing, tucked into a fork of the tree. Beyond it, she can see where the track reappears from the tree line. She can picture herself, still in her dark blue hospital tunic and pants, hair tied back, charging along the path under the trees. Her hands would have been empty. These days she rarely goes anywhere without her phone but back then it remained in her handbag, usually with a flat battery. A truck blasts past her on the bridge and Sandra closes her eyes against the heat and grit thrown up from the wheels. She walks across the bridge and down the embankment, following the riverbank past the rope swing and into the tree line where ten years ago she had come running. She walks quickly, not wanting to pause at the swing or under the trees where she'd heard that terrible noise and continues on through the swamp and the river mouth. Here, she sits to remove her shoes before crossing the sand bar even though the mouth of the river is closed now. She wants to walk along the water's edge, to feel the cold, frothy sea closing over her feet.

To her left, a white patrol car rolls down the hill from the nursing home and pulls up outside the Russells' house. Rebecca gets out of the passenger seat and turns back to speak with the driver, who has also climbed out and has his arms resting on the car as he talks to her across the roof. Sandra can't see who it is but assumes it is Keith. Can't they just leave that poor family alone, she thinks. She watches as he reaches into his pocket to retrieve his phone and take a call. Rebecca turns to look down the bay as he talks, one hand over her eyes. She sees Sandra and holds up her arm in greeting. You've got better eyes than me, Sandra thinks, waving back. The officer follows Rebecca's gaze and then looks down at his phone. He has finished the call and is making another one. Then her own phone rings, and she jumps and reaches into her pocket. It is Keith. She looks up at Rebecca and the officer, who holds his phone in the air. *Over here.* He puts it to his ear again. She needs to go home. He'll meet her there in five minutes.

CHAPTER 40

Colin
The afternoon Darren dies

Colin knew what the sound was and ducked, a reflex action that he wondered about later. Out there on the riverbank, they were all exposed, whether they were standing, sitting, or flat out on the ground. He pressed his face into the rocks, the water slimy against his cheek. Everything was silent. He couldn't hear Tim or Amy or Darren. There weren't even any trucks on the bridge. The sea breeze moved over his back, raising goosebumps on his damp, bare skin. With his eyes closed, he sensed rather than saw the rope swing pass over his head as it lost momentum. He waited for another, more sinister shadow to fall on him. Waited for another explosion, closer to his head. He wondered if his mum was home from work yet.

They'd come to the river to swim after tennis. On Friday, they'd all agreed to bring their bathers to the competition, knowing it would be a hot day. It was later than they planned when they finally got there. To their astonishment, Amy and Tim had progressed into the mixed doubles final. They almost won, losing match point with a wild forehand from Amy that arced over the umpire's head and into the fence. She'd slunk off the court, embarrassed and apologetic. Tim was unconcerned. He'd got to play more games that day than he'd had any other day in the season and losing this one was no big deal.

'Good game,' Colin had said to them both as they came through the gate, while the winning couple shook hands with the umpire. Darren hung off to the side, scowling, his hands shoved deep in his pockets. He hadn't said anything about the fight with Colin's mum.

'Thanks,' said Amy, glancing at Darren. She raised her eyebrows at Colin, and he shrugged. He figured he'd talk to him about it later.

He hadn't told Tim yet; didn't want to until he knew for sure what it was about. His mum had been pissed off last night, grilling him about where he'd been that afternoon and snapping at him to clean his room. She'd only got worse when he'd told her he'd taken Granny home. He heard her fighting with his dad about it after dinner.

'What if she'd ended up in the river, Stuart?' she'd asked, her voice raised and her vowels flattening. 'How would you feel then?'

He heard his dad say something placatory and indistinct.

'Us spending more time there won't help,' she shot back at him. 'Mum's not a puppy you can wear out and hope she'll sleep for the rest of the day. She needs watching around the clock. You are going to go up there tomorrow and ask for the next available bed in the dementia ward.'

Colin felt bad about Granny, but at least it had made his mum forget about him for a while. He still had it coming though. He could feel it. Probably tonight after she'd told his dad. Then they would both sit him down for a serious talk. He wondered how long he'd be grounded.

'I'll get into my bathers up here,' said Amy, 'I'll meet you outside.' She went to the women's change rooms. Colin picked up his bag and walked to the fence, where Darren sat on his own bag, pulling blades of grass out of the ground. Colin couldn't see his face behind his hair, but the tension rippled off him like a smell.

'Hey Darren.'

He looked up at him, his eyes black.

'Where are the others?'

'Getting changed.'

'They're fucking taking their time, aren't they?'

'They won't be long.' He took a breath. 'You alright, mate?'

'Never better.' Darren threw a blade of grass away with a dismissive flick of his wrist. He stood up. 'I'm not sitting around here forever, with my *stunted brain*. I'm off. Might as well dump my stuff home first if they're gonna take forever. I'll see you there.'

Tim came over as he stalked off and they stood there watching his back together.

'What's up with him?'

'No idea.'

'He's still got that scarf, hasn't he? Gone home to stash it.'

'I guess, yeah.'

They'd been at the river for half an hour by the time he joined them.

'Hey Darren,' called Amy from the water.

He ignored her and grabbed the rope swing. They watched him run out and launch himself across the water, swinging back to push off against the tree and out again before letting go and hitting the surface in a tight ball. Water exploded and rained down on them all. As the rope swung back, Colin reached out and pulled it to him. He jumped up, hooking his feet on the knot at the end and used the momentum to swing himself out over the water. He swung back and pushed off the tree trunk, gaining extra height. Third time lucky, he thought, and swung back again. Darren was climbing out of the water below him. Colin watched as he refused Tim's hand and hoisted himself onto his belly like a seal. Colin pushed off the tree trunk again and lifted his face to the sky as he arced back over the river. At the top of the swing, he let go and felt himself fly. It was perfect; the highest and fastest swing ever. As he felt himself slow, he twisted around, and for a moment he hung in the air. Below him, he could see the tea-coloured water, the flat rocks, and Amy's upturned face, grinning. Everything will be alright, he thought. They'd dump the gun and the scarf out past the reef, he'd confess to his mum about the nursing home prank, Rebecca would get over her sulks, and he'd get an exchange student placement in New York. In ten years, he'd be an engineer, building oil tankers and travelling the world. His stupid, small town problems will be in the past. Something to laugh about with friends in a restaurant with a view.

Colin tucked his knees into his chest and plummeted downwards, a tight, spinning ball. He felt the sting across his back as he hit the surface, then the warm water closing over him. He uncurled, pushed his feet against the slippery riverbed, and came back up into the sunlight. He looked across to his friends. Amy had turned away from him and was looking at Darren and Tim, who seemed to be arguing on the riverbank. Like the scene in the carpark, Darren had his hands in his pockets, slouching on one hip, while Tim gestured furiously at him.

'You've got no fucking idea, have you, Darren?' he shouted. 'What if someone we know is next? Did you think of that? How would you feel if we'd done nothing? What if he raped someone in our year?' He punctuated each question with a push in Darren's chest, Darren rolling with them each time, then fixing Tim with the same scornful look.

'I dunno, Tim,' he said. 'Why don't you tell me how I'd feel, you prick. Or maybe I wouldn't feel anything because, you know, my brain is fucked up.'

'Yeah, well, can your fucked-up brain consider this?' Tim stepped closer so he looked down at Darren. 'What if the guy who broke into Colin's place was actually after Rebecca? What if he comes back for another go at her?'

Amy sucked in her breath. 'Come on, Tim, that's low.'

Darren shot out his arm and grabbed her wrist, pulling her into him. She gasped and pushed him away. Alarmed, Colin struggled out of the water, slipping on the wet rocks.

'Maybe it won't be Rebecca, maybe it'll be your girlfriend.' Darren spat, squaring up to Tim.

'What the fuck, Darren?' Amy backed away from him, rubbing her wrist where he'd grabbed her.

'You're a freaking lunatic,' Tim said, dismissively, turning his back on him.

'Lunatic, freak with stunted brain, whatever.' Darren made to turn away. Colin watched as he seemed to change his mind, his face contorting, and launched himself at Tim's back, legs wrapped around his waist and his arm hooked around his throat. Amy shouted. *No!* Tim, taller and heavier, shrugged Darren off and shoved him hard in the chest. As Darren cartwheeled backwards, he seemed to receive a second blow. His chest caved inwards and his chin flipped down. Colin heard a car backfire, and everything went quiet.

The first thing Colin heard when the sound came back was splashing as Amy waded into the water. It had seemed like forever, as though time had slowed and placed them all in an alternate universe, but he knew it must have been only a few seconds. He looked up and could see her back and arms working as she pushed her way into the deep channel past the rocks and dived. There was an empty space where Darren had been standing. Amy surfaced, blowing river water out of her mouth and shaking her head. Her arms were looped under Darren's shoulders, his head resting against her throat. In front of her, the brown water churned as she kicked out and pushed them both to the bank. Colin scrambled to his feet and met her at the rocks. She relinquished one shoulder, then the other, checked he had Darren's weight, then hoisted herself out with one smooth push. Together, they laid him on his side. Blood and water pooled on the rocks around them. Amy put her fingers in Darren's mouth, searching for debris. Finding nothing, she turned him onto his back, checked for a pulse, and started CPR.

'Tim, bring your towel and press it on the wound,' she instructed. Her voice was firm and in control. 'Colin, flag down a car and get an ambulance.'

Colin turned on his heel and ran toward the embankment. Off to the right, he saw Darren's mum charge out of the trees along the river track. She was screaming Darren's name and by the time he reached the road, she had taken over the towel from Tim and was watching Amy as she counted compressions.

Colin ran onto the bridge, his arms waving over his head, as a road train turned the corner and came at him. It was too close to stop and the driver blew his horn in warning. Colin dived back to the side of the road and clutched the bridge railing as the truck thundered past. Below him, Darren lay prone on the rocks, the top of Amy's head obscuring the place where he was hit. His chest heaving, Colin looked down the river to where Amy had walked up the track three weeks ago and caught a green-and-white blur and a silver head. A figure emerged from the trees and reached out to it. He blinked and both were gone.

CHAPTER 41

Sandra

Police officers are screwing in the wheel nuts on the last of four replacement wheels on the Torana when Sandra arrives at the house.

'Forensics yard,' Keith explains in response to the query on her face. 'Probably from the car that was abandoned down by the river years ago. We were lucky; I don't know how we'd get it out otherwise.'

They stand side by side, watching as two officers release the handbrake and push the vehicle into the driveway. Keith ducks under the security tape and kicks a boot against the thick cardboard laid out flat on the concrete pad where the vehicle had been sitting.

'How long since it's been moved?' he asks, looking back over his shoulder.

'Never,' she replies. 'Greg got it when Darren was maybe nine or ten. They haven't taken it out since.'

Sandra had laughed at Greg the day he arrived home with the Torana on a borrowed car trailer.

'And just where is that going to go?' she'd teased him. The shed was full, end-to-end, with fishing gear.

'I'll make it work,' he replied. 'Why don't you boil the kettle? We'll come in when we're done.'

It was then a second person climbed out of the cab of Greg's truck and her mood had soured. Cyril Worner had been just as thin back then as he was today but moved on limbs that were still supple. They gave him a liquid grace that was more spider than cat. Sandra's throat had clenched as he silently poured himself out of the vehicle, his eyes unseeable under the brim of his hat. She held her hand up in response to his nod and turned away, holding onto the screen door until she heard the latch click into place.

Now she watches as Keith lifts the corner of the cardboard, which is stained with oil, and rotates it to one side. Her throat is already dry from the memory of Cyril when she sees what is underneath and she swallows uncomfortably. He looks back at her again.

'I'm guessing you didn't know Greg had a pit built into the floor of the shed?'

Sandra shakes her head. Lots of men, especially handy men like Greg, had pits built in so they could work on their cars, but she'd paid no attention. They'd lived closer to town while they were building the house and Sandra rarely visited the site. When she did, it was the house she was interested in; watching the rooms take shape, looking through the formwork where the windows would be, taking in the view she would have of the ocean from her kitchen. She'd climbed upstairs as soon as the second floor had been laid, to see how far she could see up and down the coast. She remembers that day. It was early afternoon and clouds had formed on the horizon, heralding the cold front that would come through later in the evening. She thought she was in heaven. She could've cared less about the shed.

Another officer joins Keith and together they slide the sheet of cardboard away to reveal six wide planks of dark wood, the colour and shape of floorboards, and laid level with the pad. They are loose, and Keith and his colleague lift one and place it to the side. They do the same with the second and the third, revealing the dark space below. Sandra can already feel that the air in there is cold and she wraps her arms across her chest. When the men return for the fourth, it seems everyone sees the crooked plank at the same time. Keith holds up a hand and motions for one officer to glove up. Sandra watches the man squat at the side of the pit and remove the wedge preventing the plank from sitting straight. As he pulls it out, the shape untangles. Sandra feels her stomach clench and a buzzing starts up in her head. Although it is stiff and coated in dust, the bright colours of the cloth square are unmistakable.

'Watch out, grab her, Simon,' calls Keith.

She feels a thick arm catch her across her back and she leans heavily into it as her knees give way.

'Bring her here into the shade.'

Sandra is manoeuvred into the shed and lowered on the floor, the officer moving slowly and taking her weight. She sits with her head between her knees. The concrete is cool, and she has an overwhelming need to put her head down on it. Someone passes her a plastic cup of water and sits on his haunches beside her. She puts her hand to her forehead, and it comes away wet. She is sweating and cold at the same time. Footsteps approach and Keith's boots come into her range of vision. She tries to lift her head.

'Best just to keep it down for a bit.' There is concern in his voice, and he squats in front of her, peering into her face.

'Sorry, I didn't expect that,' she apologises.

'Don't worry about it, we see it all the time.'

'Is it ...?' she can't bring herself to finish the sentence.

'We won't know until forensics have had a go at it. It could be anything.' His face is full of kindness and for a moment Sandra wishes she had been nicer to him.

'OK Keith, we're ready to take a look.' Above the pit, an officer wields a broom wrapped in cobwebs.

'No nasties left down there?'

'Only the big ones that wouldn't get on the broom. I shot those.'

'Good man. Alright then, Simon, get suited up.'

The officer sitting next to Sandra gets to his feet as well and retrieves a forensic suit which he steps into, then dons booties and gloves. He hooks a mask over his face and walks to the ladder that has been lowered into the pit. Sandra stands up and tests her balance before she joins the other officers watching him climb down. The boards, she can see now, had rested on angle iron embedded and bolted into the concrete, forming a ledge around the pit. It would have been easy for someone to wriggle under the car, lift one up, and push the scarf underneath. Provided you knew the pit was there in the first place. Provided you were small. The smell of cool, dry soil fills her sinuses and she peers into the hole, holding her body away from the edge. The pit is much deeper than the ones she has seen in other sheds. How do you reach the bottom of the car from way down there, she wonders? As her eyes adjust, she can see that on the floor of the pit is the ice chest that once sat against the back wall of the shed. Greg used it to store bait and as an overflow for the kitchen freezer when they had barbeques. Dread pools in her stomach. He told her he'd sold it to a fisherman south of town. On top of the icebox is a block the size of a house brick. Attached to the end is a light globe. She hears Keith suck in his breath and looks up at him in time to see him exchange glances with Simon.

'Six-volt motorcycle battery,' says Simon as he passes it up.

'Same make?'

'Don't know, I can't read Chinese.'

'Bag it up, Mark.' Keith passes the object to the third officer and they turn back to the ice chest. It has a heavy padlock on the front and Keith passes Simon a pair of boltcutters. He turns to Sandra.

'You might want to stand back for this,' he says.

She shakes her head and stands her ground. He hasn't told her what this is all about – clearly it wasn't the scarf; he was just as shocked as the rest of them – and she wants to know.

Simon sets the boltcutters against the lock and squeezes the arms closed. It snaps clean. He does the other side and passes the boltcutters and remains of the lock up to Keith, who hands him a crowbar. The lock goes to Mark for bagging. Simon wedges the end of the crowbar between the freezer seals and levers it upwards. The freezer breaks open with a sigh.

CHAPTER 42

Sandra

There was little smell, Sandra thinks later, at least not from where she stood. Just the stale, mildly unpleasant air of a closed-up freezer and a crackling sound as the rotten door seals eased apart. The four of them stood silently as they took in the contents. Sandra could hear the sea behind her back, and she leaned into it, wanting it to pull her out of the shed and its horrible secrets. At the bottom of the freezer, curled in a ball and head tucked the way the kids do when they do bombies off the rope swing, was the body of a woman. Her hair spilled across her shoulder, which was still covered in red cloth. Her face was dark, sunken, and her lips had drawn back from her teeth as her skin had tightened in death, giving the impression she was grimacing as she clutched her knees. Sandra didn't faint this time despite Keith's concerns. She'd recovered from the shock of the scarf and knew to expect something bad. Keith gave directions to Simon and asked Mark to *take Mrs Davies into the house and wait with her* while he made a phone call. She'd switched on the lights to the shed when she reached the house and put the kettle on. Mark stood silently inside the back door. She figured he was guarding her rather than keeping her company.

Keith follows them in when he is finished and leans heavily on the benchtop. He tips his head toward the door and Mark returns to the shed.

'I guess someone is taking Greg to the station?' she asks, handing him a cup of tea. Her hand, she notices, is steady, another person's hand, not hers.

'Thanks. Yes, they're on their way now. Obviously, I can't let you call him. We will need to interview you too, I'm afraid.'

She turns to the window and the ocean while he drinks his tea. Already she can feel everything moving away from her again, as though there has been an earthquake under the ocean with her at the centre, motionless as the waves roll to the horizon. She won't remember any of this afterwards, she thinks. Just like before.

Keith tells her that he spoke to Tim Patten via teleconference on the day she met him at the art gallery coffee shop. It was initially about Darren's case. He'd asked him about Arthur Zelinski, whether the boys had seen him often, whether there'd ever been any conflict. Tim had said everyone knew Arthur, that the boys often saw him at the river, at the fish and chip shop, at the video store. He said he'd heard a rumour at school about the Boyle kids giving him a hard time about being the Weymouth rapist. As far as Tim knew, he was just a harmless and homeless old man who'd lost his house in a fire. He mentioned a conversation they'd had with Arthur the day before Darren died. Jaelyn Worner had been there with her little sister, Ashleigh, and Arthur said something about Jaelyn's mum going missing about the same time as the fire at Arthur's place. As far as Tim understood, Jaelyn's dad had just taken off after a fight with her granddad. Fists were thrown and landed. Arthur told Jaelyn she was better off without him.

Keith had gone back to the remand centre and asked Cyril what that was all about. He'd laughed at him. How was he to remember a fight with his son fifteen years ago? They all ran into each other after a while. Randall, he told him, was a useless, lazy bastard and the longer he stayed away, the better. As for Jaelyn's mum, he said, the last he saw of her, she'd taken off in one of them old muscle cars from the seventies. And then he sneered and laughed, his throat rattling until he began to cough, his chest heaving over his knees, and the prison officers called the nurse.

'It made me think about the old Torana that was abandoned in the park down by the barbeques,' Keith said. 'The body – what was left of it – was still in the forensics yard, so we went over it again. Nothing there of interest except the wheels. They'd been taken off the car – stolen, of course – but they'd turned up when we raided a property out in the hills. It was a bit of a leap, but they reminded me of Greg's car up here on blocks and how there must be some way he planned to get underneath to work on it. I remembered the way that spanner thumped on the floor when it fell through the engine bay, that night Greg got Darren to crawl under the car. It wasn't the sound of metal on concrete, more a thud than a clatter. I figured there must be a pit underneath with a false wood floor. It wasn't mentioned in the first search.'

'So, the woman in the shed is Jaelyn and Wesley Worner's mum; the one reported missing?'

'Sadly, no, never reported missing. But, yeah, I think it's her. Esther Worner.'

Sandra tastes bile rising in her throat, breathes deep, and swallows it down. She feels the prickle of sweat on her forehead.

'But who killed her? Why is she in my shed? You can't think it was Greg.' She remembers the day Cyril emerged from the cab of Greg's truck, his silence, and his eyes shadowed by the brim of his hat. She reaches for her teacup but sees that her hand has started to shake and draws it back again into her lap.

'We're bringing in Randall as well as Cyril,' says Keith. 'Maybe Randall had a go at her because she was around at Arthur's place. Maybe Esther and Arthur were having an affair. Whoever killed her probably set fire to the house as well. I reckon that was what the fight with the old man was about. Cyril found out what his son'd done and would've told him to get out of town, make himself scarce. I reckon the murder weapon will be in there with the body and we'll be able to lift off fingerprints and DNA.'

'And Greg?'

'We're still working on it, but it looks like Esther was murdered around the time we think that Greg started working with Cyril ...' He stops when Sandra raises her eyebrows and shakes her head. He's lost her. 'We think Cyril was distributing meth dumped offshore in forty-five-gallon drums by freighters. We found one of them once, washed up on the beach north of town. It had a battery-powered light fixed to the top, a beacon, like the one in the pit. We think one of the ships doing the coast run was dumping the drums overboard at night so they could be picked up by a smaller boat. We never caught him with one and figured he must have had someone else picking them up for him.'

'You think that was Greg?'

'We never had anything solid, but he surfed a lot up there, on his own. He had plenty of opportunity, and his catch was lagging behind the rest of the fleet. We already suspected he was bringing small stuff in on the *Reef Walker* using the tinnie Darren had parked up on the sandbar. The beacon in your car pit doesn't look good. Maybe he wanted some extra money. Maybe Cyril offered to cut him in if he helped him cover up for Randall.'

Sandra looked through the windows at the shed, lit up against the dark. The two police officers moved back and forth across the bare concrete floor. If Greg had hidden the beacon in the pit, he would have had to move the Torana out first. Like the scarf, it could only have been slid inside with the car still in place by someone smaller and much more agile than her husband. She feels a flush of anger in her belly, rising to her throat.

CHAPTER 43

Sandra

Keith is waiting for her behind the reception desk and takes her down the corridor to the interview rooms. Nothing much has changed in ten years. Refurbishment of country town police stations must be low on the list of priorities in the police department budget, she thinks. Much like the hospitals. Even the smell is the same as before; the bleach cleaner they use to scrub the linoleum floors each night. The memory raises goosebumps on her arms. Through a half open door, she catches a glimpse of Colin and his dad in another room, hands folded around plastic cups and backs hunched. Keith reaches back and the door clicks shut.

'We're in here.'

She leaves the chair closest to the door free for Keith. She knows the protocol. And the walls are green after all. He holds a wad of papers wrapped in a blue folder and held together with an elastic band. He won't open it, she thinks. On top of the folder is a yellow-backed notebook. The vertical blinds on the windows – internal and external – are drawn shut.

'Thanks for coming in. Can I get you anything?'

She shakes her head.

'Do you mind if I finish this?' He has a half empty takeaway cup of coffee on the table.

'Go ahead. Why are Stuart and Colin here?'

'I'll get to that in a minute.'

Keith explains that the Worner property has been searched and they found no evidence linking the old man or any of the family to Darren's murder.

'No gun?'

'No gun. He doesn't even own any licensed firearms.'

'What about the drugs?'

'There were two joints in a cutlery drawer,' he says, 'Cyril says he doesn't know anything about them of course, but we've sent them to the lab. At most, it will be another fine for possession but nothing for us to get excited about. It's the trafficking charge that we're after.

'The thing is, his sister, Robyne, has confirmed he was on a plane to Brisbane on the day of Darren's murder. She even has a photo of him at Brisbane airport. He couldn't have been in town, so that puts him out of the picture as a suspect.'

'What about the current charge, the rape?'

'The hearing is set down for next month, we won't know until then but the case against him is strong.' Keith opens his notebook and underlines a date with his pen. 'Can you tell me about the night Colin and Tim slept over at your place just before it all happened? It would have been the week before. Probably a Friday night.'

Of course, Sandra remembers. It was the night someone broke into Barbara and Stuart's house. The night Rebecca was raped. Except she wasn't. It was also the night the boys startled a would-be intruder at a house near the fish and chip shop. And the night a car was set on fire at the nursing home. Not a night easily forgotten.

'The boys came over after school then went down to the beach,' she says. 'Darren had left a sports bag under the tinnie and was in trouble with his dad, so they went to fetch it. Barbara and Rochelle, Tim's mum, dropped off their sleeping bags and pyjamas while they were out. When they came back, I made them hose the sand off their feet outside. Of course, that turned into a hose fight and they all got drenched so I made them towel off under the patio and get into their pyjamas. Then we ordered pizza – Greg went out to pick it up – and we left them in the games room to watch a movie.'

'That's the big back room off the kitchen? The one that looks out onto the backyard.'

'That's right. I put mattresses on the floor with their sleeping bags in front of the television.'

'What time did they go to bed?' Keith asks, his head down in his notebook.

'I didn't check, but the lights were out, and it was quiet down there from around ten, I think. That must have been around the time they took off.'

'Where were you and Greg?'

'Upstairs. We had another television up there. I can't remember what we watched.'

'And the boys were all in bed the next morning?'

'Yes, fast asleep. I drew the blinds and Greg and I ate breakfast upstairs, so we didn't disturb them.'

'Did they ask permission to go to the fish and chip shop that night?'

'No, I told this all to the police when the story came out. They changed out of their pyjamas and sneaked out the back door. Darren would have been grounded for a month if I'd found out at the time.' Sandra had been furious when she discovered that they'd left the house. With nowhere to direct her anger – Darren was dead, Tim in Canberra, and Colin facing her alone, miserable with regret and too soft a target – she'd walked up to North Point and back, fuming and then sobbing in frustration. It was clear to her the boys' misadventure was the reason behind the shooting one week later. She'd blamed herself, Greg, the Russells and the Pattens, for encouraging their children to roam. They'd been determined not to be helicopter parents, to let their boys explore and wander, spend unaccounted-for time away from their parental gaze. So what if they came home with a few bruises and grazed knees? It was all part of learning and would turn them into resilient, independent adults who wouldn't crack the minute they faced hardship. But all it had done, she thought, was give them the confidence to sneak out at night and put themselves in the path of a violent criminal. It was their fault Darren was dead, the parents, all of them.

'And you didn't hear them come back in?' Keith is asking her, pausing in his notetaking.

'No,' Sandra pulls herself out of the spiral, 'but from what Colin said, it must have been within an hour of the shop closing.'

'So, maybe midnight?'

'I'm only guessing, I really don't know,' Sandra shakes her head.

'And they didn't go out again.'

'Like I said, I didn't hear anything but obviously I didn't hear them go the first time either, so who knows.'

Keith puts his pen down and reaches for his cold coffee. He takes a sip and grimaces.

'Barbara and Stuart Russell's house was broken into that night and their daughter Rebecca reported that she was raped,' he says.

'I know, she retracted that later.'

'Do you know why?'

'No, I don't.' She's not giving away Rebecca's secrets. That's something for Rebecca to do, not her.

'I think it was because the intruder was someone she knew, someone that she'd been seeing in secret for a while, and she was covering for him,' he puts it on the table and waits for Sandra to say something. 'I think it was Darren.'

'What does Rebecca say?' she asks.

'She hasn't. Yet. But Tim Patten has confirmed that Darren left the house again after the boys returned home. He says he only returned at dawn.'

'Did he say why he didn't tell us that after Darren died?'

'The boys were scared they would get in trouble for the car fire. Tim told me that Barbara already suspected something and had baled him up about it the day before.'

Sandra just looks at him, bewildered, and he sighs.

'You didn't know?'

She shakes her head again. There is, it seems, so much that she doesn't know.

'The boys went out that night to prank the nursing home with food dye in the windscreen wipers,' he explains, a weariness in his voice. 'Unfortunately for them, they used a flammable substance to dirty the windscreens and when one of the night shift staff came out for a smoke, the manager's car caught fire. Colin said his mum found out; I take it she never said anything to you?'

Sandra presses her lips together. If the circumstances were not so awful it would be funny. Although she probably wouldn't have found it funny at the time, even if the circumstances were different. The story explained Barbara's preoccupation in the week before Darren died. She would have been grilling the boys about what they'd been doing that night, and when she got to the bottom of it, there would have been a three-family conference and the boys grounded for longer than they ever had before. Pocket money would have been forfeited. She wonders, if circumstances had been different, if she and Barbara would have eventually laughed about it over a glass of wine, if the boys, once they had survived their youth and were comfortably middle-aged, would share a guilty smile over a backyard beer. It was the stuff of youthful legend, if circumstances were different.

'Sandra?' Keith is looking at her intently. 'I've asked for a court order for a paternity test for Sam.'

Sandra looks back at him, confused. She doesn't need to see scientific proof herself. She knows Sam is her grandson. But she doesn't understand why it is important to the case, what it has to do with Darren's death.

'Motive.' Keith's voice is soft, almost gentle as he says it. 'Darren got Barbara's daughter pregnant, Sandra. Other people have killed for the same reason.'

'But that was the world Barbara worked in,' Sandra protested, 'she saw teenage pregnancies all the time. She wouldn't have hurt him because of it.'

'She didn't tell you that she thought Darren was the father. She couldn't have been that blasé about it if she didn't discuss it with her best friend.'

Sandra bristles. 'None of us are *blasé* about teenage girls getting pregnant, Keith. Barbara knew the damage accusations like that can cause and she wouldn't have suggested it was Darren unless she was sure it was true. Rebecca wasn't saying anything. And then Darren died, just one week later, so of course she wasn't going to raise it with his grieving mother if she didn't know. She would have just let it go.' She looks out the window at the sea. She remembers Barbara being snippy with Rebecca that week, how she seemed to be stewing over something. She was in no state to have a calm conversation with the mother of a boy who might have got her daughter pregnant. Not even if she was her best friend.

'Maybe. If she thought it was consensual.'

Sandra feels fury tingle under her skin as she registers what Keith has just said.

'No,' she says slowly, containing herself. 'Darren would never force himself on someone. Especially not Rebecca. He was just a boy himself.'

'Are you sure Barbara didn't mention anything to you?' Keith asks. 'That she thought it was Darren who broke in that night?'

'No.'

'Barbara confronted Tim and Colin about it, though. They've both confirmed that she asked them if it was Darren. They said she seemed pretty convinced.'

Sandra doesn't know what to say. Did Barbara really think Darren had raped her daughter and not say anything to her about it? She didn't tell Sandra about the nursing home prank either. Sandra feels the first flickering of doubt. She didn't see Barbara walk back along the cliff top that day. It was possible she could have waited until Sandra left the nursing home and then followed her along the river or taken one of the tracks through the swamp. Down there in the thick bush, Sandra wouldn't have heard her.

'But what about the gun?' she asks. 'It had been stolen, the Russells reported it. And the DNA. It doesn't make sense.'

'There's something else you should know.'

CHAPTER 44

Colin

Colin looks up as the door cracks open. Constable Samson motions for them to come with him and he pushes himself up from his chair. He glances at his dad. He's worried about him. His face is grey and resolved, and his long, ropey limbs are loose, as though he has been out running and drained them of any further strength. Colin's own arms and legs are heavy. They feel it and look it. He has his father's height, but he must be five or ten kilos heavier and he suddenly feels ashamed. He has let himself become fat and unfit like the rest of the men in suits who walk up the city streets each morning. He has a pouch above each knee and on the day of the funeral, as he struggled with the top button on his shirt, he realised his dad's own collar sat smooth and easy against his neck. He wonders what Amanda thinks of him. His wife also has a desk job but is always on her feet. She runs three times a week, does yoga and, astonishingly to Colin, knows her blood pressure and cholesterol levels. Apparently, according to her Fitbit, her resting heart rate is 52bpm. As he walks out of the interview room behind his father, Colin resolves that he will start running again when all of this is over. Every morning. Just a few k's at first but he'll build them up. He'll tell his dad. It will make him happy.

Keith opens a door two rooms down the corridor and Colin follows his dad inside. Sandra is sitting facing the door and he drops his eyes before taking a chair on a vacant side of the table. His dad has taken the opposite side.

'Stuart, Colin, thank you for coming in today,' Keith begins.

Colin lifts his eyes and gives Sandra a half smile. He dreads her reaction to what they are about to say. It was his dad's idea. But he wouldn't have agreed come in if he knew Keith was going to make them do this. He looks back down at the table.

'Stuart, can we go back to the night of the break-in at your house?' Keith asks. 'The night before you reported your handgun missing.'

Colin hears his dad clear his throat. He can see the tops of his hands laid out on the table. They press downwards, fingers splayed the way his dad always does when he explains something and is taking care to get it right. Colin's own fingers trace around a coffee ring. It is still sticky.

'I woke up around three thirty in the morning when Rebecca came into our room. She was crying, distressed. We couldn't get a word out of her for a while, but I went to her room and saw the bedroom window open and the flyscreen removed. I checked and it was outside, propped against the fence. I figured someone must have broken in and Rebecca had seen them, so I closed the window – yes, I know that was the wrong thing to do, the forensics team already gave me a hard time about it – and went to check the rest of the house to see if anything was missing.'

Colin frowns at the table, remembering his mum telling him the intruder came in through the spare room. He hopes this will be the end of the lying.

'I think all of us here know Rebecca claimed the intruder sexually assaulted her, but after Darren died she retracted that statement,' says Keith, 'so we don't need to cover that again. Colin, Stuart, I've told Sandra we suspect the intruder that night was Darren and that he and Rebecca had been seeing each other in secret. I've also told her that I have ordered a paternity test for Sam.'

Colin nods without lifting his eyes. This will all be over soon. He assumes his dad and Sandra are also agreeing.

'What happened then, Stuart?'

'The rest of the house seemed fine, just the way it was when we went to bed, but when I got back to our – Barbara's and my – bedroom, I saw the safe was open.'

'The safe was in the built-in wardrobe,' prompts Keith.

'Yes, that's right,' Colin's dad confirms. 'The wardrobe door was open as well. I was sure it was closed when I went to check Rebecca's room, but I thought at the time that I must have just overlooked it. As you know, my handgun wasn't inside.'

'And Barbara and Rebecca?'

'Rebecca was using our ensuite and Barbara was waiting for her in our room.' He pauses and looks at Keith, stricken. 'Of course, now I think she was doing something else.'

Out of the corner of his eye, Colin sees Sandra stiffen and swing her head toward his dad. He puts his hands under the table and rubs the stickiness of the coffee against the fabric of his jeans.

'And you reported the gun stolen the next morning?' asks Keith.

Colin scowls. Keith already knows that.

'Yes, I did,' answers his dad.

'Can you tell us what happened two weeks before the break-in, Stuart?'

'I had opened the safe to check the expiry date on Colin's passport. He wanted to go on an international student exchange programme, and I was certain the expiry was due in the next twelve months or so. The passports were there but the gun wasn't.' He pauses and Colin can feel the heat radiate off Sandra's arm even though it must be a ruler's length away from his.

'That was on a Sunday,' his dad continues. 'Colin had gone off on a hike with his friends and Barbara was … well, she said she was having coffee with Sandra. Barbara had nagged me to teach her to shoot. I took her out to the range once, but we'd never found the time to go back. That was my fault. It's not easy to teach your own wife. I should have just arranged for someone else to give her lessons.'

Colin smirks at the table despite himself. He can picture his mum, all flowing skirts and frizzy hair, frustrated with his dad while he taught her to stand and aim. She'd have hated it.

'I figured she was fed up with me stalling and had taken the gun out behind the hills somewhere on her own.'

'And that didn't bother you?' Sandra's sudden outburst startles them all and Colin looks up at her. She is staring at his dad, her brow scrunched tight and her eyes narrowed. His dad looks back at her, his face unapologetic.

'You know what she was like, Sandra,' he says. 'She wouldn't have done anything to put someone at risk. I figured I would just let it go. As it turned out, I was right. Colin saw her at the gully that day the boys went hiking up there, but it was fine. No-one got hurt.'

'What?' Sandra whips her head back to Colin and he can feel the heat directed at him. She spaces out her words like a length of rope.

'You and Darren and Tim were hiking in the gully while your mum was doing target practice with live ammunition? You could have been killed.' She turns back to his dad. 'It's not *fine* at all, Stuart. Why didn't you go after her? You knew the boys were out there.'

'Actually, I didn't. They organised it at that barbeque at your place, remember? We'd all had a few that night. I thought they had planned to go up to North Point and come back through the dunes.'

Colin watches as Sandra puts her head in her hands and breathes. The three men wait.

'So, did she put the gun back after taking it out to the gully?' she asks, not looking up.

'No, I checked. She started keeping it in a basket under the bed. That's what she was doing the night of the break-in while I was out of the room; she was getting the gun.' Stuart looks up at Keith again, who nods silently. *Go on.* 'It didn't occur to me at the time, but now I think she was going to put it back in the safe before I came back and checked.'

Sandra raises her head and looks at Colin's dad as though she is very, very tired and can't understand what he is saying. Colin thinks about what he would give to be anywhere but here right now. An arm. His job. His marriage. His best friend is dead, and it is his family's fault. He should sacrifice something to make it right. But he won't be giving anything. He already knows that. He will tough this out and then he and his dad will fix it. Then it will all go away and no-one else will get hurt.

'You've got to understand, Sandra,' his dad is saying, 'she was terrified of the Weymouth rapist breaking in and assaulting Rebecca. You didn't have a girl. You didn't know what it was like.'

'So I've been told,' she says, and Colin recoils at the bitterness of the words. 'Let me get straight what I've *got to understand*, Stuart. You kept your *licensed firearm* in *a basket under your bed* for a week before it was stolen and used to shoot my son?'

'Well it was Barbara who kept it ...' he cuts in.

The look Sandra gives him is withering and her voice is clipped.

'Don't even think about it,' she says. 'Do you even know what happened to the gun? Was it actually stolen, or did you lie about that too?' She turns to Keith in disgust. 'How is it we only find this out ten years later?'

Colin swallows even before Keith looks at him.

'It wasn't stolen. I found it.' It's his turn now, and he braces for Sandra's anger to be directed back at him.

'Dad didn't know,' he says in a rush. 'He really did think it was stolen, Sandra.'

Colin makes himself look at her while he explains how he searched for the gun after the day at the gully, finding it first under the bed and then, after the break-in, in the old camping equipment in the storeroom downstairs. He feels his face heat up as he tells his – dead – best friend's mum that he hid his dad's gun in his bedroom, in his locker at the tennis club, and finally in his granny's handbag in the nursing home.

'And you, as the responsible gun owner, knew nothing about this,' Sandra spits at Stuart.

Stuart looks to Keith for help. Sandra follows his gaze.

'Where does that leave us then, Keith?' she asks.

'Well,' Keith starts, looking at each of them in turn, 'we know Darren was killed with a twenty-two calibre handgun, the type used at the gun club. Stuart's gun was a twenty-two and we know it was unsecured for two weeks before Darren was killed. We don't know who knew that, except for Colin, Stuart and Barbara, but we do know Colin can account for its location up to two days before the murder. We have to assume someone took the gun from Elsie Russell's room in the nursing home sometime between Thursday afternoon and Saturday afternoon. It is possible that person was Barbara. It is possible she then took it down to the river and shot Darren from somewhere behind the tree line, most likely as retribution for assaulting Rebecca.'

Sandra shakes her head.

'No, she was with Arthur. I left her there.'

It is not enough, she thinks. They don't have enough to convince her. Barbara might have been frightened of the Weymouth rapist, might have believed Darren had climbed in Rebecca's window and even sexually assaulted her, might have tried to cover up the missing gun from her husband. Sam might be Darren's son. But even if all those things were true, she can't believe Barbara killed Darren. Barbara loved him, just like Sandra loved Rebecca and Colin, and now Sam and Jessica. Barbara would have protected him with her life. Murder just wasn't in her blood. Sandra knows she will believe this until she dies.

Stuart clears his throat. When she looks up at him, she sees the deep grooves around his mouth and the way his eyes drag downwards.

There is sorrow on his face, but she can see a hardness too, a resolve that she hasn't noticed before.

'Sandra, Keith knows,' he says. 'He knows you and Barbara were out searching for Elsie that day. Barbara wasn't back at the nursing home; she was at the river.' He holds up his hand as Sandra tries to interject. 'Yes, I know she said she took the clifftop path, but she could easily have found her way down to the riverbank. I know it's difficult to hear this, but Barbara did have a motive, she was at the river mouth that day, and she lied about it. It is quite likely she found the gun in Elsie's room. I've thought about it for a long time, but the police were never interested in her as a suspect and, like you, I couldn't work out a motive, so I said nothing. Now we know Darren was the intruder at our house that night, well, it all adds up.'

He reaches for Sandra's hand and she snatches it away.

'But we don't know that,' she argues. 'You're just speculating on the basis that Tim said he wasn't in his bed that night.'

'We also have the scarf we found at your house this week,' says Keith. 'It's the same as the scarves found at the scenes of the sexual assaults committed that year, the ones sold at the pharmacy in town, where Rebecca still works. We believe Darren and Rebecca had planned to use it to fake an assault at the Russells' house so Rebecca could blame the pregnancy on the Weymouth rapist. Of course, we now know that the boys fought over the scarf and it was in Tim Patten's possession at the time of the alleged assault. Darren broke into Tim's tennis locker, took it back again, and hid it in the pit on the day he died.'

Sandra laughs, a sharp bark of derision, and Colin knows what she's thinking. She can't believe that her son – her skinny, pale, adopted little boy, whose development was always so far behind Colin and his friends – could concoct such an elaborate plan. Colin's not sure he can believe it either.

'There's no way Darren could have thought up something like that,' she says, 'just no way.'

'If the paternity test shows Darren is Sam's dad, it will look very much like he could.'

Colin watches Sandra look backwards and forwards between his dad and the police officer. His dad coughs and Colin squares his shoulders.

'I'm sorry, Sandra,' his dad says, 'but I do believe now that Barbara killed your son.'

Sandra shakes her head and looks at Keith. 'And the gun? What did Barbara do with it?'

'We are searching the gully today.'

CHAPTER 45

Sandra

Colin looks back down at the notebook in his lap where Sandra has written the instructions the Pilbara police gave her on the phone last week. They need to take the Nameless Valley Drive out of Tom Price and turn left onto the Nanutarra Road. There is a gravel road two kilometres along that will take them to an unmarked camp site. Sandra has already warned him that they can't stay there too long. A cyclone is coming down from the Kimberley and is expected to cross the coast in the next twenty-four hours. Right now, the sky is blue, but the camp site is next to a riverbed that will flood from rain upstream and block access to the main road. If they don't leave before the flood, the police can't say how long they'll be stuck.

Sandra has already been on this road, travelling toward Tom Price. She decided to drive herself up north, declining Keith's offer of company, and has been on the road for two weeks. She's been nervous since she turned away from the coast. She feels dry, sucked of moisture, and her pores are full of red dirt. There is no cooling sea breeze, but the best times of day, she has learned, are before dawn and at sunset, when the softer light allows the lime-coloured spinifex grass to glow against the red rocks and the sky deepens to a pure purple. The only respite during the sun-bleached hours in between is in the deep gullies of the national park. There, in the hard rock shadows, Sandra has blocked out light, heat and sound and imagined herself completely alone.

In fact, she has spoken to no-one since she left home, except for the day-to-day transactions of filling fuel tanks and buying supplies. She has free-camped whenever she can, checking in to powered sites every three days to shower and fill her water tanks. Her four-wheel drive camper has a fridge and a gas stove she has used to cook dinner each night. She has eaten solitary meals on a camp chair, her feet in the dust and her eyes on the stars. It has been six weeks since Esther's body was lifted from the pit in her shed and since then she has cleaned out the house and put all her belongings in storage. The house is on the market and the Torana will finally be restored by Teresa's brother Joe, who plans to auction it to raise money for the football club. When Sandra returns, she will buy a smaller place south of town, looking over a different stretch of coast, away from the river. There are some nice houses in the street where Keith lives. He has said he'll help her out when she's back.

She saw Greg before she left. He is being held in the remand centre waiting trial, alongside Cyril Worner, both of them charged with conspiring to pervert the course of justice and concealing a corpse. The charges carry maximum sentences of seven and ten years. Cyril's son, Randall, has been charged with murder. The police have also charged him with the rape of three women in Weymouth after taking a sample of his DNA and matching it to each of the cases. Keith told Sandra before she left that the drug squad were looking into Greg's financial records and expected to lay additional charges in the next month. He should get used to the remand centre, he said, because he wouldn't be leaving it for a very long time. Sandra knows that Greg will survive prison better than most men. He will miss the freedom of the open water, but when she visited, he was just the same Greg he has always been. Solid, sure, and undiminished. She thinks she will keep visiting him if the charges stick. She has shared too much of her life with him to cast it aside. But she won't trust him again. She has gone through her finances with Sophie and when the investigation is finished, she will remove her name from any accounts or trust funds that they still hold together.

Colin was waiting at the airport when she pulled into the carpark. There had been no flight delays in Perth and the pilot made good time with a southerly behind him. In the passenger seat of the camper, he looks from right to left and back again as they drive along the open and empty road, taking in the scenery that she now finds familiar. An old blue backpack sits at his feet; his suitcase rests on the bench seat in the back, waiting to be stowed when they get to the camp site. His camping gear, on loan from his dad and brought up in the van, is already packed under one of the bench seats. He's come alone.

'Dad and Rebecca aren't ready,' he said.

She understood. It can take a while. She hadn't gone down to the Wey River for two years after Darren died. It was Barbara who had finally taken her, insisting she needed it to heal. They had walked there together from Sandra's house, along the path down to the beach, across the sandbar, and back up the other side under the she-oaks to the flat rocks by the water's edge. It was the same time of year and the southern bank was muddy. The yellow sourgrass flowers bloomed around their legs. The water was high, and the rope swing still there, hanging straight down over the bank. Sandra tested its weight as she looked at the water thinking *this is where my son died.*

Barbara was half right about the healing. Standing there had meant something, feeling the warm rock through the soles of her canvas slip-ons and the suggestion of the sea breeze on her face. Road trains no longer rumble above the bridge, although the odd semi sneaks through. The Department of Transport deemed it too narrow and too old to carry big commercial vehicles safely and built a new bridge half a kilometre upstream. Now only local traffic passes overhead. But it didn't heal her, not completely. The pain remained and, if anything, it has only changed shape. It is just that she has learned how to carry it. For a while, the prospect that it might have been Barbara who pulled the trigger made it worse again, the tale of misconstrued events and allegations somehow devalued the horror of the death itself. But Sandra knows she will learn to carry this, too.

She will always be close to Rebecca and her children. She is not Sam's grandmother after all: the paternity test that Keith, Colin, and Stuart were so convinced would give them the answer only complicated the story. Sam's father is Wesley Worner, his grandfather is Randall, and his sole surviving great-grandparent is Cyril. When Keith confronted her, Rebecca admitted she and Wesley had met when she was on his sister's netball team. They'd dated in secret, Rebecca slipping out of parties to meet up with him before coming home long after her friends had forgotten to look for her. She hadn't told Wesley she was pregnant but had confided in Darren after she ran into him at the river mouth one afternoon. She had a secret place down there where she went when she wanted to be alone, a hideout off the main track, underneath a she-oak and up against the limestone cliff. When she pushed her way through the bushes, she found Darren there. He was upset; something about Tim Patten killing a cat. She didn't know why it was Darren she had chosen to tell that day. He was just her younger brother's friend, nothing more than that. She was ashamed and embarrassed. Her parents didn't know about Wesley. Together they made up a story to conceal the baby's paternity: Darren would break in to her room and leave a scarf behind and she would claim she had been raped. Then Darren said he had lost the scarf that she'd taken from the pharmacy, so she told the rape story without it. Keith didn't point out to her the consequences of their deception.

Colin points to a turn-off and Sandra checks the odometer. The road is not signposted, but it is the right distance from town. She slows the vehicle, mindful of its high centre of gravity, and turns in. They bump along for ten minutes, the cutlery in the tiny kitchen rattling in the drawers, until the road dips down and to the right and then opens out to flat area alongside a dry riverbed. Here, they can see where people have parked under the sparse, white-trunked trees. There are blackened stone rings and a single forty-five-gallon drum attached to a steel star to use as a rubbish bin. Sandra checks her notes again and takes a sand track that follows the left bank of the river. After fifty metres, she sees another makeshift rubbish bin under a tree. Anyone parked here would be invisible to campers at the main site.

She looks at Colin, checking in.

'It really is in the middle of nowhere isn't it?' he says, an air of resignation about him.

'How about I make a cup of tea?' she replies.

Colin wanders about the camp site, walking out onto the river sand and looking up and down the course, then goes back into the van to stash his suitcase with the camping gear. He comes out when the tea is ready, and they sit on fold-out camp chairs. He points to a breakaway on the other side of the river.

'I bet there's a great view from up there.'

'You can walk up there now if you like,' she says. 'The pot will still be warm when you come back. We aren't due to meet everyone until tomorrow anyway. Make sure you take some water with you.'

She watches him hoist his backpack onto his shoulders and trudge across the soft, dry riverbed. The breakaway is a different kind of red to the hills and gullies at home. Here, the topsoil is only evident on the plains and in the dry riverbeds, and the eroded rocks are darker and sometimes banded. The only vegetation on the sides of the breakaway is spinifex grass. The gully where Barbara had taken herself for target practice had the occasional twisted gumtree and wattle; small pockets of shade for blue tongue lizards and sleeping kangaroos. Sandra feels an unexpected sadness, thinking about Barbara teaching herself to shoot, frightened of an intruder when the only intruder was Sandra's own son. The police had searched the gully and the ruin for the gun, even sending a man down the drop toilet, but had found nothing. Without the gun, there was nothing concrete connecting Barbara to the murder, Keith had said. Even with it, Sandra thought, there would still be nothing that made Barbara the shooter.

Sandra pours herself another tea and checks her notes before following Colin out onto the riverbed. Instead of crossing it, she turns left and ploughs through the sand for one hundred metres, until she reaches the point the police described over the phone. Here, the river has changed course and carved out a hollow, exposing the roots of a tree. This is where they found her, sitting in the clean sand, her shoulders propped up between the exposed roots, a natural backrest. She faced the breakaway to the east where her son is scrambling up the rocks. Sandra already knows that the official cause of death was kidney failure caused by severe dehydration. Barbara would have sat here to rest, in the riverbed, and lost consciousness some hours before she died. The police had determined that the battery in her car was flat but couldn't say why she hadn't walked back to the highway for help.

She stares down at the hollow in the sand. In the late afternoon, it is a cool, quiet place. She curls herself into the space, resting her head against the tree roots, and cradles her cup in both hands. *I can't believe it was you*, she whispers. Every fibre inside her protests against Keith's conclusion that the shooter was her best friend, but even Stuart and Colin are convinced now. She is the last one.

The low sun lights up the breakaway and Sandra turns her head toward the rocks. Colin has reached the top and is walking away from her along the ridgeline. *I'll watch out for them*, she promises. Colin disappears down the other side and the shadows climb up the rocks. Sandra levers herself to her feet and treks back to the camp site to start their dinner.

CHAPTER 46

Stuart

The afternoon Darren dies

Stuart put the phone down, grabbed his house keys and jogged along the road toward the river mouth, his thongs slapping on the bitumen. Before he got to the sandbar, he veered right and took the track along the south bank. Barbara had said Elsie might come this way. He slowed to a fast walk. The track was drying out but was still muddy and stank of methane and sulphides. The mud sucked at his thongs and he wished he had taken a moment to put on some boots. The sea breeze had picked up, turning the olive river water silver as the ripples caught the sun. He shielded his eyes against the glare. There was no-one around.

In Stuart's mind, his mum could have gone left or right at the riverbank, it was impossible to know which. The last time she had left the nursing home – the day Colin had found her and taken her back – she said she was going out to buy milk. That day she had turned right toward the bridge. Barbara said she had taken her bag this time, so Stuart figured the odds were that Elsie would have gone the same way and Sandra would find her first. Either way, when they took her back to the nursing home, there would be hard conversations. This would be their third strike and Elsie would no longer be allowed to stay in open accommodation, the nursing home had made it clear. Residents who wander were a risk, the director had said, and the staff couldn't watch them twenty-four hours a day. The home had a locked ward for residents with dementia that could accommodate Elsie when a bed became available, but otherwise they would need to make alternative arrangements. It was for her own safety.

The first time his mum had wandered off, Stuart had met with the nursing home director and toured the dementia ward. It was like another world. The director unlocked the door with her swipe card and the lock turned back again with a distinct click as she closed it behind them. Stuart had felt his breath catch with it. The feeling of being trapped was immediate. The level of energy in the room they had entered was higher than the corridor they had just left. Stuart was used to visiting Elsie in quiet rooms, where the only noise was background classical music and the clink of tea trays. The residents that he saw, when he did see them, were absorbed in jigsaw puzzles, newspapers and televisions, or strolled along the arched verandas. In the secure ward, there was a constant background noise and movement. People muttered to themselves, tapped on armchairs and walked back and forth. A woman in a beige cardigan rocked a doll as she stood in front of a television and a tall man in brown slippers swept the corridor with an old-fashioned straw broom. Stuart watched as he got to the end and turned around to start again. The director drew his attention to the doors at the end of the corridor. They were painted with a mural, a pastoral scene with green paddocks and sheep. A smiling farmer in a red tractor crested a hill, a black-and-white collie running behind. The mural was a distraction, the director said. Before it was painted, residents would cluster at the door all day, testing the lock and trying to get out.

On the phone, Barbara had said none of the nursing home staff knew yet that Elsie was missing. If they were quick, maybe they could get her back before anyone found out. Stuart had vowed on the day he visited the secure ward that he would never put his mum in there and was prepared to tell a small white lie if that was what it took. His mum was fine most of the time as far as he could see. The police officer who took her back to the nursing home the first time might have had a laugh at her expense, but he said she knew exactly where she was and what she was doing. Stuart visited his mum once a week, on a Wednesday after work, and he never saw any sign that she was losing her marbles. There were the usual things, of course, like misplacing her glasses, not recognising faces, and going to sleep in the wrong room, but that was just a part of getting old wasn't it? Just last week he'd driven to the nursing home expecting to spend an hour talking about the royal funeral, but she'd wanted to discuss the Scottish referendum and whether the practicalities of devolution had been sufficiently considered. How many people with dementia do that? He approached the tree line where the ground was higher and drier and slowed his pace again, taking care now to look left and right in case Elsie had strayed off the path. Barbara said she was wearing green and white – her favourite colours – but they would make her hard to see amongst the trees.

Like his son further upriver and Sandra in the next grove of trees between them, Stuart recognised the sound of the gun when it fired, but also knew the calibre. Like them, he too stopped, frozen as he processed the unexpected noise, before he started running. He lost both thongs in his first steps, one falling off and the other as he kicked it away. He held his hands out in front of his face to keep the branches out of his eyes. Focussing on protecting his face, he didn't see a lump of limestone in the path and drove his toe into it. He stumbled, squeezing his eyes against the pain, and righted himself. Blood welled up around the base of the nail. He hobbled forward, testing it, and continued on, slower this time and remembering to scan both sides of the path.

As the trees thinned, Stuart saw her, a short figure in green and white, pacing toward him through the marsh grasses. She clamped her handbag to her side and was focussing on her feet. Relieved, he called out to her, keeping his voice low. She didn't hear him at first and it wasn't until he emerged from the tree line and reached out to her that she looked up, startled, and then allowed him to pull her underneath the canopy and out of sight. She was panting.

'Oh Stuart, those boys.'

'It's alright, Mum.' He hurried her along the path. 'Let's get you home.'

'They are bad boys. They were going to hurt that man. They were throwing stones.'

'They're gone now Mum, you don't need to worry.'

'I stopped them. Colin was there, he saw.' She planted her feet and looked him in the eye.

'That's good, Mum. You've always stood up for people, haven't you? Here, let me take your bag.' He reached for the handbag and she twisted away from him, clamping her arm down tighter.

'No. It's my bag. I'll carry it.'

'Alright, alright.' He stepped back. 'Let me take your arm, though, so you don't fall on the track.'

Stuart hurried Elsie along the path as fast as he dared. By the time they arrived back at the nursing home, she had turned quiet and pale. No-one was at the reception desk. He had taken her shoes off and got her into bed by the time Barbara rushed into the room. She was sweating.

'Oh, thank God,' she breathed out. 'Where was she?'

'Between here and the bridge. I walked her back.'

'Did you see Sandra? I'll text her and let her know.'

'Good idea.' He finished tucking his mum into bed and smoothed her hair away from her face. 'What was going on out there? I thought I heard a gunshot.'

Barbara shook her head. 'There were a bunch of kids fooling around by the river. It was probably a truck backfiring on the highway. I need some water and some paracetamol. My bag's in reception. Back in a minute.'

Stuart sat back in the bedside chair as Barbara left the room to refill the water jug, her solid heels marking her progress down the wood-floored corridor. He was more rattled than he expected. They'd got away with it this time, he thought, but there will be a next time and a next time after that if they don't do something. He wondered about chemical restraints. He knew Barbara disapproved but he thought he would prefer it to the horror of the dementia ward. He looked up as she bustled back into the room.

'I'm drugged up and ready to go,' she declared. 'Coming?'

'Sure, I'll meet you outside.' He stood up and smoothed the bedsheets. He knew his mum liked them over her neck even when the room was warm. As he straightened up, he saw his mother's handbag on the floor. She'd be annoyed if she woke up and it wasn't back in the bedside table. He bent to pick it up and frowned at the weight. He reached inside and his hand closed around a familiar metal shape. He looked over his shoulder at the doorway where his wife had just exited, then opened the bedside drawer, slid the bag inside, and pocketed the key. He dropped his lips to his mother's forehead and whispered. 'Don't worry, Mum, we won't let them lock you up.'

CHAPTER 47

Colin

The rocks on the breakaway glow as the sun drops lower in the sky and shadows climb the thin trees on the other side of the river. Colin sets off to the east, walking across the sandy riverbed and picking his way through the rocks and spinifex on the other side. There are kangaroo droppings on the orange dirt between the grass clumps and indentations under the trees where they have slept. They will be out feeding at this time of day. The ground climbs and Colin walks straight up to the ridge, not bothering to pick out a more gradual course. Here, there is no vegetation above knee level. At the top, he looks down over the camp site, the haphazard layout now visible, and tracks the road back to the highway. The police were right, it is not that far away. In the distance, iron sheeting catches the sun. He can't tell if it is the roof of a homestead or perhaps a water tank. He doesn't understand why anyone would want to live out here.

Below him, smoke curls upwards next to Sandra's camper, untroubled by wind. He knows she doesn't believe his mum killed Darren and, in some way, this makes him feel better about what he's doing. He had to make a choice, his dad made that clear. Send him to prison for concealing evidence or let people think his mum was a murderer. She was dead now anyway, like his granny; nothing could hurt her. Not really. He and his dad know the truth, and they're the ones who loved her most. Them and Sandra, and nothing, he knows, will change her mind.

He turns his back on the camp site and looks for the waterhole. It is further south than he remembers, at the base of the hill on the eastern side, now deep in shade. Walking down to it is harder than walking up and he scatters rocks and stones as he works out where to put his feet.

Two kangaroos startle as stones clatter down the slope, soundlessly hopping away from him. They stop and turn to look back when they reach the flat ground, their ears flipping around like radars. Colin sees the way their coats blend with the late afternoon shadow and now his eyes pick up the rest of the mob. They watch him too, waiting to see which way he will turn. He continues his path and the mob takes off down the hill. It occurs to Colin he might have an animal totem, a spiritual emblem that shares his soul and for which he must assume stewardship. Maybe it is a kangaroo or a camouflaged lizard. Maybe, he thinks, drawing down the sides of his mouth, it is a secretive and elusive night parrot.

Colin reaches the overhang above the waterhole. It is smooth and flat like the rocks under the rope swing. He sits on his haunches and looks down at the water. He wasn't allowed to jump from here when he was little and now he can see why. The water is shallow. Even in this light he can see the outlines of the rocks at the bottom. Shame wells up inside him as he thinks of the effort put into finding the gun. The police had sent divers into the river, searching the bottom from the bridge to the sandbar. Volunteers from the tennis club had formed a search party, combing the mud and marsh along the riverbank. He'd heard a rumour that a deckhand had thrown the gun overboard from a cray boat and it was now at the bottom of the ocean, ten miles offshore. A house had been searched in a police raid after neighbours reported screaming and seeing someone through a window who was waving an object that looked like a gun. The hapless newlyweds had appeared on page three explaining they had lit their barbeque for the first time that season and had been overcome by a wave of cockroaches. The gun the neighbour thought he saw was just the firelighter the husband had used when the barbeque's inbuilt switch hadn't worked.

Colin puts his backpack on the rock, removes his shoes and his jeans, and folds them into a neat pile to one side. He climbs down to the water and dips in one foot. The water is cool but not as cold as he expected. It won't matter. He won't feel it for long. He wades in and crouches at one side. Here, the underwater ledge juts out toward the centre, just as he remembered from the camping trip when they were kids. He runs his hand underneath, feeling how far back it goes. The water under there is cold and the surface of the rocks slippery. If he extends his arm as far as he can reach, he can feel a slight dip against the far wall. Satisfied, he wades back to the edge of the pool, climbs back up to the overhang and reaches into his bag.

He has only handled it four or five times, but the shape and weight of the gun is as familiar to him as a tennis racket. The suede cloth cover is long gone. Colin doesn't know when or where, but it was missing when he collected the gun from his granny's handbag using the key his dad gave him and hid it in the cave after the reporters came to his office. He guesses the cloth was dropped at the riverbank and is now sunk into the marsh. He likes to think someone will dig it up, ten thousand years in the future, and find it perfectly preserved. An archaeological treasure.

They had taken a risk putting the gun in the cave, but it had been kept hidden for another five years and might have remained there forever if Amy hadn't blabbed to Sandra at the pharmacy. Colin had texted Rebecca as soon as he left, telling her to keep Sandra away from the river mouth until he retrieved it. *Tell her that Sam is Darren's son*, he said, *it's what she wants to hear anyway.* The gun had sat in the old tent peg bag in the storeroom for the past six weeks and travelled up to the Pilbara in the back of Sandra's campervan. He holds it in front of him and looks down the barrel. His dad never taught him how to shoot and he doesn't know if he is holding it right. It doesn't matter. He climbs back down to the waterhole and wades across to the underwater ledge, where he sits and reaches down into the water. When he finds the dip against the back wall, he slides the gun under the ledge and pushes it as far back as he can. As it reaches the dip, he gives it another push and lets go. It slips along the rock and out of reach. It is gone. Colin straightens up and looks across the water into the bush. The light has faded and the cloud bank on the horizon has grown. The mob is staring back at him. They want to come in and drink. Colin wades back out again and climbs back up to get his things.

CHAPTER 48

Ashleigh

Ashleigh sits well back off the track that runs along the riverbank. She leans against the trunk of a she-oak, its bark soft and alive through her t-shirt, and runs her fingers through the spiny leaves that drape around her. The ground here is compacted and dry. People have sat here before, although there are none of the signs of smoking and drinking that are usually left behind in places like these. The sound of a happy child drifts across the tea-coloured water and she straightens her back to look through the hanging branches. The sandbar and the water are empty.

Ashleigh has been coming here since before she started school. The limestone cliff below the nursing home has an unseen spur that reaches out toward the river here, making a sheltered nook when the wind blows from the south and the west. Unlike the limestone cave on the north bank, which Ashleigh can see if she stands on the other side of the wattle bush, this green cave is hidden from view. Today, the wind is calm, and the she-oak tree makes a gentle, soothing shushing. Ashleigh leans her head back and closes her eyes, listening to the tree and the sounds of the unseen child playing.

This is a special place, just for girls, Jaelyn had told her. She said boys weren't allowed to come here. She said Auntie Robyne had brought her when Jaelyn was the same age as Ashleigh was back then. She said Auntie Robyne told her it was her job to bring Ashleigh here when the time came. They even slept here overnight sometimes, walking all the way from their grandfather's house. Jaelyn would bring sliced bread and peanut butter and, in the morning, they would eat it with their feet in the water and watch the tiny silver fish dart around the shallows.

Behind the she-oak, the layered white rocks are jagged, useless as a back rest, but they are good for keeping provisions dry and out of sight if they are sealed up well. Ashleigh has left biscuits here before, in plastic ice-cream containers she has salvaged from home. There are other things too. Private things she doesn't want her granddad to find. She knows he goes through her room when she's not there.

Ashleigh runs her hand over the pile of hard she-oak fruits she has gathered on the ground. Their spikes dig into her palm, tingling in a nice way and leaving rows of indentations. She wonders how Rebecca found out about this place. She didn't think her mum could have told her; they weren't from around here. They were from up north somewhere. Near Wittenoom, Ashleigh's granddad said. The place with the asbestos where all the people got sick. Ashleigh's face darkens. When she goes to university – and she is going to go, you can be sure of that, she thinks – she's going to study law like Jaelyn. Mathilda Boyle is coming too and they're going to live in a student college paid for with their scholarships. Mathilda's dad's in prison now, doing twelve months for beating her up after school. Serves him right, the bastard. They got the boys who touched her up as well. Two of them are under community supervision orders in the city. Mathilda doesn't need to worry about them coming back because their parents have left town. Too ashamed to stay. Ashleigh has heard people say that one of the dads had to give up a good job with the council because Mathilda didn't trust him to punish his son himself. She has also heard people say that Mathilda's a *right vindictive little bitch* who knew *exactly what she was getting into*. Mathilda said when she has her law degree like Jaelyn, she's going to come back here as a public prosecutor and put all of the lying, groping arseholes in jail. Ashleigh's not interested in ordinary criminal law. She's had enough of drug dealers, thieves, rapists and murderers. She's going to learn how to stop big companies from ripping people off. She's going to send them to prison and take away their fancy houses and flash cars, those people who poison the environment and kill their workers and launder money. She's going to fight the good fight.

Ashleigh reaches behind her into the hull of the old boat, the one Rebecca dragged here with Wesley. It is propped on its side, leaning against the jagged white rocks and you can only see it from underneath the tree. They brought it in here years ago before Ashleigh was even in primary school. She wonders now how they got it to the river. They must have used a four-wheel drive, but none of the old people would come here. Too superstitious. Although it could've been that copper, the one with the red Hilux and big shaggy dog. She heard he was the one who found Jaelyn's and Wesley's mum. The police say it was their dad who did it, and he also raped those girls all those years ago. Dad's back in town again now, but he's staying in the remand centre, with Granddad. Granddad says he was never any good, but Ashleigh reckons it would be hard to turn out right after living with Granddad. Ashleigh doesn't live with Granddad anymore; she lives with Auntie Robyne and no-one comes into her room at night anymore.

Ashleigh feels under the boat's aluminium seat for the package she has opened and resealed a dozen times and peels it free. She opens it again now and looks inside. It is just an ordinary envelope wrapped in a green bin liner, and it fills the palm of her hand, the notes inside lined up against each other. She has never been tempted to count them or take any of the money. A bad feeling in the pit of her stomach told her that no good would come of whatever it had paid for.

She hears a splash and looks out through the branches again. The wind has picked up and the child has come over to the sheltered river side of the sandbar. She is wading in the warm water. A dark stain is already moving up her skirt and her mother is hovering.

'Not too far, Jessica,' Rebecca calls.

Ashleigh watches as Rebecca tucks her own skirt into her knickers and follows the child into the water. One evening, after Jaelyn had come into Ashleigh's bedroom and whispered that they needed to go to the river again, they'd seen Wesley and Rebecca crawling out from under the branches of the she-oak. Jaelyn and Wesley fought about it afterwards. She wonders about Jessica as she runs the tip of her finger back and forth across the edges of the notes. Rebecca seems like a good mum. The little girl is chubby and smiley and when Ashleigh has seen them in the street, she is always wearing a sunhat. She has seen Sam with them, too. He is still in primary school and Ashleigh heard he got Fairest and Best for his football team this year, just like Wesley. She smiles into the package on her lap. She knows she's not related to him in a blood sense, but she feels sad that he doesn't know his dad, or her, or any of his family on their side. There is so much love he's missing out on. She has seen Rebecca's husband, though, playing kick-to-kick with him on the school oval and she figures a lot of kids do worse. And she will be able to keep an eye on him when he comes to high school. Her dad and her granddad might be going to prison, but her surname is still enough to protect the little ones.

Ashleigh wraps the package, taking care to seal the corners, and stands, brushing the dirt from the backs of her legs. She reaches high up the limestone cliff, searching for her favourite nook, and slips the package inside. Mathilda said the flood is going to be high this time, and she needs to make sure it is safe.

ACKNOWLEDGEMENTS

Thank you for picking up my book. It is my very first published work of fiction and I hope you enjoyed reading it. It was written in my home on Whadjuk boodjar and I drew on my memories growing up on Yamatji country to imagine the town of Weymouth and the Wey River. I acknowledge the traditional owners of the land of my adult and childhood homes and pay my respects to their elders, past and present. I acknowledge that this book is set on the traditional lands of the Yamatji people and that this land has never been ceded.

I want to thank the people who read early drafts of *The River Mouth* – my mum, husband, sisters, children, friends, writing group buddies – who all gave me the confidence to keep going. Katie Scott sent me to the Fremantle Arts Centre to attend a writing course and there I met Marlish Glorie who ran the course and introduced me to other writers. I am so grateful for the encouragement they all continue to give me. A cheer squad, I have found, is a very useful thing. Annie, Susan, Nicole, Liz, Ali, Fiona, Emma, David, and Dan, I look forward to celebrating the launch of your own books.

Thank you, Fremantle Press for offering to publish *The River Mouth* and for introducing me to your world. Thank you, especially, Georgia Richter, for walking alongside me and making my book the best it could be. It has been, and continues to be, a delight to work with you.

Thank you, booksellers. Over the last year, many of you have shared your knowledge of your industry with me, told me what you need from authors, and given me a whole new reason to spend time in your shops. I look forward to spending more time with you and your readers.

Thank you, fellow authors, especially those who had books published in 2020 and 2021 during COVID, for inviting me in. It is an honour to walk among you.

Thank you to my sisters, Joanne and Katie, my first friends and companions on riverbanks and beaches, on horseback, on bikes and on foot. Thank you for sharing your working lives as nurses and allowing me to use your stories.

Thank you, Mum and Dad, for making sure I was literate.

I know that I am fortunate to write at a time of my life when children are grown up, finances are secure, and I have a roof over my head and food in my belly. My husband, Ross, makes it possible for me to write by going to work each day to pay our bills. More importantly, he helps me give myself permission to take a chance and find out if this is something I can do. I will iron as many of his shirts as he wants.

I look forward to sharing my next book with all of you.

First published 2021 by
FREMANTLE PRESS

Fremantle Press Inc. trading as Fremantle Press
PO Box 158, North Fremantle Western Australia, 6159)
www.fremantlepress.com.au

Cover image: istockphoto.com
Author photograph: Amy Luckett
Design: Nada Backovic, nadabackovic.com
Printed by McPherson's Printing, Victoria, Australia.

A catalogue record for this
book is available from the
National Library of Australia

ISBN 9781760990466 (paperback)
ISBN 9781760990473 (ebook)

Department of
**Local Government, Sport
and Cultural Industries**

Fremantle Press is supported by the State Government through the Department
of Local Government, Sport and Cultural Industries.

Australian Government

**Australia
Council
for the Arts**

Publication of this title was assisted by the Commonwealth Government through
the Australia Council, its arts funding and advisory body.

MIX
Paper from
responsible sources
FSC® C001695